FAMILY!

Tony Blackreach Novels

See You On The Ice
White Dust

FAMILY!

Trevor Horsley

Typeset in 11.5/15pt Adobe Garamond by Falcon Oast Graphic Art Ltd
Printed and bound in Great Britain by ImprintDigital

War!
This ain't war, war ends

Chapter 1

Leaving the restaurant, Nadir crossed the street and headed south towards the underground; oblivious of the sounds around him, he was deep in thought. Walking down the steps onto the underground concourse, he bought a ticket and made his way to the escalators, which took him further underground and onto the station platform where he waited for the train back to Uxbridge. It was a journey he was now familiar with; the hustle and bustle of the underground and crowded train no longer worried him. The mixture of voices at this time of night were mainly foreign, many migrant workers on their way to the graveyards shifts, the underbelly of the city, the men and women that kept the metropolis going when all the businesses were closed and the general office workers were asleep in their beds, unrecognisable faces of those that cleaned the streets, swept the corridors of offices, picked the litter up from the playground of the tourists. The security guards walking the perimeters of their charges, the delivery drivers bringing in the goods to feed the city, the homeless trying to find a safe and secure spot in a lit doorway for the night and then finally, both the drug addicts and girls of the night staggering back to lay their head on whatever pillow they could find.

Getting off the Bakerloo line at Baker Street, he made the cut through and waited on the Metropolitan line for the last part of his journey to Uxbridge. His time with Tony was easier than he had thought. Nervous at meeting a complete stranger and asking for what he had was stressful; however, the man had made him feel at ease. He thought he would have asked why he wanted what he did, but Tony had cut him short, saying that he wasn't interested in what he was doing, he was more concerned, or so Nadir thought, about making sure he could pay him; in fact, he had asked him three times if he had the money. *Typical,* thought Nadir, *all about the money.* Tony had explained that the less he knew the better. He had pushed him though on whether he knew how to handle the stuff, it was dangerous and in the wrong hands could easily cause major problems. Again, thinking back to the conversation, Nadir remembered he had asked him a couple of times if he could cope. He told Tony that he was getting help to put it together, which seemed to relax him a bit. They had exchanged phone numbers and Tony had said that it would take a couple of weeks to get hold of it and he would ring him and arrange a meeting, again asking him to make sure he brought the money, and it would only be me and him, saying that if he saw anyone else, he would disappear. *Very cautious,* thought Nadir.

Thirty minutes later the train broke onto the surface, and as he left the station a light rain had started. He hunched his shoulders, slightly bowed his head and walked. The house he and his wife had was rented. They had initially decided that

2

after a couple of years if they both worked hard, they may have enough money to put down a deposit on a small house somewhere near Oxford. For now, though, this was owned by a friend, and the rent was very low, and although it took about an hour each day out to the base at Brize Norton, it was cheaper than renting near where he worked. Rounding the corner of the street where he lived, he looked at his watch and shook his head. It was later than he thought, and he had missed the last salaah of the day. Striding on towards the front door, if asked, he thought, he'd say that he had been unwell that evening. In his heart, prayer was a huge part of his life, and he believed more and more that Allah had planned a journey for him whilst he was in this world, which he knew would undoubtedly lead to a greater reward in the next one.

Opening the door of his house, he hung up his coat and walked through to the kitchen, pouring himself a glass of water. Standing by the sink, he reflected on the events leading up to his visit tonight. It was a difficult journey for him, but he had managed to get back as quickly as he could. He had been in a trance since he had heard from his father that fateful day; a day that should have been one of joy had turned into a nightmare. The funeral in his village on the outskirts of Al Diwaniyah in Iraq had been a traumatic affair. His mother had been distraught, clinging on to him every moment she could. The loss of her two sons Jamil and Malik had burned deep within the family. She had lost both her brothers in war, and her husband had lost his cousins; the family had been devastated by loss for as long as she could remember. For what reason? Had anything changed? Had life got better? Peace had evaded them, and as she cried in her sadness over her sons' graves, she felt as if there would never be an end to the suffering that the family would endure at the hands of others. His father had embraced him when he had arrived, held him longer than necessary, afraid of letting him go. His other brother and sisters were there supporting, as best they could, their grief-stricken parents. It was a sad affair. The burial was attended by over 100 people, locals who had grown up with the boys, close friends and extended family members. He didn't want to be there now. Although his family were everything to him and always would be, the god forsaken country, the country of his birth, the happy memories he had with his brothers were now fading. The country was now banging from one side to the other, with Saddam Hussain hell bent on war with whoever he could, or so Nadir thought.

On his return, he initially couldn't believe that they were no longer with him. The disbelief turned into overwhelming sadness at the loss of the two dear brothers who had looked after him, played with him and encouraged him to do well. They saw him off at the airport when he left for university all those years ago, they play mocked him at his marriage, they were overjoyed at the birth of his first child and were, along with his mother and father, eagerly anticipating the arrival of his second child. The grief had mingled with a sense of wondering: what would he do now without his brothers? His wife had tried to console him, but everywhere he looked, every thought he had, every person he saw he imagined it was either Jamil or Malik playing a game, and they would bounce around the corner laughing and joking with him again. The last few months, prayer was the answer. He felt Allah would make sense of the atrocity. He would show him the way to live without his brothers. He would provide him with the strength to go on, and he would deliver a message to him to show him how to move on with this life.

When they first moved to London, a friend of the professor who had originally put him forward for the interview and had helped him secure the position at Brize Norton had offered them a house they could rent cheaply until they got on their feet. The house, a terraced three bedroom with a kitchen and living area, was nicely appointed, and his wife had enjoyed the excitement of making the house a home for him and the children. She had made friends in the local community and was busy with the two girls. The eldest, Kala, had fitted in well at her new school and was thriving. Just born now, Polla, the baby, of course was a few years away from school but was full of fun and enjoyed being played with by a few of the other mothers' children Bahi, his wife, had befriended, spending their time at each other's houses during the day. He had settled in at Brize Norton and was astonished at the size and complexity of the base. That now changed, every day on his return after the funeral he swapped his sadness for a bright and cheerful exterior, masking the deep hurt he was feeling within. He worked a shift system, two weeks on earlies the next two lates; he'd gotten used to the work pattern and had settled in well to the routine. The job itself was challenging but was within his grasp, and early on he had picked up the internal systems quite well; the defence radar, which he was tasked with monitoring and reprogramming through software upgrades, was delicate and sensitive. The people he worked with were mostly Americans with a few people like himself who had excelled in their given technical roles. The Americans came across as helpful and were always open to explain and train as necessary. Each day, though, as he sat at his terminal working on the tasks ahead, he couldn't help but look up occasionally, his eyes filled with hatred. All of them, they had no purpose, no ideology, no history, no empathy just greed and a complete dismissal of all those who didn't hold to the American dream.

Tony picked up the cigarette packet and lighter, slipped them into his pocket and walked towards the counter. Smiling at Maria and with a wave at Allessandro, he paid the bill and walked out into the cool dark night. He had booked in at a local B & B, picking this over a hotel for the night, just in case. Running with the same hotel and restaurants was a recipe for danger; you could easily fall into a pattern that could be traced or watched. His meeting with Nadir was unexpected, unexpected in so much as to what he had wanted. He knew his name had been passed on and had waited until contact had been made. It had been several weeks, and he was beginning to think that whoever had wanted to meet with him had decided to abandon the idea. He was going to wait until the end of the week and then move on. As it turned out, the contact was made and the arrangement was confirmed; one last time he would visit his favourite restaurant, Allessandro's. He wouldn't meet anyone here from now on, a new location was needed. It was a shame, thought Tony, he had got on well with Allessandro. The authentic Italian food his wife Mary cooked was delicious but again, habits, dangerous things. Tony thought about Nadir Al Najaf. A young married man, he seemed in control if a little reluctant, or maybe it was nerves. Tony had assessed him during the 40 minutes they were together. He had wanted to know why Tony would help him, and Tony's explanation of being mercenary in his approach to business – as long as the money was forthcoming, he would supply him with anything he wanted – sufficed. He seemed reassured; they had exchanged numbers and Tony would make contact in a couple of weeks.

Rounding the corner, Tony spotted his B & B for the night. He skipped up the steps of the townhouse, let himself in and climbed the stairs to his room. Putting his coat on the bed, he carefully approached the window side on. Parting the edge of the curtain, he watched the road below. After 15 minutes, happy that it was OK, he flicked the light switch on and made ready for bed.

The following morning, up early, he grabbed a coffee from the café and ambled up the main road. Turning left and casually walking past several shops, he stopped, lit a cigarette and took a closer look into one of the shop fronts: shoes, shirts. Glancing right and looking for a reflection in the glass, he moved on up the street. Another shop front, and to any passer-by it looked as if a garment had caught his eye as he peered closer at it. Discarding the cigarette, comfortable that he wasn't being followed, he saw a cab approaching with the light on. Stepping quickly to the kerb, he hailed the cab and jumped in. The journey down to the Hilton Park Lane didn't take long. Paying, he got out and instead of going into the hotel he turned and walked up the road. Nothing appeared unusual, so he crossed over into the underground car park. This time, however, he walked straight through and out the other side, waving at a black cab as he did so. 'Whitechapel, mate,' he said as he settled back.

'Whereabouts?'

'The main drag. I'll give you a shout when we get close.'

It had started to rain as he slipped down an alleyway. Looking at his watch, 10 am, Tony took a final glance around, confident that he hadn't been followed, and entered Denham Mews. The house was the third on the left, and as he approached, the front door opened, and Rob nodded and let him in.

'Hello, mate, nice weather.'

'No kidding.'

'In the back room.'

Tony shook his coat as he walked into the room, the light rain flicking off as he did so. Leonard, Mike and Mark were there. Mike and Mark had been in the marines together,

Mike serving longer than Mark, and when he had got out Mark had introduced him to Leonard, who asked him to join the team. Rob was always quieter than the others but seemed to be the techie of the group as he had helped Tony with the cameras and radios, etc.

'Morning, chaps. How we doing?'

'Just celebrating Mike's new arrival.'

'What, nice one, let's have a look,' said Tony holding his hand out. Mike passed him a couple of small photos.

'Wow, lovely, mate, sure she's yours?' said Tony laughing. 'Dick.'

Smiling. 'She's a heartbreaker, best of luck fending off the boyfriends,' he said putting the photos back on the table. Sliding the chair back, Tony took his place at the table. Pulling out the cigarette packet from his pocket, he gave it to Mike who broke it apart and took out the slim recording tape and put it into a waiting player, rewinding it as he did so. Tony sat down; Mike pressed play.

The conversation played out. Leonard, from time to time, took some notes, occasionally requesting the tape be rewound for a minute or two then replayed. The clarity was good, but every now and again laughter from the other diners muffled the words of Nadir.

The moment everyone was waiting for was what Nadir wanted.

Nadir spoke. Mike raised his eyebrows at the request, and Leonard scribbled furiously.

'Well, that's a turn up,' said Mike.

'New one on me,' said Mark.

'And me,' said Tony.

There was a knock at the door; Rob jumped up.

'Play the last bit again,' said Leonard.

With the tape rewound, Mark pressed play as Barry entered the room. Barry, the last member of the team, seemed to be able to source just about anything and get access to any documentation they needed, and mostly it appeared to Tony that he was Leonard's right-hand man.

'Nadir,' said Leonard looking up at Barry. Barry nodded, sat down and listened.

The tape played again; they listened, Mike and Mark keen to hear that they hadn't misheard what had been said.

The tape clicked off; Leonard let out a deep sigh.

'Right, what do you have Barry?'

On leaving the restaurant last night, Barry and Mike had followed Nadir across town to his house in Uxbridge, with Mike taking photos. Barry had then returned and did some digging. Mark had been backup to Tony, and although he had looked hard, Tony hadn't spotted him on the way back to his bed that night. He knew he was there, but Mark was good.

'Nadir Al Najaf, as we know, 32 years old, married to Bahi Al Najaf. They have two children: new-born, a girl by the name of Polla, and the elder daughter, Kala. Polla was born in the UK; Kala was born in India. An Iraqi national, in fact they both are, on his visa on entry to the UK it stated that he was from a village called Al Diwaniyah in Iraq. Studied at the University in Mumbai where a Professor Dougan sponsored his application to the US Airforce. Technically very bright, he secured an IT position for the US and is working at Brize Norton, Oxfordshire. These are copies of his entry visa, job application, university qualifications, and the DVLA have thrown up his driving licence, and we expect he drives a car, but we don't have that info at the moment.'

Passing around the copies of the documents, the group scanned the information Barry had thus far been able to gather.

'Do we know if he is associated with any group?' asked Leonard.

'Not that I can find. It's early yet, but later today I should get more information. The tax office records show standard pay. I've got a line into the banks to see what his financial status is, along with Land Registry for more information on the property they are living at.'

'We have a couple of weeks. Barry, as much information as you can. Tony, you are going to be on your own with this for a while. I also need you to pick up the Italian who met with Tariq; here's his address and photo,' said Leonard leaning forward and passing a couple of pieces of paper over to Tony. 'We're stretched for the next couple of weeks. These guys. . .' pointing at Mike and Mark and nodding at Rob, 'are engaged elsewhere.'

Glancing at the photo and address, Tony put them in his pocket, looked at Leonard and said, 'We are not actually going to give Nadir the stuff, are we?'

'No,' said Leonard, 'this is new. It's probably a one off by some guy who has a minor grudge with someone at work. I can't see that it's anything major, and we've not had any indications that it will grow into an ongoing threat. Also, it's not like the terrorist bombing at the Israeli embassy that was the Palestinians and was a targeted attack, and obviously it's not the IRA, so for now, follow, gain as much background as you can. Barry will feed you with the information as he gets it. Keep in touch and we will reassess at the end of the week.'

Gathering up his papers, finishing his drink, he was about to stand up.

'I doubt it's a one off,' said Mark.

'Why?' responded Leonard.

'The amount of Semtex he wants is enough for three suicide bombs.'

Chapter 2

Tony sat at his desk, smoking. Early in the morning with no one about, he was thinking about the two meetings, first with Nadir and then with Leonard. Looking at the picture and details of the Italian that Leonard had given him, he folded the paper carefully and put it in his office draw, locking it. *That will have to wait a bit*, he thought, *Nadir needs more attention.* Switching on his computer, cigarette in his mouth, he whipped through some of the emails, responded to a couple, deleted more and then switched it off. He was lucky that he had a great deal of latitude with his day job. Based in Bristol, he covered the area from Manchester through to the Midlands, across the home counties all the way down to Cornwall and then across to Brighton. Most of the UK, in fact, apart from London and the North of England and Scotland, although his bosses were pushing him to cover that as well.

Leonard had been on at him again to join his organisation, but Tony liked being a civilian. His role, gathering intelligence and reporting back to Leonard, gave him the flexibility to do whatever and go wherever he wanted, without having to report his movements on a regular basis.

Anyway, he preferred being on the outside passing information in rather than being on the inside; in his mind it was safer. When he first met Leonard, having been introduced to him by Geoffrey Palmer-Siddley, who attracted the rank of lieutenant general and had initially recruited him several years previously, Leonard had said that he too also reported directly to the home secretary and had told him that his unit, unlike Geoffrey's MI5 section, was rarely scrutinised, and what records there were, were held securely, but after Tony's encounter with Cole a while ago, who had a photograph of him from his file, it had put him off greatly from joining. The less information of him in filing cabinets, or on any computer systems, was the better option as far as he was concerned. Leonard had said that the group had considerable leeway when they were engaged with targets. Whilst no one was above the law, what they needed, at times, was to play dirty. Their objective was to disrupt and remove from the equation the many individuals who targeted the UK with unscrupulous activities like money laundering, sex trafficking, drugs and of course, out and out terrorism. He didn't get paid by Leonard either. They had offered expenses, but Tony had refused. Again, money was traceable, and he didn't want his name anywhere near it. It was, however, getting more and more difficult to resist joining. The amount of time he spent on watching, waiting and following suspects ate into a massive amount of his time in his day job, and with weekends and many nights away, his marriage was on the rocks as well.

*

The door opened. Claire, his secretary, walked in, sniffed the air, tutting.

'I wish you wouldn't smoke in the office,' she said as she walked over to the window and opened it.

Well, we can't have everything we wish for, can we? thought Tony leaning forward and crushing his cigarette out.

'I've gotta go out, be back later.'

'Did you do that report that Jack needed for the director's meeting?'

'Yes, pretty much. I've emailed it to you. Can you just pad it out a bit, give it a polish and add the figures, oh, and shove a conclusion at the back,' he said smiling at her.

'So, you haven't then?'

'It's almost there, and you're better at typing this stuff up than I am,' he replied grabbing his coat and shouldering it on, picking up his keys and cigarettes.

'Give me a ring later if you need anything,' he said walking out of the office.

Getting into his car, he pulled out of the office complex at Bradly Stoke. Newly built, it was designed for the branch offices of bigger companies. Some had a small space attached to the office to allow for supplies distributed to local customers, or some used it as a repair bay. The area was getting busier as industry was growing rapidly around Bristol, and it was fast becoming an excellent feeding point for the south west and Wales. Picking up the M32, he dropped then onto the M4 and headed into London. He wanted to get to Nadir's house, scout the area and see what sort of make up the place had. He hadn't been to Uxbridge for a long time, so no doubt things had changed. Lighting a cigarette, he played out his plan of action for the next 24 hours. The journey to town didn't take long. Swinging onto the M25 north, he came off onto the M40 and then covered the last couple of miles before hitting the turn for Uxbridge. Preferring to walk, he parked up in the Pavilions shopping centre and headed on to the main street. Similar to many suburbs of London, it had had its day, beaten up now with more concrete buildings than necessary. He followed the street till the end and saw the Tube. Next to the Tube station was The Chimes shopping centre, and walking in he saw a café, went in, ordered some tea and toast, sat at the window and watched: shoppers old and young, nothing unusual, just another day. Finishing the tea, he strolled out, crossed the road, lit a cigarette and ambled along the street, glancing occasionally into the windows of a few shops that had remained open despite the competition from the two centres. Taking a left then a right, he entered the street where he knew Nadir to live. Looking up and down the road, non-descript like all the others, it was full of houses, no shops, no alleyways and one small park for kids to play in. The street was on a crossroads linking it to three others, which were all the same, so turning, Tony made his way back to the car.

Navigating the light traffic, he headed into Nadir's road. It was 12:30, not much activity, and as he drove, passing Nadir's house, he turned, circled around two or three other roads and pulled back into the street, pulling up about 150 yards from the entrance to Nadir's property. Facing the house, he guessed that Nadir would drive in from that direction and hunt out a parking space. Barry had told him that he drove a red Peugeot, so Tony settled in. Winding down the window, he picked up the camera, checked the film, focused on the house and fired off a few shots. Satisfied all was in order, he lit a cigarette and settled in for the long wait. Unsure who lived where in the street, anyone who approached the house Tony took a photo of; none yet, however, headed towards the door. It was approaching 3:00 pm when he spotted a woman pushing a pram with a small child in tow heading in the direction of the house. Having seen many women and children that day, he picked up the camera, focussed and took a couple of pictures. Moments later, the woman stopped outside the house and picked up the baby out of the pram. Holding the child in her arms and helping the other young girl towards the door, she opened the front door of the house and went in. Tony, more alert now, pressed the burst button, the camera capturing the event. A minute or two later, the woman re-emerged, disassembled the pram and lifted it into what Tony presumed was the hall and closed the door. *Mrs Al Najaf,* he thought. Winding the camera roll to the end, he changed the film, inserting a new one. Lighting a cigarette, he looked at his watch. *Maybe another couple of hours before Nadir arrives,* he thought.

There was no more activity by the house, and as Tony looked at his watch it was 6:15 pm. *Shouldn't be long now.* At 6:30 pm, a red Peugeot pulled into the street. Hidden, as he was, he watched, camera in hand as the car slowly drove up the street. Spotting an empty space, Tony watched as he slid in. As the driver was getting out, Tony started to take photographs. Nadir! He recognised him, slumping down in his seat, although confident that Nadir would not be looking out for anyone, better to be safe than sorry. Nadir locked the car and walked up to the front of the house, pulling his keys out of his pocket as he did so. Tony hit the burst button again; Nadir disappeared inside. It would be a long night, thought Tony, but as he had planned on staying until the next morning, he would just watch the house punctuated occasionally later by a walk up and down the road to stretch his legs. He saw the light come on in the front room. Deciding they were probably settling in for the night, he reached over onto the back seat and pulled out his flask and sandwiches. Ham and cheese. *For fuck's sake*, he thought as he looked at them, *is that the best you can do*. He'd made them, which made him smile. *Couldn't think of anything else could you, you twat?* the voice echoing in his head.

Movement at the house; Tony straightened in his seat. Nadir had come out of the house and began walking up the street to the corner. Tony got out of his car, locked it and followed. Late night shopping, he thought as he rounded the corner to see Nadir head for the high street. Crossing the road, lighting a cigarette, he too crossed further up, and then, as he entered the high street, he crossed over and began to walk parallel with Nadir. Walking with purpose, Tony guessed it wasn't shopping nor just a walk around. The street was busy with a variety of local people bustling about it, so it was easy for Tony to lose himself on the opposite side to Nadir; confident that he wouldn't be spotted, he kept pace. Nadir took a side street, walked down it, and as Tony dodged the traffic to get to the same side, he saw Nadir stop briefly, open a gate to a townhouse and walk up the path to the front of the house. Looking closely, he watched as Nadir took his shoes off, knocked on the door and moments later was let in. Tony scanned the house: three storeys, basement, no garden, a terraced property, nothing unusual. The curtains of the house were closed, and it looked, as Tony walked past, like the basement was a separate flat to the main house. He also saw that there were several pairs of shoes outside the main front door as well. Looking at his watch, it was just before 7:00 pm. He heard that Muslims took their shoes off when entering a mosque to pray, but this was a house. *Maybe they do that with their friends as well,* thought Tony. Looking around, it was going to be difficult to just stand and wait; there was no obvious place to sit and just standing on the corner would attract attention. Making his way back to the end of the road, Tony spotted a Beefeater pub with a few wooden tables outside. It seemed his best option. Quickly walking to the bar, he ordered a beer. 'Ok to sit outside?'

'Yes, sure, mate, but 9:00 pm we need the glasses back inside, OK?'

'Yeah, no problem,' said Tony picking up his pint and wandering outside.

Selecting a table, he sat and waited, taking a few sips of his lager every now and again and a couple of cigarettes; the hour passed.

Reluctant to go inside and order again, he was in two minds whether he should start to wander up and down the street when he spotted Nadir and three other men leave the house. They split up, and Tony watched as Nadir began to retrace his steps back to his house. Tony followed. A few minutes later, Nadir entered his own house, and Tony went back to his car. Settling down and looking at his watch, he wondered what time Nadir would be up for work. *Brize Norton was about an hour away, so maybe around 7 am, depending on the traffic*, thought Tony, sliding the button on his watch to wake him at 6 am just in case. He would watch the house until the early hours and then drift off to sleep if the area was quiet. Lighting a cigarette and cracking the window, he sat and watched.

Hello, he thought, *here we go again. Where you off to now?* as he watched Nadir come out of his house again. It was 10:50 pm. Nadir set off towards the high street; Tony closed the car door and followed. It was more difficult at this time of night as there were far less people wandering around, so he would have to be careful. Crossing the main road, as he did before, he saw Nadir head in the same direction as last time. A few yards behind and adjacent to him, he watched Nadir turn the corner and approach the house, open the gate, walk up to the door, take his shoes off, knock and then enter. Shaking his head, *What is going on?*

This time, he strolled past the house to the far end of the road. Darkness had crept up on them, and now he had the cover of a few street trees to linger behind. Keeping an eye out up and down the road for anyone who might think his behaviour strange, he leant against one of the trees and waited. Occasionally, he looked at the windows of the other houses in the row – no sign of life – and fortunately it seemed that this street was not a walk-through, so people were few and far between. He didn't have long to wait. Glancing at his watch, it was 11:20 when Nadir appeared, again with the other men. He was too far away to see if they were the same people, but again they split, went their separate ways, and as Nadir turned and headed home, Tony followed. The walk back again took only minutes, but this time, instead of following him down his road, he crossed over and watched Nadir open his front door at a distance. Making his way back to the car, he saw the hall light extinguish in Nadir's house. Settling back in his car, he stayed awake and watched. *Need a crash course in Islam, I think,* thought Tony.

His watch chimed and Tony woke straight away: 6 am. Checking the street for signs of life, he got out of his car and walked to the opposite end of the street to Nadir's house. There were few people around, and as he lit a cigarette, stretching, he wondered what time Nadir would leave. Tony had guessed that if Nadir went to work then he would have to turn his car around and come back up the street, past him and onto the main road. The roads that they were on lead away and would not, or so Tony reasoned, be an easy drive to get to the motorway. Hoping he was right, he waited.

It was 7:15 am. Nadir closed the front door, and Tony slid down in his seat and saw in the mirror Nadir get into his red Peugeot. 'Let's hope I'm right,' he said out loud. Nadir pulled out, went to the bottom of the road and turned right. 'Shit!' said Tony sitting bolt upright in his seat and firing up the engine. Looking in his mirror, he breathed a sigh of relief. Nadir had turned right then reversed and was now coming back down past Tony. Letting him pass, he pulled out, and they both got out onto the main road and headed towards the M40. Picking the motorway up, he headed, as Tony expected, towards Oxford, so he slotted in a few cars back. The journey was easy; most people were coming into town at that time of the day not going out, so traffic was light. Crossing over the M25, and at a steady pace, they journeyed to Oxford. Tony was able to stay close to Nadir as they went round the ring road at Oxford and picked up the A40, which would take them on to Brize Norton. Coming down the slip road of the dual carriageway, Nadir turned left and headed for the base. Tony watched as Nadir went towards the main gate, flash a badge, the barrier lifted, and he went in. Looking at his watch it was 8:40. *A 9 am start then*, thought Tony. *Ok, I'll leave you to it.* Turning his car around, he headed back into London. He needed to make a few calls and hopefully meet up with Barry.

Chapter 3

Scrunching his way up the driveway to Pittville pump rooms in Cheltenham, Tony looked around. He was hoping the person he was meeting was on time and made it obvious that he was waiting for someone. On the steps of the pump room, Tony saw a man who looked slightly foreign, so on approach he caught his eye and said, 'Hi, you Adeem?'

The man smiled. 'Yes.'

The previous evening, Tony had spoken to Barry and requested a meeting with someone who could shed some light on the traditions or beliefs of the origins of Islam and being a Muslim. Within hours, Tony took the call and was told to meet with Adeem, who fortuitously was in Cheltenham.

'He works in the area. We know him well, so he can give you the heads up.'

Works in the area, thought Tony. *There's only one place in Cheltenham that Barry or Leonard could get a man that quick.*

'Nice to meet you, and, really, thanks for your time at short notice,' said Tony.

'Hey, no problem, nice to get out of the office.' Adeem Luman, 28 years old, born in Leicester, graduated top of his class at Aston University in Birmingham and was spotted and quickly recruited. An Arabic speaker, an ideal translator embedded now within GCHQ.

'Please excuse my ignorance, but I need to understand the typical Muslim way of life. Not in-depth, but routines, essential beliefs, practices, that sort of thing. My exposure to religion is getting drunk at a couple of weddings and crashing round a cemetery after a wake, so that's about as close as I've ever got to any religious knowledge. I went to Sunday school as a kid, but that didn't last.'

Adeem laughed, 'Yeah, sure, no problem.'

'Let's walk. So, being a Muslim means your sole purpose in life is to worship Allah, the creator. The Muslin statement of faith is, 'There is no God except Allah, and Muhammad is his servant and messenger. Anyone who believes this is a Muslim. Since worshipping God, worshipping Allah, is the means of showing gratitude for having been created, anyone who refuses to believe this is a Kafir, literally "ungrateful",' began Adeem.

Continuing, as they both walked across the grass down the slight incline towards the small lake in the middle of Pittville Park, circling the lake, the information kept coming, Tony listening intently, especially when Adeem began to explain the prayers.

'You may have seen on films or TV the tall building with a man calling out. In dominant Muslim countries he is calling people to prayer. Obviously, in places like America and the UK, which aren't dominant Muslim countries, you don't see those or hear them, but Muslims go to prayer five times a day.'

'That's a lot. What about work?'

'Many work places these days allow Muslims to break away and pray in maybe a quiet office, or some companies have set aside dedicated rooms. Of course, with a lot of the younger people, they don't pray as much; it doesn't mean they don't believe it just means that they have adopted a different way of praying to Allah.'

Tony nodded.

'In Muslim communities they go to prayer at what the western world calls a mosque; we call it a masjid. Everyone is welcome, even someone like you, Tony,' said Adeem smiling. 'We welcome everyone. The masjid can take many forms; it doesn't have to be a purpose-built building like you may have seen, it can be as simple as a house, it will all depend on the local neighbourhood and density of Muslims within that area.'

Crossing the road, they continued the walk around the small lake, which contained a small boathouse. As Tony looked there were several people enjoying themselves, although some were having a bit of difficulty rowing in a few small boats.

'In the community, the main masjid will attract the majority of Muslims. Over time, more will go, donate money for instance, and then the bigger ones will be a purpose-built facility, and many will also have a school or education centre built with them. A bit like your Sunday school. The aim is to help educate local Muslim children about the religion, talk about Allah, their place in the world and teach from the Qur'an. You following me so far?'

'Yes, very interesting, thanks. Go on.'

'Sounds easy, doesn't it? Straightforward, a community praying to Allah as one.'

Tony nodded, 'I take it it's not?'

'Sadly no, it has evolved over the years and there are several different factions of Islam. The two main ones are Sunni and Shia. Most Muslims are one or the other; however, there are others, Deobandis and Barelvis, Wahhabis, Salafi and extremists and more. In real basic terms, each one has a different way of delivering Allah's message. That is really basic, but it's the easiest way I can explain it. It's such a complex and diverse religion now and would take days to understand it completely, if you ever did that is.'

'Bloody hell,' said Tony lighting a cigarette, offering one to Adeem.

'No thanks.'

'OK, so talk to me a bit about the extremists.'

'I thought that would be of interest. OK, it's very important to remember though that of the 600,000 Muslims or so in Britain it is, or would be, an incredibly small percentage that are extremist, if at all, and the ones that are, again, an incredibly small proportion of them would actually cause harm. It's always the way, the smallest always get the biggest coverage.'

'I agree with you there.'

'The way it happens is that a disgruntled person attends the local masjid, maybe for the first time, or has been a member for some time. There are people within the masjid that are on the lookout for someone unusual. Once they see one, they will approach them, not in the masjid but later maybe on the walk home. It's done discreetly, trying to identify what the issue is. It could be that they want to have that person in their group. They may be unhappy with the teachings, for instance, and want to develop the religion in a different way. There are many reasons for someone not to be happy with the current masjid. If it's a younger person, their ideals are no longer in sync with the elders etc. The person may be approached by several different sects. At some point, if he hasn't moved to another masjid etc., he may, and I stress may, be approached by one of the extremist factions. I must say again, it's very rare but may occur. He will be invited to pray at this recruit's masjid, which almost always will be a house away from the main masjid. He will be encouraged to talk about his views such as how the west is oppressing the Muslim communities, or families, or way of life, etc. It could be a deep-seated hatred for another country or capitalism, etc. In extreme circumstances, this leads to action. It is fair to say though that, let's say a young man disillusioned by whatever has already taken the step of resolving his issue in some form or another. The role of those around him feed on this, exacerbating the issues and pushing for him to come to a conclusion, dangerously, which is what we have seen in some Arabic countries; he becomes a suicide bomber.'

Tony stopped, looked at Adeem. 'It's a bit extreme, isn't it?'

'It is, but it's about belief. The person doing it believes that they go on to paradise. They become a Shahid or Martyr and live a full life with Allah. The other thing to note when

27

it comes to suicide bombers is that they are not interested in killing one person. They don't target a man or woman, it's a whole or group, as many as they can, sadly.'

'I had no idea that it was that complex.'

'It is, and I've only really given you a layman's intro to it. I've glossed over and shortened many aspects to try and give you an impression of the religion, which I hope has been of use. Please do take into consideration though that it is only a small, and I say very small, minority who can cause problems; the rest of the Muslim community, like Christians, Buddhists, Catholics, etc. just go about their daily lives.'

'I will, and thanks, that's brilliant. Appreciate your time,' said Tony.

'Gotta get back to the office now. Nice to meet you. Take care.'

Tony waved as Adeem crossed the last few yards of the park and onto the main Prestbury road and set off in the direction of the town.

'Fuck me,' said Tony lighting up another cigarette. 'Think I need to know more about Nadir's masjid.'

Walking back up the park and out of the driveway he had come into, Tony climbed into the van. It was a bit battered with an old builder's logo half scrubbed out on the side. He turned the key and headed out of Cheltenham, down the A40 and back towards Uxbridge. He was surprised by the information Adeem had given him. He'd read about suicide bombers, of course. A lot were against the Israeli soldiers and of course, Iraq, but to think that someone over here may do it was worrying. It obviously raised several questions.

Clearly, Nadir wanted explosives, and Tony guessed he was going to target the base, but the questions were why so much and who would be building the bomb? Nadir had said that someone else would be doing it. The journey took just over an hour, so Tony pulled into the street where he now assumed that the house Nadir was going to twice a night was a masjid. Midday gave him the opportunity of selecting a space in the busy street. Many of the cars had gone for the day but would be back later, all vying for that spot outside their homes. Parking on the opposite side of the road, about 75 yards down, he reversed up to part of the kerb where it jutted out a couple of yards, narrowing the street a bit to allow pedestrians to cross. This way, no one could park directly behind him blocking his view. Pushing the curtain aside, Tony squeezed between the two front seats and, half standing, walked to the back of the van. There were a couple of bench seats either side of a small, bracketed table, which he could put his camera on. Sitting, he picked up the camera, zoomed in and focussed on the house: a good clear view of the street and the house. The windows in the back of the van were one-way. He had checked when he picked the van up from Rob, getting him to sit inside with Tony peering in to see if he could make him out, which he couldn't, to his relief. The van, dirty enough but not shabby enough to arouse suspicion, was a great surveillance vehicle. As Tony looked around, he could make use of this again, he thought.

The house was similar to the one that Nadir was in; however, this street was less affluent by the looks of it, a lot dirtier. A couple of the houses were boarded up and one at the bottom had scaffolding around it. *Bit of a refurb*, thought Tony. There was no movement at the house. The street was quiet with just a few people about, a couple of mums with pushchairs but nothing else. Tony took photos of everyone who came into the street, and the houses as well. About 2:50 pm Tony spotted two men coming up from the bottom end of the road. Hitting the burst, he caught both of them and then focussed in and got good photos of their faces. He watched. They stopped at the house, opened the gate and walked towards the front door. Tony hit the burst button as the men removed their shoes and went into the house. *So, there's a least four now then, one as a minimum in the house plus these three.* Waiting, camera ready, he looked at his watch: 3:00 pm. *No more*, he thought. The men appeared to be about the same age, maybe slightly older than Nadir. When they got the photos developed, they would have a better idea.

Tony waited; 20 minutes passed then there were signs of life at the door. More photos as the men left, returning the way they came. *So, who is in the house?* The angle didn't allow him to see who had opened the door. It would be difficult, thought Tony as he looked up the road, to get a spot where he could see in but that would not compromise him. Tony pursed his lips. *There must be a way*, he reasoned.

Thinking about what Adeem had told him, he had said five times a day, so if correct, then judging by that, Nadir visited the other day at 7:00 pm and 11:00 pm. With these two at 3:00 pm, then I should see Nadir back here at

7:00 pm and then tomorrow morning at 7:00 and 11:00 am with these three again if Nadir goes to work. Four hours apart gives them the five visits. . . the questions and answers were going through his mind.

Parting the curtain to see if anyone was approaching, he pushed the curtain and slid between the front seats into the driver's seat. Opening the door and closing it carefully, he walked down the road away from the house. Halfway down he lit a cigarette, deep in thought. Earlier, he had decided that he couldn't smoke in the van. Can't have a cloud of smoke escaping when he opened the door, he'd laughed to himself. Rounding the corner, making his way up to the main road, he went into a small shop, picked up a couple of drinks, chocolate bar and a packet of crisps. He had a sandwich in the van. Stretching his legs and having another couple of fags, after having a half hour break or so, he made his way back and slipped back into his den for the night.

It started to rain. Glad that he'd gone out before it started – he'd forgotten his raincoat so he would have got drenched – he wondered if the rain would put the visits off. Dismissing the idea as quickly as it had come, doubt it, if you are that committed to religion then the weather doesn't really matter. And true to thought just before 7:00 pm, with camera in full flow, he captured first the three men, again walking together, and then a few minutes later Nadir came into view. Snapping him as he went up to the house, his shoes were taken off and he was let in. This time it was 20 minutes, and the three men left together, parting at the end of the street with Nadir heading back home.

Tony munched his sandwich and swigged one of the drinks. Activity in the street had gone quiet again, and with a few streetlamps along the pavement this was the only light that shone briefly on the walkers. As time had moved on, Tony had become adept at capturing their images in the best light the second or so anyone was under the streetlamp.

It was 10:50 pm. Both men appeared, and as they rounded the corner Nadir joined them. Again, their time at the house was around 15 minutes and then back home.

Tony waited. The house was lit, as much as he could make out, the curtains drawn but cracked enough to show a light on. Around midnight the hall light came on briefly, an upstairs light and then the house went into darkness. *That was quick*, thought Tony, *my guess is that there is only one person in there.*

Awake early, Tony nipped out for a quick fag and then settled in, camera in hand. He didn't have long to wait. Same routine, three men, no Nadir this time, 7 am, and after 20 minutes they both left. Tony contemplated. He had to leave at some point today to get the photos over to Barry and get them developed. It was midweek, so assuming they got the info back later today, maybe tomorrow, they would know who the men were. However, he wanted to get a photo of whoever was in the house. *I'll give it till 11*, thought Tony, *if he's not out by then maybe I'll get lucky later this afternoon or tomorrow.*

Time passed, the street got busy, more photos of the people, some now he recognised but took their picture anyway. The street emptied as workers went about their business. As Tony watched, a builder's van pulled up at the end house; a couple of guys got out and went into the house with the scaffolding on. More pictures of the van, the reg and the people. *Builds a picture,* thought Tony.

Approaching 11 am, and with no sign of the occupant of the house, Tony took some last few pictures of the two men, same as before entering the house. Sliding into the driver's seat, he pulled out and headed over to drop the pictures and report to Barry.

Chapter 4

The private plane landed at Geneva airport, taxied to its allocated bay and pulled to a halt. The door dropped open, and with stairs immediately connected the three men disembarked. Onlookers, if any, would not have given them a second glance. Smart suits and ties, one carrying an attaché case, distinguishing them as non-other than businessmen, who could only be detected by prior knowledge of their arrival. Ushered through the first-class area by passing customs, they were escorted to the Range Rover waiting for them at the airport arrival terminal. Settling in, the driver pulled out and wound his way through the one-way system and onto the main road. Ignoring signs for Geneva, the driver set off north onto the E62 heading towards Lausanne. On the approach to Lausanne, the driver swept up and then onto the motorway signed for Montreux. This part of the journey was one of the most scenic routes, close to the lake and in and out of many tunnels along the way. In the summer, looking over towards the mountains' endless waterfalls cascading down into the tributaries, their journey's end, Lake Geneva was a beautiful sight. The men in the car, however, were quiet, deep in thought, and the scenery passed without a glance. Passing Montreux, the driver watched for signs for Villeneuve, which was only a few miles further on. Pulling off onto the local road, he went through the town and made for Port-Valais. Passing through the port and onto a private road adjacent to the lake, the Range Rover crunched over the gravel until they emerged in front of a beautiful 14th century castle situated next to the lake. Built in 1380, it had guarded this part of the lake for centuries until falling into disrepair. Refurbished by an affluent Swiss family in 1780, it stayed in the family until just after the First World War when the last of the family line had died out. In the hands of the local port authority, it wasn't until the late 1950s when it was acquired by an international hotel chain, who spent several million renovating the property. Changing hands and refurbished again in the early 1980s, it offered stunning views of the lake, superior rooms, high class dining and full spa treatments to the discerning guests. Boasting only 25 rooms of the utmost quality, the waiting list was long; offering a discreet and professional service, it was never out of demand. Waiting on the stone steps of the entrance were two butlers, and as the car came to a halt, they stepped down, opened the doors and welcomed their guests.

Their stay would be brief: one night only. Checking into their respective rooms and with luggage delivered, dinner was set for 7:00 pm, so it allowed the men to relax and catch up from their flight. The total journey of 14 hours with a change at Dubai was tiring but comfortable. Tomorrow evening, however, they would be flying from Geneva over to the United Kingdom then onwards to the United States, which was a considerably longer journey. They had been informed that their dinner guests for the evening had already arrived. The three men, dressed impeccably, walked the short distance from their rooms, through the foyer and into the reception area, where they were guided to a private dining room. Located away from the main dining area, confidentiality was assured.

The concierge opened the door, and the three men entered the room.

'Buona sera, Signor Rostami.'

Aronne Biscotti, with a big smile on his face, walked forward and held out his hand.

'Nice to see you again, my friend.'

Kamran Rostami smiled. 'You too, my friend.' Clasping Aronne's hand, Biscotti, out of deference to Rostami, avoided the obligatory kiss on the cheeks and instead put his other hand on the man's elbow and shook his hand. Rostami introduced his colleagues. Biscotti, courteous as ever, was accompanied by two other men: Angelo Fonda from the Genoa region and Fabio Di Pietro of Rome, both of whom headed large and powerful 'Ndrangheta families. Introductions made, the six men sat at the round table in the centre of the room. A waiter had appeared and delivered a variety of drinks to the men, soft for some and a selection of white and red wine for others. Small talk ensued. All the men had known each other for about four years, so the conversation was light and friendly; centred mainly around family, holidays and sport, the meal passed. Once dinner was finished, the six men rose and selected one of the many comfortable leather chairs, which were arranged so each man could see the other but not too distant for the conversation not to be heard. On placing coffee on the small occasional tables, and a refresh of the brandy for some, the waiters left, closing the door behind them, one of whom stood in front of the door to dissuade anyone who may venture to go inside.

'And on the subject of business,' began Biscotti, 'we are happy for the arrangements to continue should that be satisfactory to yourselves.'

Placing his cup down, Rostami nodded. 'As you know, we face an uncertain future and a difficult period in our lives, once again due to the Americans and many other western countries. Our allies support us well, but as you are aware, we are constantly under pressure, both technologically and financially.'

Biscotti listened; he knew what was coming. He had no interest in international politics but knew that the man in front of him would use it as an excuse.

'I will be to the point, an increase of 7% is graciously requested from the beginning of September.'

Biscotti sat for a moment. They had discussed it between them before Rostami had arrived and they had agreed that he would do the negotiation. Nodding, he learnt forward and picked up his coffee.

'I sympathise with you and your colleagues, and your nation as a whole. Having a constant battle against your beliefs and integrity is both challenging and, in many cases, unnecessary; it can be a cruel and unjust world we live in today.' Biscotti's tone was sombre and hopefully, he thought, sincere.

'We too have seen the world change along with our markets and demand to such an extent that we would like to have an increase in our shipments, and as a sign of our friendship we would like to suggest an uplift of five percent to yourselves.'

Rostami smiled. 'How many more shipments were you considering?'

'It will be an extra one a month.'

'Well, I have to make additional arrangements, as you know, so may I suggest that we could agree on six and a half percent?'

With a few moments' pause, Biscotti nodded.

'Excellent, we have an agreement.'

Standing, both men shook hands, and with Fonda and Di Pietro standing, all six men shook hands in agreement.

'It has, as always, been a pleasure to meet you, and I look forward to seeing you again. We must retire now as our flight is tomorrow morning.'

'Are you flying back to Tehran?' asked Biscotti.

'No, not this time, we are going to America. My duty as foreign affairs minister for Iran is to admonish, in no uncertain terms, the Americans for the travesty their sanctions are having on my people.'

With the door closed behind them, Biscotti walked over to the bar and poured himself a glass of Chianti Classico. Pointing the bottle at the other two, who nodded in agreement, he filled two more glasses and passed them over. Sitting back in the chair, he said,

'Better than we thought.'

'Si, I thought he would start at 10 percent,' said Fabio. 'He makes it sound as if the money he gets goes into the country's coffers. What bollocks, into his and his cronies' pockets more like. Wonder if the big man, Mr Ayatollah, gets any?'

'Fucking unlikely. Anyway, glad he didn't link it with the new shipments,' said Angelo.

'Well six and a half percent is OK. We can pass that on, and given the amount we can now ship, it more than compensates for the extra.'

'Route's staying the same?' asked Fabio.

'I think so, no reason to change. Our drivers are familiar with the route, and I believe some of them know the border guards quite well, so an extra lorry every month won't make any difference, and when Rostami gets back he will issue the new orders, so we have plenty of time to make additional shipping arrangements,' said Aronne. A steady supply of heroin into Europe would make them the dominant player.

Rostami and his colleagues touched down at Heathrow, collected their bags and headed through the main concourse where they were collected by private car and taken into central London. He had no need to inform Biscotti of his short visit to London as it may have invited questions he did not want asked. Checking in to the Connaught that evening, they dined in the restaurant and retired early as their plane for the States left at 2:00 pm the following day. Preferring to stay at the Connaught than at the embassy, they were less likely to be spotted. Although UK customs would have documented their arrival, they attracted no attention, so little more than a cursory welcome at passport control allowed the three men through without difficulty.

The building, situated near Hatton Court, was non-descript. Apart from the cameras at the front, a standard wooden double door and a plaque on the side of the façade gave little to indicate its operation. Rostami was expected, and as he exited the cab the door opened for him

'Good morning, sir,' said the doorman.

Rostami nodded, smiled. 'Good morning.'

'This way please,' said the doorman walking Rostami the few paces to a young lady who stood behind a small high-top desk which consisted of a single computer screen and telephone.

'Good morning, sir. Welcome back.'

'Thank you.'

Placing the receiver down, 'He will be with you in a moment,' she said.

Rostami looked around the high vaulted ceiling, marble floor and ornate staircase; it was bright and glistened. The few statues and paintings on the walls were of high value and artistically placed, and as he stood back slightly from the woman he saw Graham Williams, head of international banking, coming down the staircase.

'Good morning,' his hand held out.

Rostami shook his hand.

'Please, this way.'

On the first floor the decoration was subtle and expensive.

Graham opened the door to his office and the two men made themselves comfortable.

'Coffee?' Graham enquired as his secretary entered.

'Thank you.'

Small talk passed the time before the coffee arrived, and as Graham took his first sip he said,

'The money has been deposited as usual.'

'Excellent, I would like the distribution and these amounts to go to these organisations,' he said as he pulled a small piece of paper from his pocket.

Graham looked at the list and nodded. 'Of course.'

Preferring to hand write and personally give the list to Graham, it reduced the possibility of any electronic intrusion and was substantially more deniable should the need arise.

Years ago, the list would have contained the Baader-Meinhoff Group, the ETA and the IRA; now the groups were more left-wing and anti-establishment, white supremacists such as splinter groups from Combat 18. Graham and the bank had no qualms about distributing the money. It wasn't up to them who their clients supported. They got their fees, which on occasion, thought Rostami, were quite steep, but they had always done as he had asked, so he was prepared to pay. Sanctions on his country were high and constant. It annoyed his leaders that the west wanted to push their agenda politics and rules on them, ignoring their beliefs and traditions. Fighting back by either tying up expensive police time with demonstrations and riots or overwhelming the hospital services with drug addicts was, as far as he was concerned, well worth the money he spent on these groups and, of course, allowing the Italians to prosper, as they thought, through the growth of heroin addiction.

The border crossing between Zaranj Afghanistan and Milak Iran was always busy. Wars may rage, factions may fight and ideologists have rancour with moderates, but business is business, and the two countries rarely closed the border, allowing trade to flow both ways. Checks and balances were always in place. Security was an issue, and illegal commodities were always on the agenda of the border forces, but that was the same with almost all countries around the world that bordered each other. Iran and Afghanistan were no different, the only difference was the transport; most of the lorries and containers that traversed the line were worn out, battered, old and tired. Bribes were common, heads turning the other way, and on occasions passport and documentation checks were non-existent. The world has to turn, people need to be fed, companies must generate an income; in this part of the world rigid rules don't always apply. Getting through the border was normally not a problem, the problems, should they occur, were on the journey.

Jaah Haji had done the journey many times. Him and his brother swapped each month. Along with their regular routes, this one took them from their core base at Farah. They travelled the length and breadth of Afghanistan, delivering whatever their boss got hold of and wanted moved. They knew they weren't the only ones he used, but they were both trusted, and on the monthly journey like this he needed someone who not only knew the route but had built up a rapport with the border guards both in his country and their neighbour Iran. The route took him south, out of the estate, where in the dead of night the cargo had been loaded into his container, hooked up and was ready for him in the morning. As usual, there was no one around, and as he turned out onto the dusty barren road, he settled in for an easy ride.

Approaching the crossing, he pulled behind about 15 other lorries and waited his turn; outward bound very little checks were made. Edging forward, he approached the covered passport border check, handing over his papers and tatty passport, both of which were given a cursory glance; he was waved on. Driving through, he followed the road of the gated area and pulled up in front of the Iranian border control. Handing papers over again, he nodded at the guard, one of ten different people he knew. The guard glanced at him and switched his look to the orange square sticker on the windshield before looking at the papers Jaah had given him. Nodding, he hit the button of his console, the gate lifted up and Jaah, selecting first, drove into Iran. About 200 yards further, he passed the concrete single story glass fronted building of the Iranian anti-narcotics border police division. A few cars were parked outside, but he knew he was unlikely to be stopped. Whilst the division was manned by experienced officers, border stops were rare unless they had a tip off, but even then, unless there were at least 20 or 30 of them, nothing would happen. Over the last few years, several thousand anti-narcotics police had been killed by criminals hell bent on getting their illegal substances into and through Iran, so they now only stopped trucks if there were plenty of them and they were well-armed.

A few hundred yards further on, Jaah pulled into the large truck stop and swung his lorry and trailer past several containers on beds and came to a stop next to a dull red Mack truck. Customised by Asghar Ghandchi, the father of Iran's heavy truck industry, the lorry was designed specially to conquer the Iranian terrain. Jumping out, he wound down the front frame, which held the container bed, uncoupled the wires connecting the lights, brakes and indicators and slid the cab forward, disengaging himself from the trailer. Next to the Mack was another trailer, which had been left for him. Backing into and coupling up, clipping on the lines, winding up the supporting legs, he pulled forward and headed back out of the stop onto the highway and back towards the border.

On seeing Jaar come and go on schedule, Rocio Mir finished his coffee and stepped into the baking hot sun. The day had started hot, and at this time of year he wished he had had air conditioning in his cab. Starting the engine of the big Mack, he backed it up and under the trailer that Jaar had left. Moments later, he was on the road with a slight detour north to Zabol, where he would pick up the main transient road across the mountainous region to Bam then onto Jiroft before finally heading into the city of Bandarabbass and the container shipping port. With the orange plastic symbol on his windscreen, he was confident that he would be able to do the whole journey and go into the port without being stopped. The orange symbol on the cab gave him a virtual free pass to travel unhindered. He had been stopped a couple of times over the years, but it had been mainly by new zealous cops who had wanted to make a name for themselves. They were, however, quickly reined in by their colleagues. Rocio had no idea how much they were paid to leave him alone, but whatever it was certainly worked.

Rocio had lived in Iran all his life; his mother was Italian, and he had been to her hometown of Naples a few times when he was a child. Also, when he was old enough to drive, his uncle on his mother's side had taught him and helped him get his certificate to drive trucks. His father, Malik, was Iranian and had met his mother in the late '60s, a time of great prosperity for his father's company. He'd had a carpet manufacturing plant and had sold his carpets across Europe, and it was on one of his many trips that he had met his mother in Italy. The company had suffered greatly when Ayatollah Khomeini came to power, and as his father wasn't connected in any way to the Ayatollah or knew any of his close circle, he had lost his business. Rocio and his two brothers all worked the trucks now and took it in turns to do the journey he was on. It took him all day to do the 400 miles or so to the port, and as the sun began to set, Rocio pulled up to the entry port of the customs. Handing in his documentation, the barrier lifted, and he made the familiar trip across the well-worn concrete concourse and waited in line; his container would be lifted at 8:00 pm, so lighting a cigarette, Rocio settled in for the wait.

Chapter 5

Tony took out a packet of cigarettes from his pocket, opened it and shook one out. *Must give these up,* he thought. Putting it in his mouth and lighting, inhaling deeply then letting the smoke drift from his mouth he remembered the first time he had had a cigarette. He had come home from school and didn't have a key, so he had to sit on the doorstep and wait for his mother to come at about 6:00 pm. After a couple of days of doing this the old lady next door had seen him and invited him in. She was the butcher's wife and had the shop next door to his mother. He'd seen her a few times when they had gone in for some meat. She made him a cup of tea and they had sat in the kitchen drinking. He couldn't remember what they talked about, but she smoked like a trooper and had offered him a fag, No.6, small and acrid tasting, but he'd got used to it. Every day after that, during the week, he would go into her house, have a tea, a few fags and wait. She didn't seem to care that he was smoking. He'd had one of her old man's fags once, a Players, but that was too much so he stuck to the No.6. When he was 14, he'd started a Saturday job then could afford his own. He'd seen an ad on the TV for cigarettes in a gold packet and fancied those: Sovereigns. They were small and cheap; they didn't last long though, so he graduated to Benson and Hedges and had stuck with those ever since. He glanced at the packet still in is hand. *Only a couple left, nearly out, better get some more,* he thought.

The journey up to Whitechapel was easy enough. Traffic through London was always a bit of a challenge, but the cars moved eventually, and it wasn't long before he pulled off Whitechapel high street, driving up Commercial Street, noticing the Ten Bells pub on the corner of Fournier Street as he did. Rumoured to be the watering hole of some of Jack the Ripper's victims, passing this, he turned right into Hanbury Street, catching sight of a small group of people on a Ripper tour who were just about to look at the sight of the murdered Annie Chapman, the Ripper's second victim. Just 48 years old, divorced and forced to live and sleep where she could, during the later years of her life the streets of Whitechapel were home to many like her. The murder, by slashing her throat, was immediately linked to the first murder, which panicked many in the area forcing the police to start a hunt for a serial killer. Five women in total were linked to the Ripper, and although never found there are plenty of conspiracy theories as to who the killer was, even to this day. Following the road, he turned left into Spital Road and then sharp right into Woodseer Street. Pulling up, he watched the mirror. No one had followed, so he jumped out of the van, locked it up and made his way down Daplyn Street, through the alley back onto Hanbury and then it was a short walk to the terraced townhouse. No different from the rest, he passed the house on the opposite side of the road, walked to the end and lit a cigarette on the corner. Glancing around him, he crossed over and made his way back up the steps, and as he did so the front door opened, and he walked in.

'Hello Barry.'

'Hello, mate, how you doing? We're in the back room.'

Sliding his coat off, he saw Leonard sat at the table looking through a folder with an array of pictures; sitting down, Barry joined them. Leonard offered a few photos to Tony.

'These are OK. Still don't know who they are, but the quality is good.'

'These. . .' said Tony reaching into his pocket, 'are the latest. There is a pattern to the visits to Nadir's masjid.' Tony ran through his watch on Nadir and the house he frequented, the people who came and went and also that he had followed him to his place of work.

'We know who owns the house now,' said Leonard. 'It's part of a foundation; we are checking who they are. An Arli Jassim lives there alone. We will get more information, but we are having to be careful not to rattle any cages at this stage.'

Pushing the photos back into the file and sliding the rolls of film over to Barry,

'I've not seen this Arli; he doesn't come out. What we doing about Nadir then?' said Tony.

'Arrange to meet him again and stall.'

'We're not giving him the stuff, are we?'

'No, that's far too dangerous. We may have to give a dummy package, but we are not convinced that Nadir will know what he is looking at when he gets it, so we can get away with that. What we need to know is who the bomb-maker is. We do, however, now think he is for real.'

Tony looked at Leonard.

'How do you mean?'

'Nadir Al Najaf comes from a small village in Iraq. He recently went back there for the funeral of his broth-ers,' said Leonard looking at his notes. 'Al Diwaniyah, just outside of.

His brothers Tamil and Malik were hit, we believe, by an American air strike whilst they were out delivering, or picking up, arms destined for a new Islamic breakaway group called Al Qaeda. The Americans got wind of a delivery and took them, and the supplier, out somewhere in the moun-tains near the Iran Iraq border. Al Qaeda, by all accounts, have been around for a few years, but it seems that they are becoming, or would like to become, a dominant force in the war against America. Run by a guy call Bin Laden. Anyway, we now see Nadir as a credible threat and need to know who the bombmaker is.'

'Meet with him again, and this time stall, but push for his timeline and see if he knows when and where either the bomb, or bombs, are going to be made and when and who is going to do it.'

'That's a big ask given that last time I didn't really want to know anything.'

'You can sort it,' said Leonard rising from the table.

'Tell Barry when you have the information and then we will meet again.'

Tony watched as he left; looking at Barry, Barry said, 'We need to know.'

He'd arranged to meet Nadir at the Holiday Inn at Heathrow. The huge hotel was always busy and no one ever took any notice of who was passing through. The bars, rest areas, rooms and reception were constantly busy all day and most of the night, travellers coming and going, most with a one night stop over, frequenting the bars or lounges. The lounges typically were for meetings, businessmen and women either on their way out or brief meetings for those with onwards travel. It was an ideal spot to meet Nadir. The lounge was scattered with a single comfy chaise, tables, settees, some grouped so five or six people could meet, some pairs and others, just singles, to allow the tired commuter a respite between travel to grab a coffee and catch up on the papers. When Tony arrived, the area was about a third full, and he selected a couple of chairs with a coffee table near the window and a reasonable distance from the next table. Ordering two coffees, he waited, casually making a mental note of everyone in the room, looking for any obvious signs of being watched himself. It was unlikely, but Leonard had impressed upon him that you cannot be too careful.

He looked at his watch as his coffee arrived: a few minutes to the hour. He expected Nadir to be punctual, and as he poured sugar and milk into his coffee cup, he glanced up and saw Nadir coming into the room. Standing and catching his eye, he waited as Nadir circumvented the tables and chairs and shook hands with him as he made the table.

'Hi, nice to meet you again,' said Tony amicably.

Nadir nodded, taking his hand, 'And you.'

Tony looked at him; he appeared nervous.

'I've got you some coffee,' Tony said sitting. 'Not sure if you want milk and sugar but they're here if you want. So how have you been?'

'Have you got what I want?'

'Don't worry,' said Tony as he watched Nadir looking around. 'I've checked them out. No one is watching, which is why I wanted to meet you here. It's a big place and no one will take any notice. Have some coffee,' he continued, picking up his own cup.

'How's the family?' continued Tony.

Nadir looked at Tony. 'I didn't know I told you I had a family.'

'We covered a lot when we met in the restaurant, a baby you said, and a daughter.'

'Yes, they are fine, thank you. Do you want the money now? I have brought it for you.'

'No, not at the moment. I wouldn't bring what you wanted to an open place like this. I wanted to make sure that you are still OK to have it, it's not something that is normally requested and sometimes people change their minds.'

Nadir looked annoyed. 'I thought we were doing business,' he said quietly but with a hard tone.

'We are, but I have to be cautious. Tell me, when do you need it by? I do have it,' said Tony raising a reassuring hand, 'but I don't want you to keep it lying around for several months just in case something goes wrong. When do you plan to use it?'

Nadir thought for a moment. Not unreasonable, he surmised, it's a dangerous explosive and even he was worried about carrying it around, although he knew that at some point, he would have to.

'When does your man arrive to make it up for you?' pressed Tony

'He will be here next month. I want to have everything in place by the time he arrives. I'm not telling you where I need it for,' he added quickly.

'That's fine. I don't want to know where, that's nothing to do with me. I just want to make sure that when you've got it it doesn't fall into the wrong hands. Are you sure you need this much? It seems a lot for one.'

'It's not just me.' Nadir looked at him. *The last time we met you weren't interested and now all of a sudden you want to know everything,* he began to think.

Tony saw the look and the change of posture.

'Ok,' said Tony finishing his coffee. 'Ring me in the week at any time and tell me where we meet and at what time that day. I'll bring it and then we are done, OK. You happy with that?'

Nadir wasn't expecting that, but for him to arrange the exchange reassured him.

'I will,' said Nadir standing, holding out his hand.

Tony took it and smiled.

Naive, thought Tony, *he's out of his depth.*

Pulling the van up six or seven car lengths from the opposite side of the house, Tony climbed into the van and checked the curtains were secure. Peering out, he picked up his camera and fired off a couple of shots to get the focus and to make sure the camera was working OK. He'd heard that there were some decent digital cameras on the market now, which didn't require rolls of film. *Should be interesting*, he thought. *Someone had said that you could take hundreds of pictures without running out. Will have to check them out, would save a lot of time*, he thought. Looking at his watch it was 5:30 pm. Leaning back against the side of the van, he adjusted the cushion behind his back, opened the flask and poured himself a cup of tea. He expected that the visitors would be the same as before and arrive at the same time, and true to form, a few minutes before 7:00 pm he saw the two men walking up the street towards the house. Capturing their walk, he shifted his eye line and waited for Nadir. A moment later, Nadir came round the corner, and he too headed for the house. Tony waited. *No one else visiting tonight by the looks of it, but better check*, came the command in his head. Checking the mirrors, the street was empty, and taking a quick look at the properties and the windows, there was no sign of life, so he got out of the van and set off towards the house. Lighting a cigarette as he went, passing the house, he counted the pairs of shoes, got to the corner, crossed over and returned to the van. *Just the two and Nadir*, he thought.

Looking at his watch, he saw the men leave, got off a few shots and again settled in to wait. It was 10:50 pm, and the men returned once again. Twenty minutes later all three left, so Tony focussed his attention on the house. At about 11:30, like last time, he saw the hall light come on, then the bedroom light, then the hall light switch off, and a few minutes later so did the bedroom light; the house went into darkness. Tony set the alarm on his watch just in case he drifted off: 3:00 am.

The quiet buzz: Tony was instantly awake. He'd tried to stay awake and had dozed a few times, been out for a walk, had a fag; the last hour had dragged but he was alert now. Drinking some water, he scoured the street; no sign of life, so he moved to the front of the van between the driver's seat and the back, parted the curtain slightly and again looked up and down the street: all quiet. Getting out, he walked quickly across the street and down the cellar steps of Nadir's masjid, confident that even if someone saw him, they wouldn't suspect given his confident walk straight to the house and down the stairs. The door was easy, straightforward Yale lock, which Tony picked in seconds. Quietly opening the door, he stepped into a small hallway and closed the door behind him and waited. He hadn't seen any cameras, nor any alarms, but if there was an alarm, he would hear movement above him. Breathing shallow, he waited: nothing. Pulling out of his pocket a small pencil thin torch, he switched it on and surveyed the area before him. The light picked up the corridor to a set of stairs leading to the house above. On his right was a door, and further down the passage he could make out two other doors as well. Turning the handle of the nearest door, he opened it and shone the torch inside and stepped in. Closing the door behind him, he carefully looked around the room. It was small, smaller than he thought it might be. There was a camp bed in the corner made up. A dresser, wardrobe, table and chair, a mirror. Basic furniture, enough for one person. The dresser proved empty as did the wardrobe. Satisfied nothing was there, Tony opened the door and moved quietly along the passageway to the next door; a quick shine of the torch up the stairs illuminated, at the top, a closed wooden door as he did so.

The next door was slightly ajar, so he pushed it open and went inside. This room was about the same size as the other; however, as he shone his torch around the room it picked up two long tables along the wall with a couple of chairs pushed underneath. The tables, as Tony moved closer, had several small coils of different coloured wires piled neatly together. As he moved across the table the torch light lit up a soldering iron, some tins of glue, and as he picked them up, he saw there was also an array of screwdrivers, pliers and a small hammer. Clips and elastic bands completed the assortment of equipment on the tables. Switching the beam of light around the room, Tony noticed a small carpet laid out. A prayer mat, he thought, Adeem had mentioned that if they didn't go to prayers then they would pray at home. Flicking the light around, under the table there was a large box. Carefully pulling it out, he opened it up and with the torch in his mouth he took out the first bag: it was a backpack. Looking in the box there was a second, and as he pulled this one there was a third underneath. *So, it could be three bombs then. Mike might be right*, he thought. Putting them back and sliding the box back under the table, he glanced at his watch. He'd been here half an hour already, better get a move on.

With a last look around, he went back into the passage, making sure the door was, as before, ajar, and he approached the last door. Again, quietly opening it, the door led into a kitchen, and as he shone the torch around, he could see the bathroom at the end of the kitchen through another door. Tony spotted the fridge and pulled it open; the light startled him slightly as it was much brighter than his torch. There were a few packets of food, milk and some orange. Looking at the date it was new. This confirmed his thoughts that Nadir was telling the truth about the help arriving soon. Apart from the basics, the kitchen didn't reveal anything. Tony looked at the stairs, trying to decide if it was worth it. *Of course it is*, he thought.

Carefully creeping up the stairs, the torch switched off, he tried the handle; it gave, and the door opened, surprisingly with no noise. Standing at the top, he listened, waited for 30 seconds or so with no noise. He switched his torch on and shone it up and down the hall. Picking up the front door, the layout was more or less the same as downstairs, a front room, two doors towards the end of the passage, and as he walked into the hall, the stairs to the upper floors. Carefully opening the first door next to the main entrance, the torch light swept the area. One step and he was in the room. He closed the door behind him, saw the curtains were closed, then he quickly took in the rest of the room. It was empty apart from a bookcase, and as he got closer to the half dozen books, looking at the writing on their spine, they were foreign. The only other item in the room was another large carpet arranged at an angle across the middle of the room, suggesting again a prayer mat. Satisfied, Tony left the room, crept down the passage to the next one; this door was half open revealing, as the torch flashed around the room, a couple of comfy chairs, a settee, TV and a couple of tables. Leaving the door and moving into the room, he looked at the dining table: a few magazines, an ashtray, a cup, table mats but nothing, as he leant closer, of interest. Turning his attention to the other items in the room, there was a small three drawer cupboard; this too, however, revealed nothing of interest. No letters or envelopes to give up the name of the person. Tony thought he might have a better look in the kitchen, so switching the torch off he headed towards the door. At that moment, the hall light came on.

Shit! Oh fuck! Catching him off guard, the thoughts were whizzing through his head. He stepped quietly, or so he hoped, behind the half open door and listened.

A man started coming down the stairs.

Oh, fuck me, I don't need this shit, the thoughts continued.

Arli got to the bottom; Tony waited. *If he comes in, what? What? You're going to have to fight him and try to get to the door or back down the stairs. Fuck! Fuck!* said Tony angrily to

57

himself. *Leonard will go ape shit; that's if I get out, fuck!'* The words and consequences were racing around his brain now, one more graphic than the next.

Tony readied himself. Arli passed the door, and Tony heard him go into the kitchen and flick the light on. Listening intently, he seemed to hear the clink of bottles as he opened the fridge. Moments passed, a bottle was placed back in the fridge door, the kitchen light clicked off. Tony took a deep breath and held himself, ready to pounce, as Arli approached, went past and started on up back the stairs. At the top, the hall light went out, and Tony vaguely heard a door close. He let out a deep breath. *For fuck's sake*, thought Tony, thanking his lucky stars.

He relaxed slightly, looked at his watch, controlled his breathing and took a deep breath. Ten minutes passed, and Tony slipped out down the stairs and went out of the basement door flat, locking the door as he went. Carefully looking up and down the road before climbing the basement stairs, he made his way back to the van, got in, heaved a massive sigh of relief and lit a fag.

Chapter 6

Femi swirled the whiskey around the glass. Laughing, he swallowed the liquor, feeling the burn at the back of his throat. Licking his lips, smiling, he grabbed the bottle from the table and poured another with a handful of ice thrown in. Looking down, he put his hand on the girl's shoulder.

'You come with me.' He grinned, the white teeth blazing with a small gold tooth anchored in the top row front and centre. She looked up, her glazed eyes barely recognising the figure behind her. They had been to a nightclub, and her and two of her mates had come back to Femi's room at some hotel along with four of his friends. They had been drinking and dancing, and she remembered, at some point, that she felt weird and had to sit down. She could hear the noise of the others – the music was loud, and laughter filled the room – so she wasn't too concerned and had put it down to the champagne. Her friends had partnered up, one was still dancing, and Mary had sprawled across two of the men on the large soft sofa. They were kissing her, taking it in turns to run their hands up and down her body. Her dress was coming undone and one of the men was running his hand up her leg and now under the now loosened garment.

She felt her arm being pulled up, and as Femi came round from the back of the sofa where she was sat, his hand ran down her arm and clasped her hand and she was pulled up. Her legs were like wooden stilts as she moved forward. Femi, holding her, helped her past the coffee table, over the plush carpet and down the hall; the door to a bedroom opened and she felt herself being pushed into the room. Femi downed the whiskey and threw the glass onto the bed, grabbed Michelle, spun her round and kissed her hard. She tried to back away, but it was as if all her muscles were frozen. She couldn't lift her hands or arms, and as Femi began to tear the clothes off her she couldn't speak. In a daze now, unable to control any part of her body, she fell backwards onto the cushioned bed. With her clothes now gone, she could feel the weight of Femi on top of her; unable to move or cry out, she was helpless.

The night had been long, and she vaguely remembered that her friend had been next to her at some point. She also remembered the heaviness of more men on her, their breath wreaking with alcohol, being turned over and pinned onto the bed; the morning, however, eventually came. Her head hurt as she rolled forward and up onto her elbows. Completely naked, she quickly spun her head round and looked at the room. She caught a glimpse of a foot at the end of the bed and looked over the edge: it was her friend Mary face down. Crying out loud, she dropped to her knees, pulled at Mary's arm and rolled her over seeing her face was bruised and bloody. Crying, she shook her. Mary spluttered, opened her eyes, made a gurgling sound, turned her head and threw up. The stench was excruciating. She began to cough, and Michelle grabbed her, shouting, 'Get up, Mary! Get up! You OK?'

Grunting, Mary focussed her eyes. 'Where the fuck are we?' She sat up and looked around.

'You've got blood on your face. What did they do to you?'

Mary looked up at Michelle. 'You should see yourself and the bed,' she said pointing at Michelle's hair and where Michelle had been.

Michele grabbed her hair and ran her fingers through it. The soft gloopy liquid stuck onto her fingers. She looked at it: yellow, red and white, like curdled cream with mucus in it, she thought. Looking at the bed where she had been lying, it was covered in blood, and as she wiped the back of her it felt wet. She looked at her fingers – they were covered in blood – then she winced, and the pain started to kick in.

Wiping her hand on the bed, she stood and helped Mary clamber up. The girls went to the bedroom door and carefully opening it peered out: no noise, no talking, complete silence. They held each other then groggily walked up the hall to the main room. It looked like a battle ground. Empty bottles on the floor, clothes everywhere; across the room the TV had been smashed and several chairs upturned. Michelle ran forward, crying as she did so. Diving to her knees, she had seen the hand of her friend Sarah poking out behind the sofa. On their knees, both the girls, crying, started calling to their friend.

'Sarah! Sarah! Wake up! wake up!' Shaking her also naked body, as they rolled her over, Michelle's eyes widened as she saw the blood across Sarah's stomach; she screamed.

Femi Eze had started his life as an area boy in the gutters of Lagos, scrambling around to make ends meet in the early days then graduating to petty theft, mostly from tourists. Later, he became more emboldened by carjacking and pushing drugs to locals and the occasional visitor to the city. He'd been lucky as one of the cars they had stopped to rob was occupied by a man called Bala. Unafraid of the situation he was in, he had offered Femi an opportunity to make some decent money. That was the beginning of his rise. Surrounding himself with several of his friends from the streets, Femi, under the guidance of Bala, had prospered greatly. Drugs and women trafficking were his main source of income; the latter was far more lucrative, easier to supply and with less chance of being ripped off. Bala had introduced him to some decent players in Italy and the UK, and with a tidy cut for himself left Femi to expand his empire, which Femi did with vigour. Femi had no shortage of women. Nigeria, out of the main cities and towns, was very poor. The people had little opportunity of making a living, and many families welcomed the chance to send their daughters to Europe under the guise of garnering fame and fortune. It was mostly the fortune they wanted; the idea was that the daughter would be gainfully employed and send money back to the families each month. The man who organised this was a man called Oparei. He would go to the various villages with tales of how well they were doing, showing them photos of London and Disneyland Paris, the girls all having a wonderful time, then persuading them eloquently that they should send their own daughters too. Nothing was free, of course, it would cost the equivalent of £2,000. That would cover passports, plane tickets, etc., and once in Europe, Oparei spun the story of huge sums of money being sent home to Mum and Dad each month.

The stories always ended well, and Oparei was deft at painting a beautiful picture. This resulted typically in having 30 plus girls to send over each trip. Their lives, however, would be changed forever, as once in the UK, or anywhere else Femi wanted them, they would be sold off as sex workers, moved around from one brothel to the next, doped to the eyeballs, used and abused as their handler saw fit, each one selling the girls for less money each time they changed hands. A fresh, straight off the boat, 12 to 16-year-old would fetch £30k, by the end of their days around £500 if they didn't end up dead. Like drugs, there was never enough, and Oparei had sent hundreds of girls this way, every six weeks or so a container full. Each time though, which rankled Oparei greatly, was that out of his money he had to pay off the port official in Tripoli. Around £25k for doing nothing, thought Oparei, the man was a leech and took great delight in lording it over him every time they met. The cousin of Gaddafi, the man used this as a weapon to instil fear into others around him. Loathed by all, he was, however, strategically placed to reward himself with whatever nefarious activities he chose. Oparei didn't have a choice. He had once asked Femi for the money but had received a beating in return; he didn't ask again. The money he made was considerably more than anyone he knew, but he guessed it wouldn't last forever, so for the last couple of years he had been sending money abroad, deciding that if he could escape the clutches of Femi, he had at least something to show for it.

Femi had recruited Oparei to gather the girls and arrange transport to the port of Tripoli where they would be shipped, brutally on some occasions, in a container bound for Morocco. Once landed, the container would travel to the outskirts of Tangier where they would be carried across the Mediterranean in a small boat landing in Spain. Once there, Femi's men would bus them through Spain across France into the Netherlands then onto another container that was scheduled for Tilbury Docks in the UK. Femi paid for a driver to pick the container up and ship it out of Tilbury to an industrial estate east of Barking, not far behind the Ford Dagenham plant. Here it would be met by Femi, George and Sayo, and that evening they would offload the girls and Femi would decide who would go where.

George looked at his watch.

What time Cono and Junk arriving?

Femi didn't look up from his paper. 'Tomorrow, four ish.'

George nodded. 'I'll pick 'em up.'

'No, you stay with me, Sayo will go,' he said, nodding at the man lazing on the sofa swigging a beer.

'Fuck sake, why me? Let him go.'

Femi put down his paper and looked across the room.

'OK, OK, I'll go.'

Of the men Femi had in his crew, George and Cono were heavyweight muscle. Junk and Sayo were handy but a bit thick. Femi liked them around, they were all he had that resembled a family, but they did irritate him from time to time with stupid mundane questions.

'Can we eat now?' said Sayo.

Femi ignored him.

'I'm hungry.'

Gaining no response.

'What do you want to eat, Georgie boy?'

'Fuck off!'

'When are we going to eat then?'

'You fat fuck, get off your arse and go get something.'

'Get burgers,' said Femi from behind his paper.

'Why am I going?' moaned Sayo. 'You coming with me?'

'Fuck off. I want cheese on mine,' said George.

Knowing better than to ask Femi, Sayo struggled up and put his beer down.

'So, what do you want then?'

'BURGERS!' George and Femi shouted at him.

Femi nearly threw his paper down, then thought better of it as he watched Sayo go. He continued reading the betting odds of horses he fancied at Kempton that afternoon. Ticking them off, he stood up, handed the paper to George. '£500 to win on each,' he said pulling out a roll of money from his pocket. Licking his fingers, he peeled off a wad of £20 notes and handed them across.

George stood up, took the money and looked at the paper. 'OK,' he said and left.

Femi walked over to the window. The apartment at the top of the block was rented. He had six others across town. Never staying at one for more than a couple of weeks, most were on the outskirts of London city. They had a couple of cars at each place, all in garages out of sight; these too were rented, and he had them changed frequently, going as far afield as Windsor to rent them. Bala had impressed on him for years about being cautious, not leaving a trail and always, wherever possible, using cash. As he thought about the cash, he totted up what he had easy access to. Just over four million stashed across the flats and the house in Windsor, most of it from cocaine, which he distributed to the boys in Manchester and Leeds; supply came into Hull every two months. He wasn't interested in distribution; he sold the lot to a gang of his countrymen who Bala had put into the country a few years ago. They didn't sell as much as some of the mainstream players, but it was steady, and growth was upwards, which Femi liked. Cash also was what he liked, and he collected it on delivery. Thinking about it, next month he would need to get it over to Pierre Tecky at the French advocates of Ravel & Taider. Pierre handled the payment of the drivers, boatmen and sourced any coaches or trailers they needed in Europe; he also handled the import documents for Tilbury and Hull. Pierre would bank the money in a number of accounts across France and Switzerland, transferring a small amount across to Lagos. Femi kept a few hundred thousand there for emergencies and to draw on when he visited.

*

Femi was considering looking for another lawyer to handle some of the work. Bala had mentioned to him the last time they met that he was giving a lot of work to Pierre, and he could be a weak link. Femi shook his head. 'Not yet, see how this year goes and then look at it again,' he had said. As he looked out of the window, he saw Sayo coming back, and he thought, *Now the shit Tariq was dead need to find another outlet for my girls.* Counting, he worked out that Tariq had taken about 100; fortunately, the next batch were all accounted for by the Pakistanis in Glasgow, so he had about 10 weeks to sort something out, he thought. He could syphon a few off when they get to Spain and send them into France or Italy. Femi lit a cigarette, and his mind went back to the call he had taken earlier that day from Bala; he wanted answers and had asked him if he had made any progress. The progress he was talking about wasn't mentioned over the phone. Femi remembered that when they had met in Lagos a few weeks ago, Bala had spoken of his commitment to a couple of confraternities in the Niger Delta. He knew he had ties to them but wasn't sure as to how much. The request took him by surprise though, they wanted weapons, as much as he could get. 'The Russians will supply,' said Bala.

'How can I get to them?'

'This man in London, Sergio Karnovich, is where you start. He was attaché here and has helped the guys before, go see him.'

'If you know him, why don't you go?'

'I don't know him, but he knows of me and my friends,

and your English is better than mine, and you can travel in and out of England much easier than I can.'

'What do you need?'

'These. . .' handing Femi a list, 'they have them and can get them shipped to Accra in Ghana. I can get them picked up from there.'

Femi was sceptical, but Bala had been his ticket to this life of excess, so he wasn't going to refuse him. He'd made some enquiries but hadn't, as yet, been able to get to the guy. 'Time to strong-arm my girl,' he mused as Soya returned.

'Burgers up.'

George had followed him in. 'You better have got cheese on mine, fat boy.'

Chapter 7

It had been raining all day, and she had heard on the news that morning that it would probably last all week. *England*, she thought, *typical. Oh well, at least they gave us a warning.* The trip into work was head down, brolly up, following thousands of people as she got off the Tube, went up the stairs and headed, along with all the others, across the bridge. There was no time to look at the view this morning; the boats went unnoticed as did the skyline. Taking about 10 minutes from the Tube to the office, she had welcomed the sanctuary of somewhere warm and dry. The day, like so many others, had involved an office meeting where her boss had given one of his many 10-minute updates on the state of the country, how important it was to work as part of a team and to make sure that all work was as detailed and as accurate as possible. Mistakes were not tolerated as the repercussions could be disastrous for some. Settling into her desk, fresh coffee at the ready, she unfurled the headphones, slipped them over her ears, switched the computer on and waited. A few moments later, the screen burst into life asking for her to log on. Once in, she selected the file under 'pending', clicked it and the document opened. Rewinding the tape, she decided to listen again to the report and read through what she had typed to make sure that thus far everything was as spoken. She was confident that it would be, but it was a refresher as closing the file last night she hadn't completely finished the report.

The words filled her ears, and as she scanned the type in front of her, the words and sentences tied up. Ten minutes and she was at the end. She paused the tape, took a quick drink of her coffee and hit the play button, and the typing began. She didn't really take in what she was typing as, along with the other girls in the office, she typed the words spoken in her ears but didn't really take any notice as such of the content. They did so many that most of them were the same; once you had done one you were onto the next. The procedure in place was that on completion, the file went to the boss who read the report and decided where it went. Routine stuff was filed under the designated owner or the project they were working on. Anything that was flagged was sent across to another department for clarification or action. If nothing was needed, then the report would be sent back to the original person who typed it up. They would print it off and create a precis of the subject, which would then be inserted into a physical folder with the newest report at the front with the precis in a separate folder at the front of the file. If anyone wanted to see the file's contents, the first documents they read would be the precis of the report and the others in order, and if they needed more detailed information, they could scan through the folder for the detailed report itself. After six months, the detailed reports would be removed, sent away to be put onto microfiche and then the originals would be archived off site. Some of the files contained several years' worth of precis, depending on the scope and longevity of the project. The system worked had been in place for years, but the time was now rapidly coming when the documents themselves were being stored on the central computer, slowly doing away with both the microfiche and printing of the reports. Each department in the building and their ancillary services were at various stages of implementing the changes, which in some instances had led to duplication of the reports, but IT had, at the last briefing, assured everyone that the glitches would be ironed out and everything would be fine. She'd laughed to herself on hearing this, and after chatting to her colleagues most felt the same. IT were always saying they should become more reliant on the system, but all they ever saw was it was going wrong.

The bank of filing cabinets stretched the length of the wall; every cabinet held drawers, and each drawer contained numerous files and folders. The first two filing cabinets were where details of foreign diplomats that resided in the UK were held, and all the others were ongoing projects. Updates in the first two were rare and were mainly made when a new person or diplomat came to the country or files were updated to reflect known changes within the hierarchy of an embassy or changes to personnel. Any of the three girls in the office, including Gabriella, could receive a tape with a report for any file in the system, so they all had access to everything at any time. At the end of every day, the cabinets were locked with metal bars, which straddled three cabinets at a time, and with a combination lock securing them all. Sheila, the office manager, oversaw this procedure and was always the last to leave. The office had changed; over the last couple of years, they had tightened up on security, not only on entering and leaving the building but also who had access to files. Gabriella, in the last round of changes, had moved up, along with both of her colleagues, and was focussed on the more strategic and critical reports. The other secretaries down the hall in a larger open plan office were more admin and collective report generation. The officers in the individual rooms that lined the corridors were case and informant handlers, and each had his or her own secretary and secure protocols to adhere to. They all reported to Lieutenant General Carl Peterson. Carl had replaced Geoffrey Palmer-Siddely, who had retired a couple of years earlier. Geoffrey had been the driving force behind the department in the mid-1970s and had seen it grow into a formidable division of MI5. The men and women who sent the reports into the division were an eclectic mix of individuals, all informants, information gatherers working their normal day jobs all committed to the security of the country. None were employed by MI5 or the government, they were members of the public who had come to the attention of either Geoffrey or Carl who could watch and report inconspicuously on a range of people and their activities who were of interest to the UK government.

Looking at her watch, it was twenty-five past, so she began to file away her work, switch the machine off and secure her desk. Standing, she grabbed her coat, looked out of the window, pleased that the rain had eased off. With a wave to Sheila, she walked out, finished for the day. She normally finished at five, but this week she had worked an extra half hour each day so on Friday she could finish early. She would be catching the train to Heathrow and then a quick flight to Ireland to see Peter, his wife, Jacquie, and their two children, who she was god-parent too. Peter was her cousin, the son of her father's brother. She and her mum had spent many holidays with the family, and she and Peter had become good friends. That friendship had been tested severely a few years ago when he had asked her for a favour. She had hated betraying the people around her, but it was only a small request, and she had to save the life of Peter's brother Billy, who had fallen into the hands of the wrong crowd. Coming out of the office, turning left to the top of Gresham Street, she turned right past the Lord Raglan pub, crossed the road, walked alongside the Postman's Garden, followed the road up to Albion Way, which would then lead through a short cut to the Barbican Tube.

Rounding the corner, she didn't take much notice of the silver Mercedes parked further up. It was only when a man got out of the passenger seat and walked round and opened the back door and waited, looking straight at her, that she saw him and then, recognition, her heart sank. *Oh no, I thought they'd forgotten about me*, she thought as she approached, thinking about crossing the road.

'Get in,' the man said stepping into her path, blocking the pavement.

'Get in.'

'No, I don't want to. Leave me alone.'

The man stepped forward and grabbed her by the elbow.

'Get the fuck in, bitch.'

Pushing her into the open-door space then forcing her head down, she was bundled into the car.

The door slammed, and she looked at the person next to her.

'Remember me,' said Femi smiling.

'Good, thought you might. Been a while. How've you been?'

'Let me go. I have nothing for you. I can't help you, I told you that last time,' she explained, beginning to scramble for the door handle to let herself out.

'Let me out!' she shouted.

The door locked and the car pulled away. Looking over her shoulder, she was desperate to see someone who could help.

'No one there, baby girl,' said Femi moving closer to her and putting his hand on her knee.

'Just me and you, oh and the boys.'

'Get off me! Get off me!'

With his face next to hers, she could smell the whisky on his breath. She began pushing, trying the door handle again in desperation.

'Get off me. I can't help you. Let me go or you will be in big trouble.'

Femi laughed and licked her cheek.

'Who you going to tell?' he asked, licking her cheek again.

'We are just going to have a nice drive and a friendly chat,' he continued, stroking her leg, then he slid back into his seat, grinning.

'I need for you to help me find a man.'

'I can't! I can't! I told you last time, I'm nobody. I just write stuff and file stuff. I don't see or go to any meetings. I can't help, let me out!' she said, quickly trying the door handle again.

'I want a photograph of a man,' he said reaching into his pocket and pulling out a piece of paper.

'Here's his name.'

'I can't! I won't! I don't want that,' she said pushing his hand away.

Femi slammed the back of his hand into her chest.

'You fucking will. Take the name, bitch.'

Pushing his arm harder, he lent into her, crushing her into the corner of the car seat.

'Take the fucking name. I own you. I told you last time you will do what I want or your little friends in Ballystally are finished. Take it!' he said, shoving the piece of paper in her face.

Tears welled in her eyes. 'I can't. I don't know how to get anything.'

'Find a fucking way. I don't give a shit.' Grabbing her hand harshly, he stuffed the paper into the palm of her hand and wrapped her fingers around, hurting her.

'You've got a week. I know where you live, just in case you are thinking of being off sick. I'm sure you don't want the boys to pop round and tuck you in one night, do you?' His face was now inches from hers.

Shaking her head, tears now rolling down her cheeks, the car came to a halt.

'Now fuck off.'

She heard the door unlock. Femi leant across her and pushed the door open.

'See you later, baby girl,' he said, the grin now reappearing on his face.

Femi laughed as the car pulled away; he now knew that it was a good trade. A few years ago, on one of their trips, Bala had introduced him to a Martin Flynn, a boat captain who ran out of Tangiers, amongst other places. He had shipped some coke for Bala into Amsterdam, and he wanted to send some more. They had met in a sleazy bar just off the dock, a place that Femi felt perfectly at home in. Femi had met him a couple of times since, mainly in place of Bala, delivering the odd shipment. Flynn's boat wasn't big enough to transport Femi's girls, but the two men had got along well enough for drinking anyway. On one occasion, Flynn had asked Femi if he did his own business, i.e. coke, and could he supply some without upsetting Bala. Femi had agreed and also at a decent price. The supply would be going to Ireland and would be distributed by the IRA as a side-line to make more money. They had asked if he would like something else in payment.

'They have a girl that you could use,' said Flynn.

'I've got more than enough girls, and I don't want anymore, especially a soiled one.'

'No, it's not like that my friend, this girl, works in London.

She is actually in the security services part, not the cops, and is well placed to get you information on any, let's say, people who are your competitors or maybe the occasional copper or foreign guy that you need to lean on. Let me know when you come back with the gear.'

It was an interesting proposition to have a line into the heart of his enemy, but he was unsure as to whether he would ever need such a touch. It was a couple of weeks later when Femi got back to Flynn. He'd run it by Bala who told him to snatch his hand off, so the deal was done. The first time he had met her he took her to the bar above Ronnie Scots. She was a fiery girl, but he knew that he could control her, and it was just a matter of time and patience before he could put her into play.

Chapter 8

Gabriella sat alone in her flat, head in hands, crying. She'd just got off the phone with Peter saying she was sorry, but she couldn't make it this weekend as she wasn't feeling too well. He'd wished her a speedy recovery and said not to worry as there would be plenty of other times she could come across. Of course, everyone would be disappointed, but they would understand. It had been ages since she'd seen him and the family but decided to fake illness rather than to tell him the real reason. Maybe she would on the next visit, but that was in the future, and then again, she might not. The nice kind words from Peter had tipped her over the edge, and as she placed the handle down on the telephone she burst into tears.

She flattened the crumpled piece of paper Femi had given her on the coffee table. 'Sergio Karnovich – Russian Embassy' and then a telephone number for her to ring Femi when she had the photo. Staring at it, she'd never heard of the man and couldn't remember if she had ever typed up a Russian update. Wiping her eyes, she went into the kitchen and started to look around for something to eat. Wandering around, opening first the fridge door then the cupboard, then the next cupboard, she couldn't see anything that she wanted. Turning, she boiled the kettle, made a coffee, looked again in the fridge, slammed the door shut, walked back to the sofa and flicked the TV on. Spinning through the channels, her attention was constantly drawn to the paper on the table. She picked it up, sniffed and wiped her eyes with her fingers.

I need to tell someone, she thought, *but who? I have to tell my boss, Sheila. I'll lose my job. Oh God, what if they ask me if I've done it before? What about that other bloke, what was his name, oh yes, Blackreach? Oh shit, I'm definitely going to lose my job. I'll go to jail, and they'll arrest Peter and Billy.* The thoughts raced around her head; she began to cry again. *What am I going to do? I must tell Sheila. I can't do this again, but I'll go to jail. My life is over. I can't tell Sheila. I don't want to go to jail. I could leave my job; that's an idea, I'll leave my job.* Turmoil, each thought was worse than the last. She felt sick, and her head hurt. She cried to herself, *Why me? Why me?* Then she remembered, *If I leave, he said he would kill Peter. I can't do* that.

The words on the paper never changed, however long she looked and willed the paper to disappear, the meeting with Femi to not have happened and that the initial talk with Peter didn't occur, but it didn't it just stared back at her.

After a while she noticed it was dark outside. Looking at her watch, several hours had passed by. Her coffee was cold, and she was too. Now shivering, leaving the coffee where it was, she switched the light off and went to bed hoping sleep would come. Lying in bed though the same thoughts wouldn't go away; there was no solution, no end, no way for her as far as she could see to have any sort of a happy ending to this. Tossing and turning for the umpteenth time, Gabrielle put the bedside light on, swung herself off the side of the bed, put her dressing gown on and went into the kitchen. Watching the kettle boil with a hot chocolate in the mug and several sugars, she hoped that it would soothe her and allow her to get some sleep at least. Looking at her watch, it was 3:15 in the morning. *I'll never be ready for work. I must look like a wreck.* Pouring the water in and stirring the hot chocolate, *What if, what if. . .* she thought. *What if I just get the picture, give it to him, then leave my job. I could get a job in Manchester or even Europe. Brussels would have me, I'm sure. I could get a decent reference from Sheila. I could say I needed a break. a change, I can't afford to live in London anymore. Lots of people leave. Give it to him then leave, just leave. That's it.* It seemed like a weight had been lifted from her shoulders. The solution was fast flowing in her mind. 'That would work,' she sighed, a plan in place. Taking a sip of the chocolate, she felt worn out. Tipping the drink down the sink, she went to bed.

Tony looked at his watch. He been watching the house all day, and nothing unusual had occurred. He had photographed the same men as they came and went, and at 7:00 pm he had watched Nadir come to the door along with the other two for the first of their evening prayers. *Don't think anything is going to happen here tonight then*, he thought, and pushing his way into the van's driving seat, with a last look around he drove off. *Come back maybe end of next week.*

Parking the van in the underground car park on Ludgate Hill, he grabbed a cab, set off round the Aldwych up the Kingsway and jumped out at Holborn. Lighting a cigarette, it seemed he was taking an interest in the tailors on the corner. Looking around, nothing spotted, he headed down to the Tube. Getting off at Lancaster Gate, again casually checking, he crossed the road, walked along Lancaster Gate Road and into his hotel. Changing for the evening into a nice dark blue Aquascutum jacket and trousers set off with a crisp white shirt and a pair of burgundy brogues, he grabbed his lighter and cigarettes and left the room, a circuitous route to Leicester Square and then into Bear Street, where he palmed a tenner and wandered up to the pub where he saw the large as life figure of Charles on the door. Walking past the queue, he smiled, caught his eye and held his hand out.

'Hello, mate. How you doing?'

'Good to see you, Tone,' Charles replied, clasping his hand.

The two men had known each other for years. Charles was from the Hells Angels Chapter in Reading. A tough burly bloke with more tattoos than there was ink in the world, they had first met via Winston in the nightclubs, and Reading was where Pete, Tony's best mate, used to run a snooker hall. They had all played there till the late hours of most mornings during the weekends after work. Winston, 6 ft 4, as hard as they come, was the ideal bouncer. He got on with most people and had been well respected in Reading. He'd moved to London after Pete's death.

'All good in the dark world of doormen then?'

'Hah, you're not kidding, boy, pays the bills. You here for long?'

'Couple of pints then off to see Winston.'

'Nice, well, have fun. Give the wanker my regards,' he said, laughing, letting him pass.

'Ear, mate, how come he gets in and we gotta wait?'

'Shut the fuck up and wind you neck in, you'll get in when I say so,' said Charles to the mouthy bloke who had been at the front of the queue.

Tony went through the door to the busy, lively pub. Walking along the bar, he caught the eye of Georgie, the bar manager. She nodded, and as he got to the end of the bar he watched as a pint was poured.

'Hi, Georgie. How you doing?' he said as she placed the drink in front of him. 'You on your own tonight?'

'Hi, Tone.' She sighed. 'Yes, my girl got beat up the other night, so she can't come in, and I'm waiting on another, so hopefully she'll get here soon. Oh, here she is,' she said as they saw a girl lift up the bar hatch, wave at Georgie, put her handbag behind the counter and begin to serve.

'Who got beat?'

'Michelle and two of her mates. Quite bad, she said she probably been spiked and then raped by a group of blokes.'

'For fuck's sake. She reported it?'

'Sort of, but the old bill are not really looking. They were at Mickey's night club, and the manager there said that from what he could remember they seemed OK and left with the guys without any hassle, so it seems as if you say one thing, they would say another. You know how it goes.'

'How bad were they hurt?'

'Miche said she and Mary had been spiked, raped by several of them, well abused if you know what I mean, but Sarah, when they found her, had been well and truly brutalised, blood everywhere.'

'What about the place they were in?'

'They say they didn't hear anything. The room leads onto a street balcony which leads onto the road. When Miche went back there she thinks one bloke let himself into the room via the hotel then went and undid the door for the others. No cameras, owners don't give a shit, cash paid, no cards with names, dead end.'

'Fucking hell, Georgie, does she remember what they looked like or anything?'

'Just four or five big black blokes, black, black, you know. One, she seems to remember, was a guy called Femi, had a gold tooth maybe, other than that nothing.'

'Femi,' said Tony slowly. 'Really.'

'D'you know him?'

'No,' said Tony shaking his head.

'Life, what a bitch,' said Georgie turning to the bloke next to Tony. 'What you want, mate?'

Tony picked his pint up and grabbed a seat at one of the small tables at the back of the bar, took out his cigarettes and lit one up. *Femi, big black guy, three or four mates, coincidence, doubt it*, he thought. He'd first met Georgie at the pub in Whitechapel where he used to drink when doing the rounds of pubs and bars. Most pubs had locals, and after a period of time you got to know who drank where, a little about their lives, sometimes a bit of local gossip. Tony had used these pubs to monitor any unusual activity. It was rare anything had changed, but there had been a couple of occasions when he had spotted something out of the ordinary, followed it up and reported on it. Georgie was a young girl working at one of these pubs, and he had got to know her. She enjoyed the hospitality trade and wanted more responsibility, but the pub she worked in wasn't big enough, and unfortunately, she hadn't got a great deal of experience to move up the ladder, so she was stuck. Tony knew Charles and they both had put a good word in for her, so the management had brought her on board as a manager. The pub was linked to several others and a couple of nightclubs, so if she did well and wanted to move up then there was plenty of opportunity for her. Smoking his cigarette and drinking his pint, his thoughts went back to the first time he had seen Femi. He assumed it was the same guy, and at the moment it appeared to be him, who he had seen drinking in Winston's cousin's nightclub above Ronnie Scott's. Enjoying the music and a bottle of red wine, he had spotted the brash Femi with his crew and a girl who he had recognised from Geoffrey's office. He had reported the meeting, but nothing had come of it. Winston, when asked, had warned him off the guy, who apparently was into drugs, sex trafficking and money laundering, and now it appears, thought Tony, was beating and raping white women, or maybe just any women that he and his mates came across. Picking another drink up from the bar, Tony looked at his watch. *Give it an hour then I'll go see Winston,* he thought.

'WINSTOOOOON!' shouted Tony at the top of his voice as he rounded the corner and spotted Winston at the bottom of the stairs.

'Hey, you old fucker, don't you remember me?'

'Tone, you tart. How are you?'

Winston wrapped his arms around Tony and bear hugged him, forcing Tony to wince.

'Put me down, you dick. People will think we like each other.'

Winston laughed and released Tony, who dropped to the ground.

'You don't get any weaker, do you?' said Tony rubbing his side.

'Just practicing, making sure if I need to sling some tit out of the club, I can pick him up and throw him down the stairs.'

'Nice. Charles says hello by the way.'

Winston nodded. 'Must go round and see him.'

'Busy tonight?'

'Picking up. You staying here?'

'Yeah, thought I would. Been a while since I heard any decent music. Nothing's changed, I take it.'

'Naw, all good, go up, see Damon. I'll be there in a bit.'

Tony jogged up the stairs, opened the door and walked

into the dark smoky atmosphere. Adjusting his sight, he made it to the bar and waved at Damon.

'Hey, dog, how you doing?' said Damon clasping his hand.

'Good to see you. How's the family?'

'Not bad, Mum had a turn last week. She OK now though, yours?' They chatted for a few more minutes, and Tony ordered a bottle of wine. 'Grab a table, I'll bring it over.'

The soul music crowded the air. Some in the club were dancing but most were chatting, smoking, and the place was beginning to fill up. Tony sat, lit a cigarette and looked around.

'Cheers, Damon.'

'Catch you later. Need anything, give us a shout,' Damon said placing the bottle and glass down. He wasn't the only white person in the bar, but everyone who came in apart from the girls were treated with suspicion, but being accepted by Damon, the ones who had taken any notice of his arrival in the club turned their attention back to the people they were with. Tony poured some wine and took in the clientele: a mixture, as expected, all here for the music. The Ronettes 'Be My Baby' filled the room and was swiftly followed by a Wilson Pickett number. The mood in the club was easy, and Tony smiled as he looked around and saw some girls were dancing, handbags on the floor. An hour passed.

'How's the wine?' Winston had sat next to him.

'Grab a glass,' offered Tony.

'Can't, working, maybe later.'

'Good tonight. Can't beat a bit of Motown and reggae.'

'Too right.'

'Notice your wise guys are not in then, you thrown them out?'

'Who's that then,' said Winston looking at Tony.

'That bloke with his mates. What's his name, Remi, Demi, something like.'

'Oh, you mean Femi Eze. Nah, they don't come in here no more, they pissed some of the girls off, so we barred them.'

'Good for you, bothering another club now I've no doubt.'

'Hah, yeah, let old Stringfellow deal with them. They go there on a Saturday from what I've heard.'

Tony nodded. 'Good riddance, you working all weekend?'

They chatted for a few more minutes before Winston stood.

'Got to go, closing at three tonight. You staying?'

'No, I'll shoot in a bit. Cheers, my friend,' said Tony raising his glass.

Winston smiled and worked his way back through the crowd to the door.

The following day, Tony parked up. It was early, just before 9:00 am. The one-way street offered little in parking, so to get a space, Tony had had to drive round three times before one had become available. Settled in now, he got out, placed a construction worker's permit on the dashboard and set off past Stringfellows and onto Covent Garden. Breakfast was in order. The day passed slowly, and as darkness fell, he returned to the van, pushed the curtain back between the front seats and the back and made himself comfortable, or as comfortable as he could, peering through the curtain with his camera focussed on Stringfellows. The activity in the street got busier as the hours passed by. He watched as the doormen erected the barrier for entry to the club, and by nine the first people began to queue. It had opened at eight, but few had been in. Tony photographed the few that did, fortunate that the area was lit up well so those pictured could be easily identified. About 10:30 pm, a black Mercedes pulled up outside; there had been a string of cars over the course of the evening with Tony capturing each one. As the doors opened four black men got out. Tony zoomed in to the front passenger and clicked the burst mode on the camera. It was Femi, behind him three of his men. As they slammed the car doors shut, he made a note of the plate and watched as they made their way into the club.

'Got ya,' he said out loud. Looking at his watch, he reckoned it would be several hours before they left. Photographing several other people over the next few broke the boredom of waiting for Femi to leave. He had spotted another of who he thought was Femi's men, probably the driver, going into the club.

It was 3:00 am. Tony yawned and looked at his watch. He had seen many leave the club and was now waiting patiently for the driver to leave, when on cue he spotted a lone black man leaving the club, and as he zoomed in, he recognised him as the bloke who had arrived late. Fifteen minutes later, Femi and his men began to leave and congregate on the pavement by the road, smoking, laughing and obviously waiting. Tony took a few quick photos and then scrambled into the driver's seat, switched the engine on and waited. The Mercedes pulled up, Femi got in and the car sped off. Tony pulled the van out and set off. They made a left and then came to a halt at the lights, enabling him to catch up. Turning, they crossed Waterloo Bridge. Traffic was busy, which worked in Tony's favour a few cars behind them. They picked up the A23 and headed south. The journey took just under an hour, and they pulled off Streatham high street, Tony following cautiously. A few more turns and they pulled up outside a large block of flats overlooking the common. Tony drove past and watched as the car was parked and all the men got out and went into the building. Finding a suitable space to park, Tony decided to stay the night and get a better look at the place in the morning.

After a few hours' sleep, he swigged on some water left over from the night before; the place was quiet. Checking around before he got out, there were a few dog walkers on the common, but that was about it. Leaving the van, Tony lit a cigarette, walked past the flats and onto the main road about half a mile away. Spotting a petrol station, he picked up a few bits and pieces and went back to the van. Finding a better vantage point, he took some pictures of the flats and the car. It was still early. *Doubt they will be up and around for a while,* he thought. *I'll come back tomorrow.*

By the Wednesday afternoon, apart from watching some of his men come and go, Femi had not been seen, and he was beginning to wonder if he had missed him on the Sunday after he had left. Watching one of the men jump into the Merc, the driver reversed and sat waiting outside the block. Tony immediately got into the driver's seat and waited. Femi came out, got in, and the car headed for the main road. Tony in pursuit, the car headed towards London, this time over Wandsworth Bridge then right onto Kings Road, a short left, then right, another left, and they were on Earl's Court Road heading for Kensington, and then, as the car slowed, it turned into Kensington Palace Gardens and pulled up halfway. Tony passed the car, crossed over the junction into Clanricarde Gardens, U turned and sat at the entrance of the street overlooking Kensington Palace Gardens. If the Merc came to the end, then he could follow either left or right. *Strange*, thought Tony. *What is he doing here?*

Getting out, he edged along the road and looked down the road. He could see the Merc still waiting, it had come up the road a bit further and he could make out that both men were still sat in the car. Tony looked around: directly opposite the junction was a café. Tony went in, ordered a coffee and was able to sit in the window where he watched and waited. He didn't have to wait long: the door opened, and Femi got out and walked quickly towards the end of the road. Taking a left, he picked up his stride. *Shit!* thought Tony. Quickly getting up and out of the café, he began following on the opposite side of the road. Femi had caught up to a man, and as Tony watched they were clearly talking to each other. They stopped, turned slowly and walked back the way they had come. *For fuck's sake,* thought Tony. Watching the two men, fortunately they were in conversation and didn't see Tony turn and begin to follow again. On the corner of the Gardens, the two men parted. Femi headed back towards the Merc, and the man went through the gates into the building. Unable to get back to the van without attracting attention from the now fast approaching Merc, he buried himself into a doorway until the car had gone.

So, who are you? said Tony to himself as he crossed over the road and slowly walked past the impressive, gated building the man had gone into. 'Fucking hell,' said Tony under his breath.

The plaque on the wall next to the high iron gates read, 'Embassy of Russia'.

Chapter 9

The two CH-135 twin Huey helicopters rose in unison from the Pratica di Mare military airbase. Situated a few miles southwest of Rome, it was an ideal location for the military to fly to areas in either the north or south of Italy with ease. The flight, now routine, had been active for two weeks. The flight path would take them south, initially across the Tyrrhenian Sea, and then they would come inland at the coastal town of Briatico, flying slightly to the east of the town then continuing south until they were over the Aspromonte National Park before sweeping west and onto the Sigonella Air Base in Sicily. Flying at 5,000 ft with no sense of urgency, they had become a relatively normal sight in the skies across Calabria and attracted little or no attention, which was exactly the purpose of the regular flights. The two helicopters always maintained the same route and altitude and would continue to do so for the next week. If anyone had spotted their departure flights over the last two weeks, they would have noted that it seemed strange to fly helicopters that distance whilst empty; today, however, that changed. As a helicopter of choice for the Italian military, today each craft had a complement of special forces operatives from the 4th Alpini Paratroopers Regiment, who specialise in mountain combat. One of four special forces regiments of the Italian Army, their pedigree is highly decorated, having served with glory since their inception in 1882. Having changed little over the years, they have seen action in both World Wars and in recent years, distinguished themselves, supporting NATO on several occasions.

As the helicopters approached Santa di Christina D'aspromonte, the lead helicopter altered his course slightly to fly a few degrees east of the town; the second altered to a few degrees west. Maintaining a height of 5,000 ft, the lead helicopter pilot hit the red button on his console. A light came on in the cabin behind him, and the four men, two either side, moved into place, each holding a rope. Spotting the clearing about a mile south of the town and in a valley, which hid them, the pilot dipped the stick, the Huey dropped forward and fell out of the sky. A practiced move of coming in hot to a site, the four highly trained special forces paratroopers braced themselves. Within a moment, the green light came on and two members of the air crew, one either side, heaved on the retractor handle and the doors flew open. Without hesitation, the four men threw their ropes out and began fast roping down. Without a pause, the pilot, true to his absolute skill, had dropped the Huey 4,925 ft in seconds. One of the aircrew, on opening the door, then swiftly turned his attention to the deployment bag, and as the paratroopers descended the bag followed. Within a matter of seconds, the men were on the ground, and they watched as the helicopter crew disengaged the ropes, which fell to their feet. The Huey, with doors still open, cranked, upped its speed and rose quickly back to the skies and with the doors closing headed back onto the prescribed route as if nothing had happened. The second helicopter had dropped its team of paratroopers to the southwest, about a mile apart. On securing the craft, it too swept up back to 5,000 ft, raced and within minutes had caught up with the first helicopter. The valley and drop zones where the men had landed had been scoped out many weeks earlier. A placement of scouts had been in the area for a while and had reported that no one came to either drop zone, so both would be relatively secure to use for this operation.

Dragging the ropes in, coiling them and running them to the tree line, they were hidden, covered in loose bracken. The four men who made up the unit, a primo capitano, sergeant and two senior corporal majors, quickly checked their equipment and spread the load from the deployment bag between them: four small foldable shovels, telescopic lightweight aluminium poles, three plastic sheets, food, 10 gallons of water, which one man shouldered onto his back, spare ammunition, communications equipment, along with several other items needed. The men set off. It was 7:00 pm, and they wanted to cover the five miles or so within the next few hours. The difficulty, of course, was the terrain; however, after years of training in mountain exercises and combat, the four men, along with their colleagues in the other valley, were more than up to the task. Making sure his night vision goggles were correctly sighted on the top of his helmet, not needing them just yet as dusk was about an hour away, as point, checking his compass, he headed into the dense forest with the team behind him, all on high alert, visually scouting the area as they walked.

Tough, with a few challenges, but not unduly so, the four men crept over the last tor, the top of which was a barren rocky outcrop, before slipping back into the trees where they spread out. Cautiously now, with night vision goggles on, the four men slowly made their way down the hillside, stepping over broken branches and jagged stones, which were scattered across the floor of the forest. Checking his compass, the lead man hit the button on his radio once, and the other three men closed in as he knelt. On joining them, a brief, quiet conversation followed. Two of the soldiers pulled off their packs, got out the shovels and began to dig. Of the other two, one went 75 yards or so to the right and slightly higher, the other to the left and slightly lower. Finding a suitable patch of ground, one of them began to dig whilst the other knelt and scoured the area, watching for any signs of movement, his light machine gun at the ready. Taking it in turns to watch and dig, it wasn't long before the three hides had been dug out. Unstrapping the aluminium telescopic poles, which served as a roof support, the plastic sheets were interleaved through them, covering the top of each hide. Loose earth, leaves and a few branches covered the roof of each. Satisfied they were hidden, water and food were split between the men, and they descended into the hides. Three of the men immediately slept while the fourth stayed on watch. A few hours later, as dawn broke, one man emerged carefully and inspected the roofs of the hides. Making a few adjustments and crawling away, he was confident that non were visible; in fact, you had to walk on them to know that they were there. They settled in for a wait. The two soldiers in the front hide had fashioned a couple of spy holes through which, using the telescopic sights, they could see the valley below them and the courtyard in the centre of the small village some 300 yards further down from their location. On the other side of the village, and again some 3 to 400 yards up in the tree line overlooking the area, the other four paratroopers had dug in, and they too watched and waited.

The light knock on the door was perfunctory. Opening the door, the man walked through into the opulent first floor room. Vittorio De Luca was behind the mahogany desk. Elegant and beautifully polished, adorned by an ornate desk lamp, the writing pad of soft leather with the sheaf of papers were the only items in front of him. Putting down his Mont Blanc pen, hc looked up.

'It's done. They've got Genet.'

Vittorio nodded, 'And the other one?'

'Not yet, but they will find him.'

'Ok, it's that time of year again. Have the bags packed. We fly to Rome tomorrow morning, 11:00 am flight.'

'Si, signor,' said the man, and with that he turned and closed the door behind him.

Vittorio pushed himself back in his chair, button padded chestnut leather of the finest quality, and looked outside. The road below was quiet: this part of London was affluent and attracted few tourists. The four-story townhouse, merged with the property next door, now provided eight bedrooms, several bathrooms, guest rooms, servant quarters and luxury dining and sitting rooms. Typical of the grand design built by Thomas Cubitt in the early 19th century, Belgrave Square was a most desirable residence. The room had been designed by Sheila Covetti, an admired Italian interior designer, based in Milan. Vittorio had contracted her when he first purchased the house four years ago. He wanted both a traditional Victorian appearance, given the age of the house, but with an Italian neoclassical feel provided by the high ceilings with intricately carved cornices, which reflected the Victorian age, with a central light moulding from which hung an 19th century classical glass chandelier. The walls, fair in colour, were offset by the striking art: a huge picture by Carlo Bellosio entitled *The Battle for Naples* and on what would have been the fireplace wall, a picture by Andrea Celestini who, born in Naples, spent most of his life depicting religious subjects. Finally, as you entered the room, a sculpture of Ferdinand VII by Antonio Canova held pride of place.

Each room throughout held similar art and furnishings and had cost Vittorio over £10 million pounds, but it was, he thought, a small price to pay as it gave him great pleasure each time he walked into a room. Art was his passion; however, the works on the walls in these rooms were nothing compared to what he had securely locked away in the temperature-controlled basement. A large room encased in a metal framework, alarmed and with 24-hour surveillance, these works of art were his main pride and joy, rarely seen other than by himself. He had accumulated them by various means over the last few years. Standing, he walked over to the Venetian bureau, selected a cigarette from the small silver tray and lit it. Walking back to the window, he opened the room height balcony window, stepped through onto the small veranda, leaned on the rail and inhaled. With Tariq dead, his gang in jail, he hadn't really needed to have Tariq's brother Genet killed, but he wanted everyone to know that a debt was a debt and it had to be paid. The millions of pounds were gone, a small dent in the bank balance but gone non-the less. He'd been told that the other brother and the rest of Tariq's gang would be in jail for a long time. Genet had got out on bail as a smaller player, but crossing Vittorio was a mistake.

The last one associated with Tariq's organisation would soon be found and face a similar fate to Genet. The shortfall in distribution would be picked up with the pizza takeaways of the Pakistani and the Tyneside boys. He may look at Scotland and Wales, but for now the two and a half tons a year of heroin he brought in each year was sufficient. Anyway, he wanted to develop the Irish operation, albeit it a bit of a pain as he preferred to be more hands off. That, however, he thought, may change considerably over the next few days. Blowing the smoke out, he walked back inside, closing the balcony window. He crushed the cigarette out in the marble ashtray on the coffee table. The yearly meeting at the Sanctuary of Polsi would give him the opportunity to demonstrate his control over the UK's drug trade, thus making any changes easy. The Sanctuary of Polsi had, for decades, been the safe meeting ground for the families and affiliates of the 'Ndrangheta. Held in secret, the meetings gave everyone the opportunity to resolve any differences and discuss strategy and tactics to benefit all, plus any new opportunities that any player may wish to take advantage of. This meeting, however, was closed to just a few of the bigger players in the organisation. Whilst they would heed the others, from time to time, international considerations were more important than local disputes.

Checking into the first-class lounge at Heathrow, Vittorio and his companion Ciro sat in the comfortable seats, Vittorio pulling the *Financial Times* from his valise while Ciro ordered coffee and appetisers. At home with Vittorio, the two men had grown up together in Corsico, a province of Milan. Ciro was the muscle whilst Vittorio was the brains. The pair had made headway very quickly. As the son of the major crime family that ruled the area, Vittorio wanted more, broke away then quickly became a wholesale supplier of cocaine to the family. With the money they made he was able to consolidate his position, strong-arm out of business the opposition and become the dominant importer in the north of the country. As with any business, however, intelligence and the ability to compromise saw him partner with the Biscotti family, another highly dangerous but efficient member of the 'Ndrangheta, and a major player in the importation of drugs into most of the south of Italy. His alliances with the Camorra and Sicilian groups had allowed

Biscotti to negotiate high value import contracts for both cocaine and heroin from several sources.

Letting Biscotti take over his business in Milan made sense to Vittorio as the plans they had for the UK and Ireland would lead to greater profits pushing heroin, both of which were lucrative markets. Thus, with Biscotti handling wholesale imports from Italy, moving it into the UK was simple and secure. Dealing with everything at arm's length when he could gave him a cushion between the drugs money and the law. The distribution of heroin through the restaurants worked well. Never getting close to most of it, the cash came into his banks then onto Italy and the France. Laundering the money through several companies, the trail was difficult to follow and even harder to break. The money that came back into his bank in the UK was via an offshore account in the Cayman Islands, which in turn had come from another one that had links into Bahrain then Saudi Arabia. In turn, that money had come from Switzerland, which had been deposited in several banks in Italy and France. With so many twists and turns, any law enforcement agency would have to spend months trying to track down the source, which, from Vittorio's point of view was excellent as it had enabled him to buy several properties in London and a villa in the Bahamas, all of which, it appeared, were legitimate. It was time consuming and involved a quick and agile brain to keep track of everything, and he was constantly thinking of ways to make this part of the business simpler.

The money they made was always split equally between the two of them. Ciro had a passion for cars and now had some eight supercars in his collection, including a Ferrari, Lamborghini, Maserati and Bugatti. The Bugatti EB110 and the 1987 Ferrari F40 were his favourites. All Italian, he had considered buying a McLaren but felt it would spoil the collection if he introduced a non-Italian make. When he wasn't needed by Vittorio, he spent most of his time cleaning each one, rarely taking them out as it could damage them, and he thought, of course, with more mileage on them the value would also go down, though not that he had any intention of selling them. He had also bought a few properties in London, one of which boasted an underground car park, which was the main reason he bought it. Most of the time though he spent and lived in Vittorio's house, as it was easier as the two always had something to attend to.

Landing in Rome, the two men exited the plane, and on picking up their luggage walked through the spacious glass tunnel corridors following the onward travel sign. Having completed the journey many times and knowing where they were going, it was only a few minutes before they entered the Air Italia lounge, settled in and waited for the flight to Lamezia in Calabria. They would stay in a local hotel that evening and be picked up and driven the 80 or so miles to the sanctuary. The journey would take over two hours, as the church in the heart of the Aspromonte mountains was difficult to get to and required local, knowledgeable drivers to make sure that the correct route was taken, otherwise, many lost hours could be spent driving around the mountains. The car that took the two men had arrived early at the hotel, and as they got into the back, greetings were made and bottled water provided.

As they drove up the mountainous road towards the church, Vittorio noticed, as usual, that there were a few cars parked every couple of miles or so with the occupants leaning casually on the bonnets or sat by the roadside smoking. There were only two roads into the valley that contained the church and the monastery, and at this time of year there were no tourists. Anyone approaching the area was either a local who lived in the small village that housed the church or were part of this meeting. Security was paramount; anyone approaching from either direction would be discouraged and suggestions made that they should leave the area. As they got closer, more vehicles were parked, and this time the occupants were openly armed, many with machine guns, all with handguns holstered, several had walkie talkies. No one was taking any chances.

Sweeping into the cobbled square, the car came to a stop, the doors opened, and the two men stepped out.

Through his powerful scope the lead Alpini paratrooper watched the greeting and clicked the button twice on his radio.

'Ciao, benvenuto, benvenuto.' Scipio Sorrentino grasped Vittorio, kissing him on the cheek.

'Ciro.' With a big smile he hugged Ciro.

Scipio had been in Corsico and was a family member and had known both men for most of their lives. The greetings were genuine, and as they walked up the steps to the big oak double doors that guarded the entrance to the old building the talk was of Scipio's new grandson.

Chapter 10

The Sanctuary of Our Lady of Polsi is a Christian sanctuary in the heart of the Aspromonte mountains in Calabria. At the bottom of a gorge surrounded by high mountains, the church and monastery were built around 1100 AD, and since the 16th century it had housed a beautiful carved statue of the Madonna, which was the centre of the religious festival every September. Extremely difficult to find, the small village had barely changed in hundreds of years. With a dozen or so small houses for local people, a couple built on the sides of the mountains, several large houses, which initially were used as refuge for travellers who fell on hard times and were housed by the monks, were now in the hands of local villagers and had been turned into family houses. Two of the largest though that had been built around the courtyard offered a place for meetings. Ownership was uncertain, according to the records, but someone had unearthed some historical paperwork in the Reggio archive that linked the houses to the church, but it wasn't too clear. A local man and his wife kept the houses clean and tidy and made sure that they were habitable. When used, they proffered a large kitchen, two very large reception rooms, an old what some thought was probably a library and several bedrooms. The second house, similar in structure, generally housed any guests of the first house's occupiers.

Vittorio walked through the large wooden double doors with Scipio at his side, giving him a rundown on the recent birth of his grandson and saying that it was such a shame that he and Ciro couldn't make the christening a few weeks ago. His wife understood, of course, and he stated that, as always, they had an open invitation to come and see the family at any time.

'On our way back.' Vittorio smiled. 'We will come and celebrate with you and the family.'

'Bellisimo, bellisimo. Maria will be over the moon.'

Through the large hall they walked into the main reception room on the right-hand side of the house. A large square room, a polished stone floor, a simple yet practical room, the door was open, and as they walked in, Aronne Biscotti put his hand up in welcome and came over. Greetings were made, hands were shaken, token introductions carried out. The space was busy; about 10 men were already in the room. Chatting amiably, they smiled at the newcomers and waited for Vittorio to do the rounds. There was a large round table in the middle, a bar on the one side serviced by a man who provided a small glass of red for Vittorio. Ciro took a glass of orange.

'I'll have a drink later,' he said to the barman.

Vittorio greeted the men traditionally with Ciro next to him, Ciro hugging a few he hadn't seen in a few years. They all knew each other, and respect for one another was there, but behind the smiles, handshakes and pleasant words there lay, for many, a deep-seated wariness of each other. Over the years there had been many family feuds resulting in deaths, mainly over territory, supply and money. No one had ever won the wars that had raged between them, and for most in the room, whilst distrust was still lingering in each one's mind, business, or more to the point money, was the calming factor these days. It had been several years since the last all-out war between families, and few wanted a re-run.

Mancuso Calabrase walked over to the table and pulled out a chair. Putting his drink down and lighting a cigar, he waited momentarily as the talk quietened down and men began to either leave the room or take a seat. The bar tender placed his final glass on the bar, and he too walked out followed by Ciro, Scipio and a few others. Six men sat down at the table and looked at Mancuso. Mancuso was a boss of the Calabrase cosa nostra family in Sicily. It was under his protection that this meeting took place. Well respected across the country and with a wealth of international contacts, many had prospered from his intervention and assistance.

'Gentlemen, welcome.' Raising his glass and sipping his wine, he continued. 'I know some of you have a few concerns, which is why we are here today. Our guests, if you agree, will join us later. If you cannot agree then I think you will have missed a great opportunity to expand your respective organisations, but it is your choice not mine. My business is not affected by whatever choice you make, I am only here to make sure our friends are greeted with cordiality, which I'm sure they will be.' Putting his glass down, 'Aronne,' with a wave of his hand, 'Over to you,' he said sitting down.

Placing his cigar in the ashtray, Aronne looked at each man in turn.

'Don Calabrase, grazie. Thank you for your hospitality. Gentlemen, we know why we are all here, this is the last time we will meet to discuss this, and I hope we will all collectively agree on the right decision. Each one of you, including me and our representative families, has seen how the world is changing. Our customers and those we help are changing too, and we need to adapt to this, which if we do, I believe will be good for all of us. This deal allows us to focus on our core businesses and not get side tracked with what, whilst lucrative, is a small part of what we do. 'With exception,' nodding at Vittorio, 'we have other areas that we can grow, which, dare I say, are far less hassle and more attractive.' Picking up his cigar, he drew on it, watching the men in front of him, trying to gauge their initial reaction.

'We met with our Iranian friend and have agreed increased shipments each month. Delivery will still be into Genoa and then sent on to the respective countries, and on arrival we will gain payment from our friends. They will be responsible, from that moment on, for distribution. This will allow us to free up our network, use our own guys in other projects and, more importantly, we will have instant cash in our pockets without the wait for it to filter through.'

He watched as a few of the men started to nod in agreement.

'How will we know that the money is right?' growled Giovi Bossio. As head of the family in Turin, his territory covered a fair chunk of northern Italy from Turin across into Germany and southern Switzerland.

'The money is the same as what you received last year and will continue to be the same with a 10% increase each year. As it is with all of us, whatever we moved last year will be the same revenue for this and the coming year with an increase of 10%. The extra shipments, which we have now negotiated the money from, will be split equally between each family sat at this table.'

Giovi nodded.

With revenues approaching €6 billion a year and assets worth over €25 billion, the 'Ndrangheta had become one of the most profitable criminal organisations in the world, and if they could agree and keep it together with no more in-wars then their income could become limitless.

'I have met many of these guys and they are very similar to us,' said Vicenzu Minniti, whose family was in the heart of Calabria and had been a dominant clan since the turn of the century.

'They have the same values as us, they are only family based, brothers, cousins, fathers, uncles. Like us, blood is blood, and you can only trust your own blood. We have Omerta, the code of honour, and they have Besa, their code of honour; these are the bonds that our two people embrace with the old traditions that we believe in so much. In our hearts, we are the same: vengeance, honour and respect. This is why I am for this deal: they work and live like us.'

'I agree,' nodded Fabio sipping his wine. 'It is time for us to build a relationship with these people.'

'Si, si, our exposure is minimal. They don't get the gear until we get paid. We control the transport to Genoa and beyond, and if anything goes wrong, we can stop it and divert if needed,' said Angelo Fonda, the boss of the Genovese family.

'Don Angelo is right. Also, the networks that buy heroin do not buy anything else, so our other activities are secure. May I suggest that if we all agree and this goes well then we could consider letting them take other areas of our business. Let them take the risks. We control the supply and have the money quicker, which I have no problem with,' said Fabio.

Aronne looked around. The discussion continued for the next half an hour or so. Each one had their say; others answered the questions for him. He wanted this deal, as did Fabio and Angelo. It made perfect sense. They would increase the imports, up the cash and stay at arm's length.

'I would also like to propose that Vittorio continues with the movement of money. Vittorio. . .' said Aronne nodding towards the man from London.

'The increased amounts will pose no problem. This time the money will come locally, depending on the country, and via Durres into the Cayman Islands, transferred across through several other banks, into Switzerland, across to France and then into the banking system in London. This cleansing allows me then to forward you payments to wherever you want. If you wish to stay the same as now, that's fine, if not then I can easily arrange other accounts for you to access your money. The process will take no longer than before. Once I have received notification that the money has landed, the goods can be realised into their control and the transactions across the banks can take place. I personally guarantee that your money will be safe, on time and correct,' said Vittorio looking at each of the men in turn.

The conversation continued for a few more minutes. Aronne, smoking his cigar, looked at Fabio and nodded slightly.

'Shall we vote?' said Fabio. Looking at each man in turn, 'Si, Si,' came the replies from around the table. Vittorio smiled; his life was about to get so much easier as money was much simpler to move around than vast amounts of heroin.

'Let's have a drink,' smiled Aronne, standing.

'Our friends will be here in an hour or so.' Patting Fabio on the shoulder as he walked round the table, the men stood and shook hands with each other.

Stopping next to Mancuso, 'Grazie, my friend, it has gone well. We are indebted to your hospitality.'

Opening the doors to the room, several men walked in. The barman had a pot of coffee in his hand and went over to the bar where a few had congregated. Pouring the coffee in prepared shot glasses, the hot coffee aroma filled the room. Vittorio walked over to Ciro, who had come through the main doors.

'You need to make a phone call for me,' said Vittorio quietly in Ciro's ear.

Ciro nodded.

*

Rinori Kodra and his cousin Genti sat in the back seat of the car. They had been picked up from the hotel a couple of hours ago and had another hour to drive before they arrived. The other four men who had come had all travelled separately, each one making his own way from a different hotel and waiting to be picked up. Caution was the name of the game. Rinori, along with the others, had many enemies, and whilst they occasionally fought each other, the threats from outside were greater. Each man controlled considerable areas. Spain, France and Germany each had its own army, supply chain and customer base, built on initial aggression, and then any deviances cracked down hard on; it was the Albanian way. However, all had realised over the years that as a family group, albeit extended, they were stronger and had more buying power if they pulled together than as a single entity in their own right.

The car pulled onto the cobbled courtyard; the door opened and Rinori and his cousin got out.

'Benvenuto.' Scipio Sorrentino was waiting and greeted the two men cordially. Handshakes followed and they were escorted into the main building.

'Let me introduce you,' said Scipio.

'Fabio, you know,' he said as Fabio shook Rinori's hand.

Introductions made, the men went into the room where Scipio walked over to Aronne, waiting, and with a smile he welcomed the two men.

The table in the room had now been extended, many more chairs were placed, and as the two men made their way around the occupants of the room, several more people had arrived. Rinori looked over as he saw the rest of the party being showed the same courteous welcome that he had.

'Don Calabrase,' said Rinori, 'thank you for the hospitality.'

'You and your men are both welcome and safe.'

The two men had been introduced a few years earlier by the Columbians. They had formed a good relationship, and he had supplied some cocaine to Rinori when there had been a mix up at the docks. In return, Rinori had provided Mancuso with an array of weaponry, which had proved very useful to him in the intervening wars that had raged between his own countrymen.

The two men clinked glasses.

'Let's sit,' offered Aronne.

The room went quiet, some left, and once again the doors closed.

The meeting this time was started by Aronne. Standing so he could see everyone, he outlined the proposal to Rinori and his countrymen. They were fully aware of the nature of the arrangement, and all had been in broad agreement.

'It is important that we all agree,' said Aronne. 'We do not want for there to be a misunderstanding as to how it will operate, who is responsible for what and also when. If anyone has questions this is the time to ask. If we disagree, there will be no comebacks on anyone. This. . .' Aronne waved his hand across the room, 'is under the house of Don Calabrase and respect will be given.'

Aronne looked around the men sat at the table; many

were smoking, and all were listening to him. He knew this was a potentially dangerous situation. All outside were armed, and possibly some of those around the table were armed as well. A cordial and constructive meeting was on the agenda; it would be a catastrophe if anything kicked off. He hoped that sense and business would prevail.

'This is what we. . .' Aronne pointed at his own countrymen, 'have agreed.' Aronne ran through the details. They would supply the tons of heroin directly to the port at Genoa. The consignments, once delivered to individual countries and paid for, would be then in the hands of the Albanians. They would distribute it as they wanted, and each Italian family that sat around the table would provide them with the methods and customers that they were using to move and use the drugs. Individual meetings would take place across Italy, France, Germany, Spain, Poland and England, where information and control would pass to the Albanians. The Italian families would direct, strongly if necessary, to their supply chain and customers that the Albanians were now their source of supply and no longer the Italians. Prices and quantities would be set by the Albanians. Once control had passed then each Italian family would walk away from any further contacts they had in the supply of heroin in that country. The only exception would be Sicily and the USA and Canada.

Aronne sat down, opening the floor to anyone who wanted to speak. A few questions were asked about the supply out of Genoa, and an agreed route was taken. Aronne would provide support for the transport out of Italy into Germany, just in case. That seemed to please everyone. Two or three trips a month wouldn't cost Aronne anything, and it was unlikely that they would encounter problems, but he saw it as a token and was happy to provide it.

The conversation in the room died down.

'We will leave you now for a few minutes to discuss what we have said. Don Calabrase will be here.' Nodding to the others, the Italian family's leaders stood, closed the door and went into the room, which had been laid out for dinner that night.

It didn't take long. The door opened, and Aronne was beckoned back into the room. The men took their seats and waited for one of the Albanians to speak.

Rinori stood.

'We have agreed, and we would like to do business,' he said simply.

Aronne stood, walked round, shook his hand. Taking their lead from Aronne, the men all stood and began congratulating each other. Prompted by the noise that was coming from the room, the barman entered with an assistant and laid out glasses of wine in front of everyone.

Don Calabrase stood.

'Gentlemen. . .' the room went quiet.

'It is a moment that binds our two countries. I know we will all do well. Thank you for coming; the future is in your hands. Let me raise a toast,' he said holding his glass in the air, looking around the room.

'Partners, brothers, famiglia.'

Chapter 11

Walking over to the bedroom window he carefully and slowly parted the curtain and looked out. He was on the fourth floor of the tower block. Occupying a corner flat, he could see both the north and west approaches. The road below was getting busy with the locals beginning their day, a normal Saturday morning. Some kids had already started to play outside. The weather wasn't great, but kids were kids and they preferred to be outside than in. *The little shits*, he thought. When he first arrived, he had stayed with his aunt and uncle who had come over in the mid-seventies. His uncle had run a small café, and a couple of years ago, he had retired. It was nice to stay with them, but eventually Lorenc had got his own place, nothing fancy, just basic and convenient. He owned a car not a decent one, he would soon but not in this neighbourhood. The local brats on their bikes routinely scratched the sides of the new cars that appeared from time to time, people visiting, those that wouldn't stump up the five quid that they charged to 'protect' the vehicle from vandals. *Enterprising but annoying*, he thought, staring intently for any changes that had occurred overnight. Satisfied that nothing was untoward, he let the curtain close and stepped the yard or so to the other window, facing east, and did the same. Nothing. Looking at his watch, a beautiful gold Rolex, he nodded to himself: time to leave. Picking up the Glock from the kitchen table, checking the magazine, he tucked it into his belt, pulled the coat over it and fastened the two of the lower pop buttons on the jacket. The coat, waist length, covered the gun, but if needed, access to it could be swift.

He favoured the stairs and dropped down the four floors with ease, and before going outside through the front double doors of the block of flats, he waited patiently. Moments later, a taxi drew up. With another quick look, he pushed the doors open and stepped quickly into the taxi, getting in the back.

'Shabani's, mate.'

'OK.'

The drive took the taxi through the estate and into Barking town centre. Barking, an east London conclave, was once renowned for its fishing industry and boat building, both of which, like so many across the UK, had died, which left the likes of Barking with nothing. As the years progressed, with a lack of investment in the area, the concrete-built shopping centres and high street shops all fell into decline, the population mix changed to become ethnically extremely diverse, and with the only major work in the area being provided by the Dagenham car plant, unemployment was rife, fuelling not only crime but drug addiction, a perfect location for the man in the taxi. Pulling up outside Shabani's, paying the cabby, he walked into the café and sat down.

'Morning, Lorenc. Usual?' said the man behind the counter.

Nodding, he lit a cigarette and waited for his breakfast.

Ali walked over with a coffee in his hand and placed it in front of Lorenc.

'Sad day yesterday.'

'Yeah.'

'How's the mother? She OK? Not many there, which was a shame.'

'She's OK. Gutted, as you can imagine.'

'Do you think she'll go home?'

'Not sure. Her other son is still in Durres, so she might.'

Ali nodded. 'If you need anything. . .' leaving the question hanging.

'Thanks.'

Lorenc drew on his cigarette, letting the smoke choke his lungs. He liked a deep bitter taste; the English fags, in his opinion, were weak, preferring his own country's brand. Sipping the coffee, he thought about the funeral, the second one in the space of four weeks. First was Tariq and then his brother Genet. Tariq Shehu had been the leader of the tightly knit gang of Albanian drug dealers. Run by Tariq, with his brothers and cousins, they had ruled since Tariq's elder brother Agron, who had originally set up the gang had been murdered a couple of years earlier. Tariq had been taken out along with one of his men by someone suspected as being a rival gang member. On his death, the remainder of Tariq's men had been rounded up, most of them charged with the usual: drug dealing, trafficking and possession of guns. Tariq's brother Genet had been released on bail, but last weekend he had been targeted and shot dead outside his flat by a couple of guys on a scooter. It was too much for their mother. The grief was overwhelming her, so it was highly likely that she would go back home to Albania and her close-knit family.

Lorenc had come over when Agron had been murdered. In the attack, Besnik, Agron's right hand man, had also been shot and killed. Besnik Kodra was Lorenc's brother, and although no one had talked about Besnik as Agron was the main man, to Lorenc he was blood and it had hit him hard. Tariq had asked him to join the gang, but he wasn't interested, preferring to stay on the outside biding his time, both for revenge and to establish his own presence when the time came. Tariq had taken care of the dog that had killed Agron and Besnik, so Lorenc had just sat and watched to see how events played out. With Genet and Tariq now both dead it provided him with the ideal opportunity to step in and take over a drug network already established. Two more of his brothers and several cousins would be arriving in the UK soon, and there were more on the way, after which it would make them a dominant force in the area.

Sipping his coffee and eating his breakfast, he had picked out several places over the last few weeks that would make good supply houses. Clean and in the middle of a housing estate, one of them would become his cutting lab; the other, in a quiet cul de sac, would not attract any attention. He didn't agree with Tariq's view that they should be out on industrial estates, he held the belief that hidden in plain sight was the best way. As initial drop points for the coke, the units were ideal, but after that then they would use houses for the small amounts that they kept for themselves and any favoured customer who wanted to deal direct. Most of the coke they were bringing in they would sell straight on and left the local distributer to cut it anyway they wanted. They wouldn't make as much money as they would if it was on the street, but they wouldn't have the hassle of bagging it into small quantities; let the next layer down take that strain. Initially, he would use his cousins to bag up their own supply, but as they got more established, he would use girls. Tariq had told him about some Nigerian guy who could supply labour. He had watched Tariq's patch unravel as the days and weeks had gone by. The druggies didn't care who supplied them as long as they got their little packets every day. Yardies, Pakistanis and a few local small fry had stepped up and were on the ground regularly. Easy for him, he thought, once his crew were with him to move them off. He had seen who the players were, in his opinion, easy meat. A truck was coming in next week from his brother that had an assortment of nines, which meant they all would be strapped with some decent gear.

Finishing his food and pulling out a few notes, he waved at the counter, pointing to the money he left on the table. The owner, Ali, acknowledged him and Lorenc walked outside. Pulling a packet out of his pocket, selecting one, he lit up, took in a lung full and walked towards the crossing. His plan for the day, as always, was to walk to the station, catch a Tube into town and get to know the city's alleyways and walkways around Soho, Leicester Square, Covent Garden and up to Whitechapel. This was the area that he wanted to develop, a lot of homeless people, clubs, bars and strip joints, all good targets for pushing. He'd been here a couple of years now and knew the ground all the way from Lewisham up through Bermondsey, across the river and into the city down to Soho. Watching everything and everyone during the day, and during the night, sometimes late into the early hours at the weekends, he had the feel of the underbelly of the place. Every month, his family had sent him money, so he was able to travel, stay, eat as he needed. Knowing the competition was key to him, crowding them out and taking control, he had expected trouble at some point from Tariq, but the light had shone on him brightly, and neither Tariq nor his gang were going to be a problem. So, as far as he was concerned, he could have all his territory as well. It was a route to market they had used before. He had seen some tear into a place and try and control it through violence, but it never worked, you needed to know your enemy and plan. Violence was a common denominator, but there was no point shooting soldiers if you didn't know who the captains were, which was why so many gangs failed. Albanians always planned, and when they struck, they struck hard, and it worked.

The scooter pulled up a hundred yards from the lights and came to a stop by the side of the road. The pillion passenger adjusted his helmet, pulled his gloves tight, squeezed his knees together to anchor himself to the bike and slid his hand inside his leather jacket, feeling the butt of the gun. The pair waited. They had seen their mark a couple of days previously and watched his routine. The rider switched off the engine and looked at his watch: less than 10 minutes. Looking around, the traffic was light, a few pedestrians, a couple of buses, an ordinary day. It would be quick and simple, a well-practised manoeuvre. As they watched the café, they saw Lorenc come out, look up and down and then light a cigarette. The rider clicked the start button on the scooter and got ready to push off. The pillion passenger slid his hand into his coat and clutched the butt of the gun in readiness. Lorenc walked up to the lights and hit the button. The rider slowly pulled out into the traffic. *This is going to be easy*, he thought.

The pillion passenger felt a buzz in his pocket and tapped the driver on the shoulder who, surprised, pulled over.

'Be quick, otherwise we'll miss the lights,' he said.

The man pulled out the pager from his pocket and glanced at the display. The rider revved the scooter's engine as he saw the lights turn red, and Lorenc stepped onto the crossing. Not waiting, he pulled out onto the road.

The man behind read the message and quickly hit the rider's shoulder twice.

'Pull over.'

'What?'

'Quick!'

The passenger shoved his hand in front of the rider's eyes, showing the display on the pager.

'Fuck!' he said.

Pulling back onto the road, he drove to the lights. Lorenc was halfway across.

Turning his head, Lorenc looked at the scooter and the two on board. A moment of recollection shot across his face: this was how Genet had got hit. He slid his hand into the jacket and quickly gripped the Glock on his belt. The scooter just stayed still, engine turning over quietly, neither man really looking at him.

Lorenc made the other side as the lights turned green and the scooter raced off. The pillion passenger looked once more at the display on the pager before putting it into his pocket.

'FARE ABORTIRE! FARE ABORTIRE!' it read, cancelling the attack.

'Are we done then?' said Bill Blake, her DS, sighing, looking at Izzy. The two of them had spent the last week or so tailing Lorenc. After the first funeral, Tariq's, they had spotted Lorenc and had decided to watch him to see if he stepped up to take Tariq's place. The funeral was only the second or third time they had seen Lorenc. In their surveillance of Tariq and subsequent arrest of the gang, Lorenc had never figured in any of the photographs or had been observed at any meeting between Tariq and his gang members, so he had been left out of the gang round up. DCI Paul Jackson, who headed up the taskforce, had given them a few weeks to follow and report just to see if he would be making any headway onto the turf. The second funeral, the other day, Genet's, had again seen Lorenc, but nothing had been out of the ordinary. They had been following him around London, during the day and then on their own time during the night and on weekends, but he was always alone and had shown no interest in what they would have determined suspicious activity.

Today then was the last day of the follow.

'We might as well,' said DI Isabelle Taylor, watching Lorenc from the passenger seat of the Peugeot as he crossed over the lights and headed towards the Tube.

DI Isabelle Taylor, or Izzy as she was known to her friends, had been deeply involved with the Tariq gang, suffering a brutal attack by Tariq just before his death at the hands of an unseen assailant. She and her team had gathered massive amounts of detailed, incriminating evidence against the gang, resulting in their arrest. Tariq's death had been a surprise but was the catalyst to make the arrests and put to bed another London drug gang. Genet had been at the heart of the operation, and his untimely death was seen as either revenge or another drug syndicate vying to take over. DCI Jackson was keen to make sure that they would nip it in the bud early if Lorenc was following in Tariq's footsteps. However, after watching him for the last few weeks nothing had transpired, and they had decided their time was now better spent on other toerags in the area.

Absent mindedly touching her forehead where the bruise had remained for some time, she thought about Tariq, his death and the unknown killer as Bill started the car, slipped into the traffic and headed back to base. There were still many questions unanswered as far as Izzy was concerned, but everyone around her had congratulated themselves on a good job and now it was time to take the fight to the next group. *I suppose*, she thought, *I'm still alive. I wasn't shot. I still have a job, and most of the gang are going down for a very long time,* and as her thoughts drifted towards the remaining members locked up, she pulled her diary from her bag and looked through at the court dates that were coming up. All the reports had been done; it was now a matter for the crown prosecution to secure sentences for them all. Her and her team would be appearing in court for a while, but as long as they got a decent outcome then it would have been all worthwhile. They were tasked with targeting drug gangs and sex trafficking in the city and surrounding suburbs and had nailed the Shehu gang with great success. The turf wars, however, were constant, and trying to keep up with the major players was time consuming. They were given considerable latitude by their bosses so were able to be more proactive than reactive when it came to players in the lucrative drugs market.

'You up for an Indian tonight?' asked Bill, bringing her back.

'Yeah, why not.'

Chapter 12

Couple of days later climbing the stairs two at a time, she reached her floor easily, and she was pleased with herself. *Not out of breath, or well, not quite*, she thought. Preferring the stairs to the lift, it gave her some exercise. She had belonged to a gym a while back but having piled 10 months of money into the place and having been only twice she'd called it quits. They still wanted the rest of the money though, which had pissed her off, so on her last week of membership she'd gone and spent an hour in the gym, swam in the pool and used the sauna. Relaxing in the sauna, she almost changed her mind and signed for another year, but then the nag in her head decided against it as most of her time was spent at the desk or just recently, in court along with late nights scouring the endless amounts of information that the team and she were gathering. The team, her team, had been praised by the DCI, and the previous Shehu case had made them stronger, and they worked well as a group. The team comprised her, acting DS Bill Blake, DC Craig Dawson, who had replaced Mike – he'd taken on a job in the drugs team in Liverpool – DS Claire Southam, DC Wayne Johnson and DC Simon Carrs. Their office was several floors up at Scotland Yard, and they occupied a small area on one corner overlooking the Thames, overseen by DCI Paul Jackson.

The court case she had given testimony at today was on one of the lower ranked members of the Shehu gang. As usual, she had to hang around for three hours before being called, but on giving her evidence, apart from a couple of cross examination questions, she got out quite quickly. Looking at her watch, it was coming up to four. Having nothing planned for the night, which, sighing, wasn't a surprise, she sat at her desk, nodded to Bill and picked up the daily sheets and began to wade through them.

'Anything?'

'Not really,' said Bill. 'Couple of muggings, nothing from the stabbing at the weekend, and that bunch of dicks who crashed their car with some hash in it a couple of weeks ago have been cautioned and sent on their way. The paperwork's there,' said Bill pointing at a separate pile on her desk.

Izzy nodded. Her main target now was the Yardies. They had been seen several times on Shehu's turf, and from what they had heard were mopping up his smackheads. There had been a few reported beatings but nothing out of the ordinary. *Consolidating their position*, she thought, picking up another file.

'It's Sihana's case week after next. Is there anything the CPS asked for that is outstanding?'

'No, she pleaded not guilty at her pre, which was expected. It's going to be hard as we don't have a great deal to pin on her, apart from gains from prostitution, and because of the women that we found there, exploitation as well, which should run in our favour. Jeremy was saying yesterday that if we had hard evidence that Tariq had delivered the girls then it would be clearer cut, but he's dead, so that's a non-starter. He also said that because you didn't have a one hundred percent clear view of what was happening then he can't use your statement either, as you know. We'll get her, well, we'll get her on something, but I can't see it being a lengthy sentence, prob probation.'

Sihana was Tariq's sister and had been caught with several Nigerian women at her alleged brothel in Soho. Izzy had witnessed the delivery of the girls, but as she tried to get closer, she had been attacked and knocked unconscious.

'My guess is that he bought the girls from someone. He never left the country when we were on him, so he must have known someone here, and I reckon he'd done it before. Get a bus load, sell a few, keep a few then move them on after they've served their purpose,' said Izzy.

'I agree, but that trail is dead.'

Putting the file back down, vowing to follow up, she leafed through some more of the papers on her desk.

'Izzy, got a minute?'

Looking up, DCI Jackson had poked his head round the corner at the far end, beckoning her. She walked over.

'What's up?'

'Upstairs. DSUP wants us.'

'Oh,' she said, feeling slightly nervous.

'It's fine, a briefing that's all.'

Izzy sighed, relieved. It was rare that she saw Detective

Superintendent Arnold Cartwright. Typically, it was never a good thing to be called to his office. *Must be the Shehu trials*, she thought. *Shit, hope I haven't forgotten something.* She desperately tried to remember if every bit of paperwork, statements and files were in order. The last thing she needed was for a trial to be thrown out down to an error, especially an error from her or her team.

They took the lift to the eleventh floor. His secretary was waiting for them, and as they approached her desk, she picked up the phone. They waited.

'You can go in,' she said, her face bland.

'Afternoon, sir,' said Paul.

'Sir,' said Izzy, nodding as she closed the door behind her.

'Hi, grab a seat.' Rising from behind his desk, he picked up a file and sat at the long table in the middle of the room. Selecting a chair, they both sat opposite Arnold.

'Hear the trials for the Shehu gang are going well,' he began, looking at Izzy.

'Yes, sir, we will get them all, and hopefully the sister as well, in the next few weeks.'

'Good, good.'

Opening the file, he pulled out some photographs.

'And it's that theme I want to talk to you about. I've whizzed this past Paul and we both want you to cover this, given recent events.'

Izzy looked at Paul.

'Yes, sir.'

'These,' said Arnold pushing well over a dozen pictures towards her, 'were taken a short time ago.'

Izzy looked. Some were long range, others were close ups of faces, men's faces. Staring at them, 'I don't recognise any of them,' she said, slowly going from one picture to the next.

'Now as I explained to Paul, we have been given these by our friends in the Italian government. What you are looking at is a gathering of the 'Ndrangheta mafia and known Albanians. The meeting took place in some small village deep in the heart of southern Italy. The Italian operation was mounted by their SISDE, their equivalent to our MI5. As everyone knows, the Mafia are a massive problem for the Italians, so disrupting their flow of money, drugs etc. is a priority over there.'

The pictures were in colour and of good quality; each man was easily identifiable. The pictures showed arrivals and departures of the group. They also showed that the men departing were shaking hands, which Izzy assumed were their hosts, the Italians.

'Blimey, quite a group, but. . .' looking at Arnold and then Paul, 'what have they got to do with us?'

Arnold lent forward. Sifting through the photos, he picked a few up and gave them to Paul. 'These,' he said. 'You explain.'

Paul put them in front of Izzy.

'This guy,' he said, pointing at one of the men, is Rinori Kodra. We have been told that he is a major drug trafficker in Albania along with these other three.' He pointed at another couple of photos.

'So?'

'So, we believe that the Italians and Albanians have struck a deal of some sort. We think that they are going to let the Albanians, this man and the others. . .' said Paul pointing at Kodra, 'have control of the import and distribution of either cocaine, heroin, or both, into Europe and the UK unhindered; the thought is that it will probably be heroin. Not sure how the Mafia profit, but clearly there is a reason for them doing it, and I'm sure they are not doing it out of the goodness of their hearts.'

'OK, OK, I get that, and I know the name Kodra,' she said in recollection.

'Rinori Kodra is Lorenc Kodra's brother.'

Izzy began to nod. 'That's why he hasn't gone home.'

'That's what we think, plus the other factor that has swung it are these men. . .' he continued, leaning across and picking up three other photographs, 'Vittorio De Luca and Ciro Massimo. These guys are based in London.'

Rinori hadn't been to London before, so watching the flight over the outskirts of London and into Heathrow would have been of interest if, of course, it had been sunny, but it wasn't, so he didn't. Genti, next to him, and three other cousins were aboard the flight and were going to be the first group to establish a base using the flats that Lorenc had earmarked. He was disappointed that he couldn't attend his brother's funeral, but on balance they had discussed it and it was decided that Lorenc should go on his own. The fewer photos the cops had the better. Gathering the bags, the men went through customs, and

Rinori was delighted to see Lorenc waiting for him. It had been nearly three years since they had seen each other, and the welcome was genuine and for Lorenc a much-needed boost from his family.

The two cars crossed over the M4 joining the A40 at Northolt and then onto the North Circular at Hanger Lane. The journey, dropping them into Barking and onto the estate where Lorenc lived, wasn't far and took about an hour and a half. Lorenc was driving, making sure that the cousins in the second car didn't get left behind. Rinori, in the passenger seat next to him, spent most of the time talking about the family back home, filling in Lorenc with the various births and marriages in the family since he'd been away. Pulling up to the block of flats, Lorenc let them in and pointed out the bedroom that Rinori would be using that night and settled in the kitchen, making drinks.

'I've got you a couple of flats; these are the keys. A bit later we'll go across. I've got you a car each as well; here's the keys,' he said handing them over to the three cousins.

'Rinori will stay here with me tonight and then later we can decide who goes where, OK?'

'Great, thanks. BMW, nice,' said one. The others laughed.

'Only the best for my family!'

Smoking and drinking, the conversation turned quickly to business.

Pulling out a map of London and spreading it out onto the table, Lorenc, using an ashtray to hold the corner down, began to explain where they were.

'So, we are sat here,' he started, pointing out Barking. 'Heathrow is here and this. . .' drawing a circle with his finger, 'is mainly the boundary of London,' he said, explaining where the flats were, the two industrial units and houses that he had earmarked for the gang and then about the territory.

'All along here, these places. . .' he continued, with more finger pointing, 'are up for grabs. Easy distance from the house, and in the city here, here, and here are drop off points.'

The conversation continued with Lorenc explaining where he had seen the Yardies and Pakistanis operate, the pushers on the street and where some of the middle guys were.

The formula worked all over the world, a major supply came in, cut, if necessary, bagged and given to the main distribution guys. These were then siphoned off to the middlemen. The middlemen dropped it at certain houses or shops, or sometimes drove it to the pushers, who then sold it on to the users, money changing hands all the way. The higher up the chain you were, the more money you made, but the initial outlay was greater as were the risks with such a huge quantity of drugs in one place for a short period of time. A pusher, or user, would get a caution, slapped wrists, maybe a month or two behind bars, the middlemen a couple of years, the main distribution guys substantially longer plus the seizure of assets and at the top, the likes of Rinori and Lorenc, many, many years banged up and total seizure of everything the police could find. Laying the drugs off quick was the name of the game. Getting the money and hiking the price was down to violence, or the threat of violence; however, once established, violence was perceived.

Opening the map fully, Rinori looked at the UK. 'So, what's what here then?'

'London, Birmingham, Manchester, Scotland, Wales,' said Lorenc. 'Apart from Bristol and Cardiff, nothing down from there,' indicating the southwest. 'Fuck all along this coast,' he continued, pointing at the South coast. 'Same again up here,' he said, drawing a line from London to Newcastle. 'Hard work here. Apparently, they are fucking nutters,' he went on, circling Tyneside. 'Fuck Scotland. The one or two I have met I can't understand, so bollocks to that. This area, Liverpool, Manchester, etc. across to here,' pointing at the M1, 'is good, and so is Birmingham.'

'Good. OK, well early yet, but looks like we can split it once we start getting the gear in. You go up here with some of the boys,' he said letting his finger fall on Liverpool and Manchester. 'I'll take here, London, and Genti can get Birmingham. Supply won't be a problem now we have an agreement with the Italians.'

'Oh yeah, so it's for real, is it? We get their chain then?' said Lorenc.

Rinori outlined the meeting he had had and the agreement that was now in place.

'I met their London guy Vittorio, and we've arranged to meet. He'll intro to his distribution setup, which we will take over. Also, the sooner we get more girls in, the sooner we can get a couple of chop shops up there,' he said pointing to the north of England. 'Then we can control the whole lot without any aggro from our friends. Expect the others will be a problem, but we can sort that.'

'Yeah, the Pakis don't tend to go north, but the Yardis have quite a reach, so could be a bit of bangin' there to do. Not sure about the chinks up there though.'

'OK. We'll use the Ital's setup for the H, and I've got a load of smack coming in in a couple of weeks, which we will throw out to the guys. That gives us a hook into that market straight away.'

The conversation continued, and they agreed that a lot would have to wait a week or so until Rinori and Lorenc had more people on the ground.

'I'll go up to Liverpool at the end of the month and take the Agfa cousins with me.'

'OK,' said Rinori.

'What about picking up some of Tariq's boys if they get let out?'

'We'll see, doubt it though. They fucked up with Besnik. If they push, we'll just get rid of them.'

Lorenc made some more coffee and lit a cigarette. 'What about hardware?'

'The box should arrive tomorrow morning; we get it late tomorrow afternoon. I've got enough nines coming to spread between the houses for each of us and a few spares, a couple of heavy-duty bangers just in case. We go strapped at all times. Fuck the polici, we stay quiet for a week or so, get to know the area, and no fucking about,' said Rinori looking at his cousins. 'We can do that later, OK?'

'OK,' came the nods.

'Week after next the others will be across. By then we should have our first load. Do we need anything at the chop shops?' said Rinori looking at Lorenc.

'All there, bags, powder, safe, nothing needed. OK. Right,' said Lorenc, 'let's go. I'll show you the flats and cars, and after that, me and Rini will go over to the houses and the units.'

Chapter 13

The meeting had been arranged at an old house south of the river near Waterloo station. Tony hadn't been there before but knew roughly where it was. The journey from Paddington was simple; he had caught a cab down to Russell Street, walked through Covent Garden, pausing every now and then, casually looking in a few shop windows or stopping to light a cigarette. Dropping down to Charing Cross, grabbing the Tube, he got out at Waterloo. Working his way around to the entrance of the main station, he walked across the concourse pausing briefly to look over the wall at the Eurostar trains. To anyone watching he was just a casual observer. A moment there, and then past the main boards, he headed down the staircase, which took him to the ground floor. Turning left, he crossed over and took the road next to the Wellington Hotel, through the cut and under the railway arch, then a brief walk past The White Hart to the house. He made one last check before getting onto the path to the door which, as he approached, was opened by Barry.

'Hello, mate. Found us then?'

'Yeah, no problem. Been a while since I was at Waterloo,

but I remember the area. Used to have a beer in The White Hart from time to time, not a bad place but nothing special.'

'Not been in there. Leonard's in the kitchen.'

The house was deceptively big. An extension had been put on the back, which was where the kitchen was, a long, large kitchen with, Tony saw as he entered the room, a dining room table where Leonard was sat. Pulling up a chair, both he and Barry sat down. Tony pulled out his cigarettes and offered one to Barry, who took it and they both lit up watching Leonard looking through some photos.

'Our friend has made some new acquaintances by the looks of it,' said Leonard glancing at Tony as he passed the photos across.

'Vittorio De Luca and his sidekick Ciro,' said Barry pointing at the faces on the photo in Tony's hand.

'Where was this?'

'Our friends in the Italian SISDE got wind of a meeting between some of the 'Ndrangheta and what they now know are members of an Albanian mafia gang at a meeting in the hills of southern Italy,' said Leonard.

'Their information is that the two groups have made a deal. The Albanians will take over the distribution of heroin from the 'Ndrangheta across Europe and importantly, for us in the UK. We are not sure about cocaine as yet, so we are waiting for updates. It seems that that they can make more money sub-contracting their business than doing it themselves.'

'Makes a bit of sense,' said Barry. 'They keep their noses

clean while the Albanians take all the risks of supplying the pushers. It also gives them a much bigger share of the market, and with the blessing of the Italians they won't be facing any turf wars with those guys.'

Tony nodded. 'Bloody hell, must be worth a lot. How does our man fit in?'

'Our initial interest in him was money laundering and art theft. We know he's got some decent art on his walls, but we were told that he buys art from various fences in Europe. It's a stretch to find out more, but that was the reason I gave you the guy in the first place. The money laundering, we now think will be on a much bigger scale if he is providing that service to the Albanians, but we don't know for sure.'

'I could possibly make headway with the art, but as for the money laundering, I've no chance.'

'We know that. I've got a section tracing some money, which we think is, or was his. It's a slow burn, but the techies are hopeful. Your task now has moved up a gear given this meeting.'

'Why?' asked Tony.

'This bloke. . .' said Leonard pulling three other photographs from the pile and laying them out on the table, 'is Rinori Kodra.'

'I don't know him.'

'His brother Lorenc is in London and has been since the death of his brother Besnik, who was Agron Shehu's right hand man. Shehu, as you know, was replaced by his brother Tariq.'

'Small world,' said Tony.

'Absolutely, it's too coincidental that Lorenc is still in London. Our information is that he's not done anything since he's been here, which suggests he's been waiting. This, we believe, is probably what he has been waiting for.'

Picking up the photographs, Tony looked at each one in turn. The handshakes, the pats on the backs, the familiarity of the men in the pictures, a deal was done. *Wonder just how big it was,* thought Tony.

'Our guess is that de Luca will be asked to move more money about once he offloads his distribution arm in the UK to Lorenc, which means he will have a lot more money to float into the art world.' Tony nodded.

'Get close to Vittorio. We've created a backstory for you because I expect him to go looking. Keep an eye out for Lorenc, but don't go near him. We think the Met might take an interest, so I don't want you caught up in that, OK?'

'Yeah sure.'

'Where are you with Nadir?'

Tony replayed the conversation he had had with Nadir at the hotel.

'Well, he can't have the stuff now, so you need to tell him. Handle it so you can get back to him in a month or so. We need to find the bombmaker first, so delay him, OK. So, anything you need?'

'Yes, £35,000,' said Tony.

The call had come at 10:00 am on the Wednesday morning. The number Tony had given Nadir was monitored and routed through to an answering machine at Leonard's

138

offices. The message was brief and requested a meet at 6:00 pm the following day.

Listening to the message, it was clear to Tony that Nadir had decided to trust Tony with the location, giving him plenty of time. Tony thought that if it were him doing a deal like this with money and explosives, he would give the guy a couple of hours; however, it would be simple enough to meet. He knew Barry knew of the meeting, and it was decided that Tony should go on his own as it was unlikely that Nadir would have someone with him. The location of the meeting was just outside of Denham, not far from Uxbridge and Nadir's house. Slightly south of Denham aerodrome was a small industrial estate that housed the Martin-Baker factory, the original pioneer of ejection seat development. Since 1946, the business, renowned throughout the world, employed many of the local people. They had succeeded where many manufacturing companies had failed during the '70s and '80s by concentrating and mastering, with considerable expertise, their niche market: ejection seat technology. As the main company on the industrial estate, towards the end of the day it emptied out and around 5:30 pm was quiet. Nadir had picked this location as he had been detoured past there one day when there had been an accident on the main A40.

Tony was early and had scouted the area. Pulling up near the entrance to the estate in a large layby he waited. Glancing at his watch, he had about 50 minutes before Nadir arrived. Where he had parked would give him the opportunity of seeing anyone who came onto the estate. He doubted they would be much earlier if there was going to be trouble, but he erred on the side of caution anyway. In a plain, slightly dirty Vauxhall Cavalier 2LT Sri, a popular car on the streets, it attracted no attention, and as Tony smoked, he planned his story to Nadir. Time passed quickly, and Tony watched as the red Peugeot came into view. Driving past him, he saw Nadir look at him, go up the road a short distance, turn and drive and pull up behind him. Tony quickly jumped out and got into the passenger seat beside Nadir.

'Do you have what I need?'

'I've hit a bit of a problem,' said Tony looking at Nadir.

Nadir's eyes widened. 'What do you mean, you said you had the stuff?'

'I did, but I had another buyer the day after we met, and he needed it. I hadn't heard from you, so I moved that on and have got some more on the way. So don't worry, you'll get. . .'

'Are you taking me for an idiot? I told you I needed it soon, and I've got your money. What am I supposed to do now?' said Nadir angrily, cutting him off.

'Don't worry,' said Tony calmly. 'I will get it to you, but it's going to take a bit more time that's all.'

'Fuck off! Get out!' said Nadir. 'I'll get some somewhere else. Go on, get out!' he said raising his voice.

'It's fine. Don't worry, I'll. . .'

'Get the fuck out!' Nadir was trying to reach Tony's door handle, his voice getting louder.

'Get out! Go on! Get lost!' now shouting.

Tony raised his hand. 'It's OK. I'll get. . .'

'Just fucking go! Get out!' Nadir slammed the car into reverse and went back a few feet.

'Get out!' he continued, shouting wildly.

Tony opened the door and was just able to get out when Nadir roared away, shouting and waving his fist in the air as he did so.

'Shit! Shit!' cursed Tony. *Now what?*

The conversation with Leonard hadn't gone well. Slamming the phone down, Tony kicked open the door of the telephone box, lit a cigarette, inhaled deeply and spat on the floor. 'What the fuck did he expect? Telling me I should have handled it better. Well then you do it, Mr Dickspook,' the conversation continued, partly out loud, partly swirling around in his head. Getting into his car, he headed to Bristol. Midday, he was lucky to find a spot in the car park. Grabbing his bag he went inside, muttered a greeting to Claire, his secretary, slammed the door to his office, chucked his jacket on the back of the chair and punched on the button, which lit up the computer screen.

'Meeting went well then,' said Claire as she came into the room.

'I'll open a window,' she continued, watching him light up a cigarette.

'No, we didn't get the contract.'

'Which one?'

'The electric down in Torquay. They are going to wait; fuck knows what for. Fucking idiots!'

Claire stood in front of his desk and looked at him.

'Sorry, didn't mean to swear. It's just annoying, that's all.'

'Ummm, here's your post. I'm going for a late lunch, be back in an hour.'

'OK, thanks, Claire, and sorry again.'

Leaving him to scan through his emails, she put her coat on. He glanced up and smiled briefly at her as she went out.

Pushing himself back from the desk, losing interest in the dozen or so emails on his screen, he smoked his fag. Noticing the coffee machine still had some coffee left, he poured himself a cup and calmed down.

Pulling himself towards the desk, he whizzed through the emails, signed some letters and added a few notes to a presentation which was going to be needed next week. He looked at his watch: a quarter to. He sat back, thinking, *If not me then someone else will supply. It's not over.*

'I told you to keep with our own. You can't trust them; they don't believe the same as we do.'

Nadir apologised.

'Go home, do what you normally do. Go to work, come back for prayers. I will take it from here, don't worry,' said Arli laying a reassuring hand on Nadir's shoulder. 'It will be fine, trust Allah.'

Smiling, he led Nadir to the door.

'Prayers later?'

Nadir nodded and walked home.

He knew he should never have left Nadir to get the Semtex, thought Arli, but he didn't want his name or prints anywhere near the stuff, just in case. That now had changed, and to keep to their schedule he had phoned his cousin in Iraq and had cagily explained the situation. The next message he got a few days later was an address in Reading. Collection on Thursday the following week, the money had changed hands and assurances were given that he could go and collect. The name of the man was Eugene.

Pulling up outside the Coach and Horses in Tilehurst, he looked at the pub. From what he knew it was a typical pub selling mostly beer with very little, if, any food. He'd been in a couple around where he lived just to make himself familiar with them just in case he had ever needed to go in them on business. Well, that time was now, he thought. Glancing at his watch, it was just approaching 6:00 pm, and as he sat, he saw several burly looking men in overalls and donkey jackets go in. Having no idea what Eugene looked like, he hoped it would be simple. Locking the car, he pushed open the pub door and was met with a cloud of smoke. The bar was close, but as he walked over most of the people in the place stopped talking and stared at him. Ignoring them, he lent on the bar and waited for the barman to approach him. The slap on the back made him jump.

'Hello, my fine friend. How are you today?'

Turning, the man next to him patted him again on the shoulder.

'Over here, come on.' Arli was not expecting the thick Irish accent but was relieved that he didn't have to start asking for Eugene or waiting around. As a devout Muslim, drinking was not allowed, and Arli had never been tempted.

When he'd been in foreign company before, drinking Coke was his choice.

The noise in the bar resumed. 'You found us alright then?'

'Yes, thank you. I hope you have what I need,' said Arli quietly.

Eugene nodded, looked around the bar, swigged the last remnants of his Guinness and said, 'Let's go.'

The two men left the pub with Arli following Eugene into the car park and down the side of the pub to where a white beat-up old van was parked. Arli heard footsteps behind him, turned and saw two other men closing in on them. Eugene saw the look on his face.

'Don't be a worrying about them,' said Eugene opening the van and picking out a large black sports bag and another smaller bag.

'These are yours. Keep them separate, OK?' Thrusting them into his hands, slamming the door, Eugene nodded at the two others who got into the van with Eugene, and with a rev of the engine drove away.

Arli felt the weight; it was heavier than he expected, and he was slightly shocked at the immediacy of the trans-action. No questions, no invitation to look at the goods, just, 'Here's the stuff,' which as Arli drove back to London, he thought, was probably a good thing. The less people know the better.

Back in the basement, Arli placed the bags on the table carefully. Unzipping the larger one, he peered inside: three square blocks wrapped in what appeared to be greaseproof paper lay at the bottom of the bag. Pushing the bag to the back of the table, he picked up the second much smaller bag, and although not necessary, this bag he put at the other end of the table and breathed a sigh of relief. Unfamiliar with how explosives worked, he knew enough, he thought, to keep the detonators and Semtex apart. It had taken less than two weeks to get this after Nadir had told him that Tony couldn't deliver.

Having picked it up from Eugene, he had speculated on the drive back where it came from. He guessed, given that Eugene was Irish, it had probably come at some point from Libya. Gaddafi, he knew, was supplying the IRA with Semtex and had a good smuggling route into the UK. Gaddafi, he also knew, was a supporter of Al Qaeda as two of his brothers had been in the desert training camps about 100 miles south of Tripoli a few years ago. Either way, as he closed the door to the basement flat, he walked up the stairs and made himself some aromatic tea in the kitchen. Sitting at the table, he sipped the hot liquid. They now had what they needed. Just a few more days and they could strike at the heart of the infidel's capitalistic world, he thought. It had been eating away at him for three years now, the death of his friends and half of his village in Afghanistan. He was lucky to get out alive; they had died, and he had vowed revenge. Allah had provided him with the path to follow.

Chapter 14

'Let's go,' said Femi looking at his watch.

George stood up, grabbed his fags, adjusted his coat and slid the 9 mm into his belt.

'Stay near the phone,' said Femi to Junk, nodding also to Sayo.

Leaving the flat, the two men bounded down the stairs, through the concourse, out the front door catching Cono flicking his cigarette into the gutter next to the Merc.

'We on?'

'Yeah, let's go,' said Femi getting into the back seat. With George in the front, the car revved and pulled away sharply and onto the main drag into London.

The journey didn't take too long, and as Cono pulled up outside The Ram pub just off the Aldwych, George and Femi got out. The entrance had two doors; the first went into the downstairs pub, which at this time of the day was full mostly of the city boys and girls after work drinking, some celebrating the success of the trades they had made that day, others drinking just to keep up appearances. The counter behind the bar was laden with credit cards of every colour, each one pushing the limit to the max. The second entrance was just a solid oak door, no signs, no windows, with a solitary handle which when opened revealed a set of dark stairs. Those who opened it by mistake typically assumed it was the wrong entrance and didn't venture any further. Femi climbed the stairs, passing the first floor and onto the second. He'd been told to just keep going until he reached the top, which he did quickly. The door at the top gave way to a large room. The oak floored room had half a dozen tables set for dinner with a few nice chairs near a very small bar. As Femi walked through the door, a man approached.

'Good evening, sir, this way.'

He escorted Femi across the dining area to a table near the corner overlooking the Aldwych where Sergio Karnovich was sat, who rose as he saw him, holding out his hand.

As Femi looked around as he crossed the floor, he could see why Sergio had picked this location. It afforded both men anonymity, whilst the pinch point was the door to the front of the building. Femi surmised that a back entrance was available, as neither man wanted to be seen, or worse photographed, together, and this, thought Femi, was a venue that suited both: neutral, quiet and discreet.

'Femi, good to see you again,' he said in a rich Russian accent.

'Hey, man,' he said, returning the handshake.

Water was served to the table. 'Anything else, sir?'

'No, that's fine,' said Sergio.

Set for food, neither man, however, would be eating, the

table gave both men a view of the complete room, and as Femi had walked in, the only other person, apart from the waiter, he saw was a man sat at a corner table several feet away. Far enough, Femi thought, not to hear the conversation but close enough to come to Sergio's aid should he so wish. As Femi sat down, he unbuttoned his jacket, watching Sergio closely. He was unarmed apart from George, who had remained downstairs as it was unlikely that trouble would be coming their way.

'I would like an answer to my question from last time. How did you find me?'

'I was given your name by my friend, who knows you have helped with the cause in our country before. It's a small request, and we are willing to pay you for your trouble, as I said. So, will you supply?'

'I don't need the money, and it's hardly worth the risk. If you see things from my point of view, it's a lot of work. Whilst we sympathise with your struggle, I doubt our contribution would make much of a difference.'

'How much do you want? My friends back home are relying on your support and are looking to me to give them good news.'

'It's not about the money. The quantity you need is, in the scheme of things, minute, and the risks of getting it undiscovered far outweigh any strategic advantages we see in your country at this present time.'

Femi picked up his glass of water and took a sip.

'I can see how this could be a small request in your eyes, but we would be in your debt, which I'm sure that as regimes

148

change, you being in a position of influence, shall we say, would be of benefit to your country.'

'That's as may be, but we are a long way from that,' said Sergio leaning back in his chair.

'Much as we would like to help, I really am sorry.' Sergio glanced over to the man at the other table. The meeting was going to be drawn to a close.

'I have something, something more than money, something I think will change your mind.'

Sergio shrugged, 'And what would that be?'

'You asked how I found you.' Femi reached into his pocket and slid the paper across the table.

Sergio picked it up, raised an eyebrow as he opened it and saw a picture of himself.

'So, you took a photo of me. So what, there are plenty of those about,' he said passing the paper back to Femi.

'There may well be, but I got this from your file in MI5. Just imagine what sort of information you could get if you had control of that person on the inside.'

Sergio leant forward and picked the paper up again and looked closely at it. The photo had been taken about a year ago, just after he had arrived in the country. He remembered the hat and coat he had worn at the time. Still owning the coat, he hadn't worn the hat in a very long time, the winters in England were not as cold as Moscow, so it had been languishing in his wardrobe.

Sergio smiled. 'I would want to meet them before I agree to anything.'

'Once you have them, I have nothing. I'm sure you can

arrange delivery before I introduce you. As you say, it's a small request we need, but I think the returns now outweigh any risks you may have.'

Sergio looked again at the picture. He knew Femi had not taken it, and he was certain that it could have only come from an inside source, but was that source in the UK? *Was that person, as Femi had said, in MI5? Was it worth the risk? What they needed was a pittance,* thought Sergio. *What was the downside to me? Very little.* The train of thought continued.

'I can do this for you, but to be clear so there is no misunderstanding between us, if this person is not real, then. . .' Sergio glanced over to his companion.

'I do not lie,' said Femi.

'Consider it done then.'

The two cars moved swiftly onto the M25 heading north. Picking up the M1, the cars powered themselves into the outside lane, hitting a steady pace of around 85 mph, fast enough to cover the distance in an adequate time and slow enough not to attract any attention from any waiting police car poised to nick speeders. The second car was several lengths behind the first, music blaring out, Sayo behind the wheel with Cono enjoying a spliff. The lead car was driven by George; next to him was Junk with Femi in the rear, passing another spliff between them. The journey, taking about three and a half hours, would see them arrive around 7:00 pm.

'Burgers?' George asked over his shoulder to Femi.

'Yeah, why not.'

Indicating, George watched the mirror and saw Sayo clock his change as the two cars slowed and pulled into the services at Tibshelf, filled up then headed into the drive thru of McDonald's. Sayo followed, and with a handful of cheeseburgers, fries and drinks, the cars set off on the final part of the journey, crossing onto the M18 then dropping onto the M180; their destination, Immingham, was less than an hour away. Jettisoning the leftover fries and paper wrapping from the burgers out of the window, Femi lit a cigarette. Moving the latest consignment of girls had gone well. The Pakistanis had paid on delivery and had arranged for several cars and a couple of busses to pick the girls up from the container. The handover had been easy, and apart from a couple of the girls whining, a quick slap around the head for some, they had been whisked away. The £1.2 million, mainly in twenties, had been counted, wrapped and put into three separate boxes destined for France.

'Have you booked your tickets?' said Femi.

'Yeah, pick them up Wednesday. Got Sayo to stick a mixer in it,' said George.

'Femi thought through the process; it was the third time they had used the van.'

'Get rid of it when you get back.'

'That's a pain in the arse, man.'

'Don't give a fuck, you know the rules.'

George sighed. 'OK.'

This is how we get caught, thought Femi. *Why the fuck can't they think for themselves? The van with the builder's gear in it was a good cover for taking the money across to France, but this would be the fourth time, and any more might raise eyebrows. Day to get into France and drop the money, two-day layover and then back to the UK. Looks like a bit of spare time work for a couple of builders. Good idea, but time to change,* thought Femi.

'Buy a carpet fitter's van when you get back. We'll use that for a couple of runs. Go to that auction place in Wembley. Should be a few old vans with the signs still on them. Make sure it's got an MOT and works.'

'OK,' said George.

Taking the exit for Immingham, George slowed. The road took them through the main town towards the river. Turning right past the docks, the two cars bore left onto a single track, followed this for a few hundred yards and turned into the entrance to a derelict site. It had been an engineering factory for repairs to the British D-class submarine in the First World War and had sited anti-aircraft battery during the Second World War. Long since removed and abandoned, the dilapidated buildings now were wind torn, rusty and being taken over by nature. Several ways onto the site allowed for a number of vehicles to congregate behind one of the buildings without attracting any attention. Femi had scouted the place out on a month-long tour of the northeast, picking the best spots close to the main commercial docks from Tyneside down to Ipswich. He favoured this as it was close to Hull, so if he couldn't get a delivery into Immingham then Hull would do, the changeover site far enough hidden from prying eyes and not a track for walkers.

They parked; Femi looked at his watch. They had made good time. Getting out, he stretched his legs. Sayo and Junk started smoking. George was checking his gun. Trouble, thought Femi, was unlikely, but he checked his own. Best to be ready, just in case.

Hearing the sound of some vehicles, he slid the 9 mm back into his belt and covered it with his jacket. Three cars approached, swinging round and pulling up near Femi.

A man jumped out of a Range Rover, waved and walked across to Femi.

'Hey, man.'

Femi smiled, his gold tooth shining.

'Hey, bro,' he replied putting his hand out, and with a finger snap handshake the two men relaxed.

The conversation was light; Femi looked at his watch.

'Not long, about 10.'

'Yeah, cool.'

Casey looked across: his men were smoking and chatting with Femi's guys. Some of them had known each other from the streets of Lagos, all had done well coming to England and all had benefitted from Bala's help. Whilst they were wary, this was business; they all had a lot to gain.

'Here we go,' said Femi flicking his fag away as he saw the truck come onto the ground. Slowly picking its way through the potholes, it came to a halt between the cars, and the driver killed the engine and the lights. Sayo jumped into the Merc, reversed and came up behind the trailer and switched the headlights on. It wasn't too dark yet, but the light helped. The driver jumped out, went around to the big steel flanged doors, pulled a pair of clippers out and cut the seals. His job now over, he returned to the cab.

Cono pulled the heavy doors open, and Junk heaved himself up into the trailer.

Femi had considered when they first started to distribute the coke that he would unbag, check and then call Casey; however, he felt it was a sign of faith and honesty that if they were all there when the cargo was unloaded any mistakes could be seen by all and with no blame attributed to either gang. So far, the deliveries had been OK. His people had always delivered the right amount and on time, and Femi had no reason to suspect anything was going to change.

Junk pulled a couple of small lightweight pallets out of the way and with a crowbar George had chucked him prised open the large box. Turfing out the plastic sheeting, he lent in and pulled out the first package, giving it to Sayo, who had got in behind him. Piling them up on the tailgate, the first 50 were neatly stacked. Femi pointed at the stack and looked at Casey.

'Pick one.'

Meanwhile, Junk jemmied open the second box and started to repeat the process.

Casey took one of the packets over to a man who had already opened the boot of the Range Rover, and with a flick of a knife pierced the package and dropped a small globule of white powder into a vial. Shaking it, he held it up to the light.

Nodding affirmative to Casey, Casey waved at the driver of the second car, who pulled forward, popped the boot and called Femi over.

Femi counted the money.

'All good, bro?'

'Yeah, cool.'

George swapped the money to his Merc whilst a couple of Casey's men split the load between the three cars. One hundred packets, 2.5 kilos each of cocaine, and with £2 million in Femi's car the deal was done.

Chapter 15

Vittorio settled into the leather chair, and with a swirl of cloth the barber floated the white sheet across his body and tucked it in. Lathering up the brush with a liberal amount of soap, he brushed the warm liquid around Vittorio's chin and cheeks. With a deft hand of a skilled craftsman, he preceded to shave. Idly watching the barber at work in the mirror, Vittorio enjoyed this daily routine. He could shave himself, of course, but he liked the way he was treated here. It was quiet, the furniture and fixings were stylish and fashioned in a 1920s Art Deco style. The four red leather chairs, each one adjustable by a foot pump, were luxurious, the mirrors edged in the classic style, and the small waiting sofa was again leather and extremely comfortable. The three barbers were draped in uniform, each with their own distinctive hairstyles and moustaches and performing like an orchestrated ballet around each client, soaping, shaving then a warm towel to the face and then oil as required through the hair, some clients enjoying a cut and trim.

With the towel placed on his face, a few moments later, moisturiser applied, the process was finished for the day.

'Grazie, Simon,' said Vittorio as the chair was lowered

slightly, allowing him to stand. Pulling a £50 note from his pocket he placed it on the counter in front of him.

'See you tomorrow.'

'Have a good day, sir.'

Leaving the shop, Vittorio crossed the road and walked the short distance around Grosvenor Square to the Italian coffee house just off Mount Street. As always, Ciro had driven him to the barbers, and if it was a pleasant day then Vittorio would stroll back to his house in Belgrave, stopping first for an espresso. The drink, thought Vittorio as he stood at the counter inhaling the fine aroma of the Italian coffee, was just delightful. The pleasant walk back took a few minutes, and as Vittorio was approaching his home, Ciro came down the steps.

'Ciao, il capo.'

'Ciao, Ciro. Where you going?'

'To wash the cars. They got a bit dirty over the weekend so need a polish.' This made Vittorio smile. 'Do you need me?'

'Not until 11:30.'

'Si, OK. See you later. Ciao.

'Ciao, ciao.'

Vittorio let himself in. The opulent hallway led to a drawing room where he would spend most of the day reading. David appeared as he settled into the chair behind the desk.

'Good morning, sir. May I get you anything?'

'No, I'm fine, thank you.'

Nodding, David closed the door behind him. His duties included the day to day running of the household, kitchen deliveries and of course as valet to Vittorio. Unplugging the

Blackberry, Vittorio scanned the message and some abstract emails that had come through. He had invested heavily in encryption on the device and had been assured that as long as he kept his software up to date, anything that was on there was secure.

The message was simple: Salt 10M.

Vittorio smiled; he had been waiting over a year for this. The message was from Genaro Salucci. Salucci meant salt in Italian. Genaro was a renowned Italian art dealer. Based in Milan, he had several galleries across Europe and in the States. He was, however, a fence, a fence with a difference. If you wanted anything he would get it for you. It was rumoured that he had had a hand in the huge art theft in Detroit several years ago. Art to the value of nearly £600 million had been stolen; none of the pieces had been recovered and many had passed through the hands of Salucci. Vittorio knew this because in his basement were several paintings he had supplied, one of which was a Rembrandt, which had gone missing in 1990.

Replying to the message, Vittorio put the Blackberry down, stood and went into the hall. The hall led past the staircase and at first glance would be a door to the kitchen. Opening this, Vittorio stepped through, closed the door behind him and pushed the adjacent wall in the corner. A click was heard, and a door popped open revealing a staircase down to the basement. This was the second entrance to the basement, which had been cleverly created and hidden. The main basement stairs would lead to a wine cellar where Vittorio stored his vintage wines. This staircase was different; lighting came on as Vittorio walked down. At the bottom he was faced with a steel door. The camera took a picture, and he placed his fingers on the pad; the combination complete, the door swung open. Closing the door behind him, he was in a small corridor. Three steps and he was at the second door. This wasn't locked, but as he opened it the air swished around him, the lights in the room came on and Vittorio quickly closed the door. An ambient temperature had been set; the air conditioning in the room constantly changed the air to ensure that the paintings on the walls were kept in a pristine environment.

Slowly walking to the wall, on his right he looked at the first of the paintings, and by far the most expensive, a Picasso. *Just wonderful*, he thought. Looking at each painting in turn he knew that the next in his collection would fit perfectly with these. On the opposite wall were several gaps; the one from Salucci would make 11 with room for a few more. The value of the paintings, as he looked around, in an auction house would be close to £400 million, not that he had paid anywhere near that nor was he going to sell any either. All had been stolen to order, and the latest was a beautiful painting by Titian. It would cost him £8.5 million, but was worth every penny, thought Vittorio. He could haggle with Salucci and get down from the £10 million he wanted.

The journey didn't take long, out of Belgrave Square, down The Mall, along Fleet Street, past St Pauls and then a left into Victoria Street. Ciro pulled the car into a small alleyway and stopped. The two men got out, walked back to the main road and entered the restaurant. The Genovese Spaghetti House, a chain of over 628, growing by the week, Vittorio had a controlling interest via a third party in the house. A booth was set towards the back. Vittorio sat down and poured himself a glass of water.

'Ciao, Orsino.'

'Ciao. Capo, stai bene,' 'said Orsino.

'Si, grazie.'

Sitting down, Orsino too poured some water and looked at his watch.

'12:15, si?'

Vittorio nodded.

And as if on cue Rinori and Lorenc walked into the restaurant.

'Gentlemen. . .' Vittorio had stood, held his hand out.

'Vittorio, good to see you again, man.' Rinori said taking his hand. 'This is my brother Lorenc.'

'And this. . .' said Vittorio with a wave of the hand, 'is Orsino.'

'Please sit,' said Vittorio after introductions were made.

'I have spoken to Orsino here and explained the new routine. The shipments will arrive as always from Tilbury, be collected by his man, brought to the plant and then distributed as per normal.'

Rinori nodded.

'You can supply your own driver if you wish or continue to use Orsino. That's up to the two of you to decide, OK?'

Rinori again nodded. 'OK, how is it brought in?'

'The shipment is brought to our warehouse in Genoa. It is then transferred onto a container and delivered into Tilbury, picked up and taken to Orsino's distribution warehouse. The container is sealed by customs in Genoa and labelled 'food'. It has on board kilo bags of pasta, bulk wheat and several drums of olive oil. The pasta etc. is offloaded along with the oil. Some of the drums are emptied; these contain your packages securely wrapped. There are several olive oil drums; the real ones are emptied into vats, and Orsino has a small bottling process in the warehouse which then are filled each with one litre of virgin olive oil. These bottles, along with pasta, wheat, mozzarella, etc. are boxed along with however many packages are required onto a pallet, which are then distributed across the UK to the Genovese Spaghetti House chain. There are 628 outlets, all taking, every two weeks or so, the heroin. That is how we float our produce into the UK market, which is what you are taking control of.'

Rinori smiled. *This is going to be good*, he thought. The distribution channel already in place, the dealers in place, all they had to do was to make sure that the supply was continuous.

'What about the money?'

'On delivery at the warehouse, you pay Orsino for the shipment. That then comes to us, and after that it's up to you. At the moment, the delivery drivers bring back the money to Orsino, who checks, counts and stacks the cash ready for onward transport. That part is now for you to do with as you want. You may send your own men to each location to pick up the money, or you may want to leave this process in place and collect the money from Orsino and bank it yourselves, or, of course, Orsino could bank it, and as we discussed at our meeting, I can launder the money across several countries and banks for you.'

'At a fee, no doubt.'

'A modest administration charge, I would call it.'

'OK, well for now we'll think about that.'

'Nessun problema; no problem.'

'What about new outlets?' asked Rinori.

'Orsino is over-seeing a role out of another 35 houses this year with growth on the cards. The houses are purchased via a French company who, shall we say, can assist with the most delicate of matters. They provide a range of services ideal for losing track of both company ownership and people. Each house manager is personally appointed by Orsino and is part of several extended Italian families from back home; this keeps it tight with no loose ends. The day-to-day operation of each house is left to the managers; there is no need to interfere, it runs like clockwork. Each manager places an order in the box, which is brought back each time. Orsino will provide you with all the ledgers where you can see how much is taken and how much each one has increased over time. The local manager creates his own chain in the area that he is in. The amount of money each manager makes is exactly the same, which is 4.5% of the sell price, which is set by us, or I should say now, set by you.'

Rinori smiled, and the conversation continued with more of the drilled down detail coming from either Orsino or Vittorio.

'OK, we would like to go see the warehouse where the gear comes in and how it is sent.'

'Fine, I'll leave you with Orsino. We will not meet again unless you want the service I can provide. If not, then everything will be in Orsino's hands, OK?' said Vittorio.

Rinori nodded.

The knock on the car window caught Simon by surprise; the face of Craig was smiling at him. Simon pointed to the door, and Craig quickly got in the back.

'You're not very good at this, are you? I spotted you when you arrived.'

'Fuck off! What you doing here? Thought you were tailing Vittorio.'

'I am, he's in there,' said Simon pointing to the restaurant.

'Fuck, so you saw Rinori and his brother go in then?'

'Yep, best tell the boss.'

Simon picked up the radio connected to the centre.

'DC Simon Carrs. Put me through to DI Taylor, please.'

A few moments later and the familiar voice of Izzy came across the loudspeaker.

'Go ahead, Simon, what's happening?'

'Hi, boss, I'm here with Craig. Both Vittorio and the Albanians are meeting now.'

'How long they been in there?'

Simon looked at Craig. 'Five minutes?' Craig nodded.

'Five minutes at the most.'

'Copy that. OK, I'm on my way. Keep me posted on any changes.'

The line went dead.

'I'll get back to mine, parked over there, and Vittorio's is over there,' said Craig pointing to a row of cars.

Putting the phone down and grabbing her jacket and bag, she called out, 'Bill, Craig and Simon are watching a meet between the Italians and our friend Rinori. Take Wayne, and Claire. . .' she shouted across the room, beckoning her, 'come with me.'

The four offices ran down the stairs into the car park and jumped in a couple of cars. With Claire driving, she led them out and onto the embankment.

The road was busy as usual. 'Step on it,' said Izzy.

Claire hit the sirens and lights and pulled ahead; taking their lead Bill followed suit.

'Twenty-eight, twenty-eight, any change?'

'Twenty-eight here, no change.'

'On way.'

'Copy that.'

With a flurry, the cars sped along the embankment right into New Bridge Street and then on to Ludgate Hill. Most vehicles got out of the way on hearing the sirens, a daily occurrence in the busy city, the two cars hardly attracting any attention from pedestrians. Passing St Paul's, Claire switched off the lights and turned left into Victoria Street.

Spotting Simon's car, Claire pulled in and waited as Izzy got out and jumped in beside Simon.

'Hi, boss, they are still in there. What do you want to do, go have a look?'

'No, we'll wait. So, who's in there?'

'De Luca and his man, plus Rinori and his brother Lorenc. We don't know if anyone else is.' He picked up the camera. 'Got them entering, but no one else. Craig said he followed Vittorio as usual from his house. He went for his daily shave, he then went for a coffee, walked home, and then Ciro came at 11:30 and they drove here. That's their car over there,' said Simon pointing to the alleyway where Ciro had parked.

'OK, we'll wait. Sit tight, any movement get them on camera, OK?'

'Will do, boss.'

Not wanting to attract attention, Izzy got out and went back and sat in Claire's car. She had turned around and now faced the restaurant on the opposite side of the street, a suitable distance away to not be noticed but with a clear enough view so the boss could see anyone coming and going.

'What we doing?' she asked.

'We'll wait.'

'Thirty-two, Bill.'

'Thirty-two, go ahead.'

'Bill, sit tight, all four are in there plus maybe more. Let's see what they do.'

'Copy that.'

The four cars with their occupants sat and waited; Izzy looked at her watch. They had been there nearly 40 minutes; no one had left, and no one had gone in. It was difficult to tell at this distance if the restaurant was open, but no one had tried to go in for lunch so maybe they were shut, thought Izzy.

'Movement,' crackled the radio.

Eyes now focussed on the door. Ciro had come outside and lit a cigarette, lent against the window and was casually looking around. Sliding down a little in their seats, the four waited. Flicking his fag into the gutter, Ciro opened the door and held it open. A few seconds later, Vittorio walked out and the two headed back towards their car.

The radio buzzed. 'Boss, shall I follow or wait for Rinori?' said Craig.

'Wait, one,' said Izzy.

Watching the two men get into the car, Izzy was in two minds as to whether to send Craig on a follow, but what were the odds of him going back to his house? *Can't risk he's not.*

'Twenty-nine, follow him.'

'Copy that,' said Craig. Watching Ciro back out onto the road, he waited until he was sure which way he was heading and then pulled off the kerb and dropped in a couple of cars behind him.

'Here we go,' came over the radio.

Simon pulled the camera up and began burst shots of the men leaving; there were three.

'We've got target one and target two with an unknown.'

'Copy that.'

'They are heading for target one's car,' said Simon over the radio.

They watched as the three men got into Rinori's car, Orsino in the back. A moment later the car set off up Victoria Street.

'All units follow; I'll lead,' said Izzy on the handheld.

In unison, a tail was in progress. Rinori went onto Leadenhall and then the car picked up the A13 and set off out of London.

'Bill, take my place,' said Izzy into the radio indicating to Claire to let Bill take the lead. Pulling over slightly, Bill got past Claire and settled in behind Rinori, a couple of cars back.

'Twenty-nine, twenty-nine, where are you?'

'Back home.'

'OK, leave them and follow us, Tower Hamlets direction.'

'Copy that.'

The cars swopped places a few times over the next 20 minutes or so as they continued along the A13.

'Passing Barking.' The call on the radio was for Craig. He wasn't far behind and had made good progress. Lights and sirens had cleared a decent path for him, and it wouldn't be too much longer before he caught them up.

'Off, off, off.' The junction of South Stifford had come into view; Wayne had seen Rinori indicate.

Sweeping up the slip road, Rinori turned right and headed down towards the river. Wayne followed; checking his mirror, he saw the others not far behind.

'Take over, Claire.' Wayne slowed and dropped back as both Claire and Bill overtook him.

Not knowing where they were going, it was going to be difficult to keep a tail without being seen, but so far, thought Izzy, so good.

Seeing the car in front.

'Back off a bit, there's not much here, so this must be near to the end.'

Claire nodded.

'Where to, man?' said Rinori.

'Take a left after this one. See those buildings over there?' Orsino said pointing to a group. 'Take this one. OK, now left, right. Here we are, go round the back.'

Rinori entered the gated compound and drove around the back of the buildings.

The tail had proved successful; they hadn't been spotted.

'Pull up over there,' said Izzy.

'Simon, get as close as you can,' she said into the radio.

Bill pulled up 100 yards from the entrance and waited for Claire to come close. Getting out, he jumped into the back.

'What do you think this is?'

'Got to be a distribution point.'

'Want to go have a look?'

'No, not yet, it could be a handover, you know, some sort of this is what we have, this is yours, etc.'

'We need to pick a spot to do an all-nighter.'

'Yes, get Wayne set up. Give him Simon's camera and then let Simon take over later. Sort the shift out.'

'OK, will do.'

'We'll wait to see what happens, OK?'

'OK, boss,' said Bill getting out of the car and quickly driving his to Wayne, who had parked further up the road.

Chapter 16

Getting out of the BMW, Rinori looked around: there was an abandoned warehouse next to this factory, but that was all. The site backed on to the river with a fence surrounding the property. There was a one-way system in place, in via the front gate, then either park at the offices or go right, as he did, round the back of the warehouse. There were four loading bays; one, he saw, was occupied by a container lorry. Once filled or emptied, it continued around the building and then out onto the main road again. Looking up, he saw several cameras mounted on the corners, and as he looked closer, he saw three on the ring fence as well.'

'They work.'

'Si, my friend, I will show you into the office. Come, come with me,' said Orsino heading towards a door adjacent to the loading bay.

Following Orsino, Rinori was surprised at the size of the building as they entered next to the loading bay.

'This is just the first part,' said Orsino climbing the small set of stairs and waiting for the brothers.

'We have three deliveries a week. Over there. . .' he said pointing at a large room within the building, 'is the freezer.

Our ice cream comes in on refrigerated lorries, it is offloaded and then straight into there.' Walking into the large warehouse, Rinori saw rows of shelves all packed with some produce or other.

'Fresh vegetables and fruit come in, stored briefly over here,' he explained, pointing to another section. 'When the orders come in, the guys fill a pallet, ice cream, mixture of vegetables, then from over there. . .' he said pointing as he went deeper into the building, 'wheat, boxes and tinned goods are also taken and added to the pallet. The final part comes. . .' as the men continued alongside the rows of stacked shelves, 'from here. These all contain olive oil, vinegar and any other items each restaurant may want. Once on the pallet or in large boxes, depending on what's been ordered, it is wrapped or crated. . .' he continued, pointing at the high box fillable metal creates, which had a base and were on wheels for easy delivery, 'then onto the vans who then go out and deliver to each restaurant. Each van normally has six stops; the process is continuous, five days a week.'

'This is massive,' said Rinori.

Lorenc, catching up, having taken time to look up and down some of the racks in more detail, said,

'They have everything here, man. We're not taking this on, are we?'

'No, signor. If you are happy after today with the distribution, as I show you, then I will continue to manage this operation. All the men and women here are normal employees from around the area. Shelby looks after them on a day-to-day basis. Her office,' said Orsino, 'is next to the canteen, which is through that door over there.' Pointing, he continued, 'She handles the workforce, pays the wages, etc. She is my cousin's sister so knows what's happening, but she is the only one on this floor who knows how detailed our service is.'

Rinori nodded. 'How long has this been going on?'

Orsino smiled. 'I can't remember, a little while now.' Getting to the end of the large warehouse, he entered another set of small offices.

'These offices lead to the side of the building where you would come in and out. The main warehouse and distribution come through the front, but if you use these, very few people will see you, and it leads directly into here,' said Orsino opening another door. Rinori and Lorenc followed. It gave way to another large area, and this one had, as Rinori looked closer, machinery.

'Is this a bottling plant?'

'Si, si, this is where we bottle our own olive oil.

The factory area was quiet. Orsino closed the door behind him.

'When the container comes in it is offloaded and the various goods are stored in the racks and fridges you have seen. The drums of olive oil are rolled into here, through the loading bay,' pointing at the metal rollup, 'and put into this lift here,' he said walking across the floor to a commercial lift shaft.

'Please, follow me.'

Next to the lift was a door that had a security numbered lock, which Orsino pressed. The door clicked open, and the two brothers followed Orsino down the stairs. There was another locked door at the bottom, and the three men entered a large holding area. Lights came on as they moved into the underground room. The smell of olive oil was intense. Next to some machinery were cases of empty bottles, all ready to be filled.

'That is a fire exit, which leads back up to the loading bay,' he explained further, pointing to another set of stairs. 'It can be opened by a number lock from the outside, so you could use that as your entrance should you so wish.'

'This place is enormous,' said Genti.

'It is, but you will get used to it. Don't forget, we serve hundreds of restaurants every week, and there is an enormous amount of food coming and going daily. Olive oil, however,' nodding to Genti, 'is only sent every four weeks or so.' Turning, he pointed.

'The olive oil is emptied into these vats and then pumped through these pipes into the system, which fills the bottles, screws on the caps and pastes the labels. They go up that conveyor belt and into the room above where we just were. It is then packed into boxes and delivered onto the pallets that are all ready for each restaurant.'

Rinori looked around.

'Clever, so how about our gear?'

'The drums that are marked are cut open. The olive oil is tipped into this drain here. . .' he said, stepping over to a large grate in the floor, 'floats away and the packages are collected. There are normally three drums at a time with the heroin, the rest are full of the real olive oil, which we use.

The packages are collected. Follow me,' said Orsino opening yet another door, which revealed a lab. 'You may be familiar with the set up.'

A long chrome table with stools and several cupboards were in view.

'The packages are weighed, opened, checked, verified and then passed to the women, who sit here. They cut, weigh, repack and send them upstairs.'

'This is one set up, man.'

'This is what you wanted, yes?'

'Yes,' said Rinori nodding.

'The men and women who work in this area are family. They start at midnight; they never see anyone other than my brother Mario. He lets them in; they come in from the fire exit, which makes it easy for them. The men start the bottling, and the women do the cutting. They finish around about 4:00 am.'

There were cameras everywhere: each stool had a camera above it, the door had a camera, and there was also one, Lorenc noticed as he looked around, covering the main room.

'Where do the cameras feed to?'

'They all go into the office; everything is recorded. The main alarm is with the security company. If it goes off then they call my son, who is the main keyholder, and they come to site and wait for Mario to attend. They call the police just in case they are needed when they get here. The cameras record all the time and are changed daily; if there is a break in then we would look through the tapes. If there is a problem with supply at one of the restaurants, then we can look through the tapes and see which girl bagged what. The TVs and recording equipment are up in the office, which I will show you before you leave.'

Lorenc nodded. 'And that door there?' he said pointing at a small door at the rear of the room.

Orsino smiled.

'That, my friends, is what I call the business end.'

Punching numbers into the keypad, the door opened. The three men went inside. Another camera was present, and the lights came on automatically, revealing a nicely carpeted room with an office table and chairs and filing cabinets by the back wall.

'This is where we do the ledgers, collect the money and allocate the powder to each restaurant.'

Orsino walked past the table to the three filing cabinets at the back wall. Opening the first drawer, he pressed a button; with a whirl of a motor the two other cabinets began to move forwards.'

'What the fuck!' said Rinori.

'Watch.'

Rinori and Lorenc peered forward as the two cabinets slid forwards across the carpet; a staircase came into view.

Lights came on.

'Follow me.'

Making his way down the stairs into a small passageway and on to another, this time electronic door, on opening it Orsino stood back.

'Signors, please,' he said with a wave of his arm, allowing the two men to go ahead of him.'

As they went through the door the light came on.

'Fuck me!'

In front of them was a large room, but this time it was caged. A few paces and they were at the steel barred door. Peering through the bars both men gasped.

'Our money,' said Orsino.

Unlocking and swinging it open he walked in. There were several shelves on each side.

'Signors, the money room, safe and secure.'

'Fucking hell!' said Rinori. 'How much have you got in here?' he asked looking around.

Lorenc was picking up bundles of notes, flicking them and putting them back and picking up another wad.

'Thousands, I'll bet,' he said.

'Each week we collect about £3 million. In here, currently, is £18.5 million. Next week we will be taking delivery of your first cargo. This will all then be out onto the container and shipped back to Genoa.'

'Three million pounds a week,' said Lorenc.

Rinori looked at the money. This was probably a good place to store his coke money as well, nice and secure, out of the way of prying eyes.

Looking at Orsino, he asked, 'How does the money get through here?'

'The delivery drivers have a black box, which they swap each time they go to a restaurant. There are two keys, I have one and the manager has one. The delivery driver has been told that it contains the order book for the following time. They have never questioned it and have no reason to either.

When they arrive back here, they give the box to Shelby, who then stores them in her safe until the night shift arrive. They pick it up then bring it down here to the room we have just been in. The money is counted, checked, ledgered and then put into the cage. The system works well, and we have never had a single problem in all the time this is being done.'

'This place must have cost a fortune,' said Lorenc.

'Signor Du Luca spent a lot of time and money several years ago to make sure it is as tight as possible,' said Orsino nodding.

'So, signors, please let me show you the ledgers, they are upstairs,' said Orsino making his way out of the vault.

Working their way back up the stairs, Rinori turned to Lorenc.

'Go see Vittorio before you go to Liverpool. Make sure there is no problem for us expanding into that area with coke and get him to set up a money chain for us. We will use him for now. Might cost us, bro, but at least it's a simple way of moving our cash about. Also, you need to get some new papers. Make it hard for them up there if you are pulled. Have a word with Vitty boy, see if he can help.'

Lorenc nodded.

'Morning everyone,' said Izzy entering the room and taking a chair. Sitting next to Bill, she opened the folder in front of her.

'Morning, boss.'

The door opened and DCI Jackson came in. 'Morning people,' he said, and he too took a chair.

'OK.' Izzy stood up and walked over to the wall chart where several pictures were hanging.

'What we know. De Luca and the two Kodra brothers were seen meeting at a Genovese Spaghetti House. We tailed the two brothers and this guy. . .' she said, pointing at one of the pictures, 'the manager, Orsino Santoro, across town to this location here,' she continued, pointing to a map, 'a gated warehouse/factory compound just outside Grays, near the river. Wayne has been swapping with Craig since then, keeping the building under obs. Wayne?'

'After they left, nothing has happened the last few nights. The place gets locked up at six and then the guy arrives and about twelve workers around 8:00 am. Craig has reported that they have had a couple of containers in. Several lorries and vans have left on a regular basis. We tracked one; it was delivering to a few of the spaghetti places in town. We watched them unload, seems like a usual food delivery from what we have seen, nothing unusual. Neither of the Kodras have been back, and neither has the Santoro guy.'

The DCI nodded.

'Claire, what have you found out about the building?' asked Izzy.

'The property was bought in 1986 by a French company called Ravel & Taider. They are a firm of solicitors based in Paris. Land Registry has provided a copy of the title. I've been on to the local council and searched the property register. They had some building work done soon after they purchased and then they had more work done late in 1989, some electrics connecting to a bottling machine, but that's all. The company has 628 locations throughout the UK. Accounts filed for last year has them showing a turnover of about £522 million a year; all taxes are paid up. De Luca is not shown as a director, in fact, he's not listed as a director anywhere,' said Claire.

'Bill?'

'The brothers have spent most of their time at the house. They have been joined by several other men. Photos matched to passports have shown they are cousins, and one other brother Genti tailed them several times, but they have split on a number of occasions. The best I had was a tail to a house on an estate in Wandsworth.' Leaning forward he took out several papers from his folder and began to pass them around. 'This is the house, it appears empty so they may be using it, or will be using it, either as a live in or a place where they can store some gear. Nothing has been seen being taken in, so at the moment it's a blank.'

'Craig?'

'Nothing to report. Since the meeting at the restaurant, De Luca and his man have spent their days in their house, back and forth to the barbers and coffee house. He went to the opera last night, but that's it. My guess is that on the face of it he could no longer be involved with the Kodras.'

'OK, my suspicion is that they are now gearing up to take control, if they haven't already done so, of the Italians' supply chain. If that warehouse/bottling plant is the main depot where the drugs come in, are cut and packaged then are sent out by the lorries to the restaurants across the UK, this is a extensive operation, which means we are looking at some serious amounts of cocaine or heroin, or both. Sir,' said Izzy looking at DCI Jackson, 'I think we've struck lucky for a change, and if I'm right we are at the beginning, which means we are going to need a lot more bodies.'

'I agree,' said Jackson. 'I need your report on my desk by tonight detailing the options, manpower and course of action,' said Jackson rising from the table. 'Thank you, everybody.'

'Will do,' said Izzy. 'In the meantime, Claire, can you double up with Bill on the Kodras, and Simon, drop De Luca for now and help out with Wayne and Craig, OK?'

Chapter 17

Abbas Karzai set off in his pickup truck. Taking the road north out of Asadabad, the journey would take about a day. Travelling during the day was easier as the route took him over the mountains, and as parts of the road became a track it was also in places single and treacherous, so daylight was in reality the only option. Once through the mountains he would then travel south, skirting Marden and then on to the airport at Peshawar in Pakistan. A veteran member of the mujahideen, he had been fighting all his life. When the Russians eventually were seen off, out of Afghanistan, his skills were in demand. Initially, the Taliban had wanted him to join them, but he was indebted to Omar Hekmatyar, who had saved his life when they were under a heavy attack from the Russians. He had dragged him out of a compound and into the desert. His only injury was the loss of a finger on his left hand and a slight limp where a piece of shrapnel had pierced the bottom of his right leg. Hekmatyar was a close ally of Osama bin Laden, who was the founder of al-Qaeda, an Islamic group whose doctrines were closely aligned to his own, so following Omar was a way to repay the debt he owed and to continue the jihad against the western world of non-believers.

*

He had benefitted greatly from the Americans, especially the CIA, who had not only provided arms and money but also training in the use of mines and explosives and how they were assembled and triggered. He had become adept at creating the vests, which many of Omar's men and some women had used against the Russians. He was, however, one now of a very few. Many had died in the conflicts, but Osama, he had been told, had promised more, more money, more training and more weapons. So, he believed that his friend Omar would provide the true course of action for him, and as a servant of Allah he would gladly give his life in his name. He had taken the opportunity to learn as much as he could from the Americans, including how to speak English. Each time he met them he would speak to the Americans, learning more on every encounter to such an extent that he was now almost proficient in reading, writing and speaking the barbaric language. He had hidden his contempt and disgust as Omar had said for him to use them, abuse them and take as much from them as he could. This had now put him in a unique position. Although he would have preferred to fight at home, he knew that to break the will of the non-believers, striking at the heart of their easy, comfortable lives would one day lay the world at the feet of Allah, which then he could truly rule over, like he once did.

Crossing into Pakistan was simple. The border wasn't monitored where he crossed as it was an old but well used

181

mountain pass between the two countries. He picked up the main road once through the pass, which would take him onwards to the airport. He could have gone from Kabul, but the risk was too high. Travelling out of Peshawar was easier and fewer checks were made. Arriving at the airport, pulling into the car park, he got his case out of the back of the vehicle and made his way into the main airport concourse and spotted the check in desk he needed. His flight was in two hours' time, so once through customs Abbas waited. His journey to Dubai was scheduled at midday and would take about three hours. The journey was straightforward and easy, he had flown before but on internal flights, so he was a little familiar with what to expect. On landing at Dubai, after collecting his bag, he went into departures to see what time his flight was to Brussels. Checking his watch, he saw that he had made good time and he would only have to wait four hours. Walking along the concourse, he went into the men's toilets and closed the door on one of the cubicles. Removing his perahan tunban and scarf he pulled from his case a pair of jeans and a shirt. Swapping over, he stuffed his old clothes and passport into the case. He pulled a new passport from a pocket inside the case. Looking at it, the photo and name were the same but a different nationality. Opening a zip pocket, he pulled out a wad of notes, a few for Dubai, some for his onward transit in Brussels. He leafed through them; pounds and dollars were also there. He had been told if he needed more then it wouldn't be a problem; bin Laden, he thought was as good as his word, plenty of money to travel and buy the required essentials. Leaving the bathroom, he walked along the main thoroughfare, selecting a jacket from one of the many shops. Paying, he put the coat on and caught sight of himself in the shop mirror. He was surprised at his appearance; he now looked similar to many around him. Finally, approaching the check-in desk, he gave them his passport and boarding ticket. The passenger list that day showed an Abbas Karzai, a Saudi national boarding the 11:00 pm flight to Brussels.

Arriving in Brussels, he had been given the address of a local family who he could stay with for a day or so. Picking his way out of the airport, he got into a cab and gave the driver the address. The journey took him out of the main airport, along the main route into the city and then into one of the suburbs. He had no interest in talking to the driver nor any interest in the myriad of office complexes that closed Brussels in, his focus was on his mission. Paying the driver and knocking at the door of the small bungalow, a man opened the door.

'As- Salam-u-Alaikum wa-rahmatullahi wa-barakatuh,' he said as he saw the man.

'Wa Aliakum Assalam wa Rahmatullah, please come in.'

'I have prepared a room for you,' he said in Arabic.

Abbas nodded. 'Thank you.'

'Once you have rested, we will eat. I am alone in the house, so we will not be disturbed.'

Opening a small bedroom door, he gave way to allow Abbas to enter.

'I'm at the end of the hall,' he said, leaving Abbas.

The following day passed quietly. Abbas was able to maintain his prayers at the normal times and slept in between. The train for Ostend would leave at 6:00 am the next day and catching the ferry to Ramsgate would see him on the shores of England at around midday. He had been given directions on how to get from Ramsgate to central London and also the phone number of the person who he would be staying with for the short time he was there.

Entry into the UK as a passenger on a ferry from Europe, as far as he could see, did not raise any suspicions as he disembarked and went through customs and then on to the railway. The journey took him into St Pancras where, as he looked at his detailed directions, he made his way to the Underground and caught the train to Uxbridge.

Tony got back to Uxbridge late and parked up just in time to see Nadir walk down the street and enter the house. Not sure if the others were in there, he decided to sit tight and wait. They had decided to keep the house under surveillance, rather than Nadir, as if they were to get some Semtex then whoever was in the house may arrange it. *I'll give it a few days, over the weekend and maybe next Monday, Tuesday,* he thought. The following few days dragged; Tony, up early every day, sat and watched. He alternated between his car and two different vans he had access to. Both the vans allowed him to watch and photograph, with impunity, the car; he had to be more careful. Documenting the visits, they were regular as clockwork, frustratingly though, no one had come out of the house. He did notice, however, once or twice one of the men had a carrier bag with him. *Maybe it's food*, he thought. He watched Nadir and the others come to prayer over the weekend, and by Tuesday night Tony decided that he couldn't stay any longer as work needed him. Sliding into the driver's seat after the last few photographs of Nadir, and his companions had made their way home for the night, he started the engine and drove back to his B&B. *Back Saturday first thing,* he decided.

He hadn't got the parking space he wanted and had ended up further down the road than he liked. He could see the house, but he had no chance of catching a glimpse of who-ever opened the door, even if they stuck there head out. Sitting in the back, armed with the camera, Tony watched and waited, deciding to risk a move closer should a spot become available. The three men, like clockwork, had come and gone for their first morning prayer session. The street, as Tony clicked a few photos, was busy, Saturday morn-ing shopping for many, and as they came and went, he recognised quite a few of them, taking their photos anyway; it all built a picture. Tony shook his head, *How can one man stay in a house for such a long period of time and never come out?*

Still no movement on car spaces, and the morning went by quickly enough, photographing the three men again as they reappeared for the 11:00 am prayer session and again on their departure. Feeling the need to stretch his legs, Tony surveyed the street. Picking a moment when no one was on his side of the road, he slipped out of the vehicle and walked towards the end of the road, went around the corner, lit a cigarette, crossed over and returned to the street but on the opposite side. Slowly walking, idly looking at the houses and the occasional person, he smoked as he walked. Nothing unusual, he glanced at his watch: 2:15 pm. Having a bit of time before the next visit he decided to go up to the main street and buy a few things for the rest of the day. On the opposite side was his target house, and as he walked past nothing, as far as he could see, was out of place. On his way back he would be on the same side. *I could have a quick look to see if the basement curtains are open or maybe even a light on,* he thought. Flicking his cigarette onto the street, he began to cross over diagonally to the road that led towards the high street.

Most people, when walking, will look at the person approaching them. The initial glance is to see if they recognise them and may exchange a nod or greeting; more often than not it's to make sure that you are not going to bump into them or if you are worried, that they are not a threat. Eye contact is brief; the brain assesses the situation, and you carry on walking.

About 10 yards before the end of the road, Tony had made the pavement as two men rounded the corner and came onto the same street directly in front of him. Neither changed their pace, and as a courtesy Tony moved slightly to the left to allow them to pass. Tony checked them out in detail as they approached him: the first man 5 ft 6 ish, walking with a slight limp, carrying a suitcase, normal clothes, the second slightly taller, beard, baggy clothes, sandals, neither man speaking. Making brief eye contact, the men passed each other when something stirred in Tony's head. Having photographed dozens of people in this street for some time now he had not seen these two before. In that millisecond, on passing them, Tony slowed, pulled the cigarettes out of his pocket, stopped and half turned and began lighting as he watched the men continue to walk down the road. Moments later, to Tony's surprise, they walked up to the front door of the target house.

Throwing the cigarette down, Tony quickly walked into the high street. The phone box was empty; he placed the call and described what he had just seen.

'Please come in,' said Arli.

Allowing Abbas space to come into the hall, Arli closed the door quickly.

'Please, follow me, I have arranged the basement for you.'

The two men went below, and Arli showed them the rooms. 'Everything you need is here,' he said, walking over to the tables.

Abbas put his case down and began looking at the items placed neatly for him.

'These are the two main bags,' Arli said pointing at the first, which held the Semtex, and then the other.

'We have prayers at 3:00 pm. Nadir and the others will be here; we can talk after, as you wish.'

'Thank you, leave me now. I need to check everything.'

Arli nodded. 'The basement door is locked. The key is

on the table should you wish to go outside. There is food and tea in the kitchen. I will be upstairs if you need anything else.'

'Thank you.'

Leaving Abbas, Arli closed the door and went upstairs where he finished reading the twenty first chapter in the Quran.

Abbas walked over to the table. Switching on the standard lamp, he sat down and looked at the items before him. Carefully selecting some wires, he began to assemble the connections to the detonator. Twisting the long wires, he clipped the end, exposing the bare copper. The soldering iron he tested on a metal plate: hot enough. He screwed the detonator into the vice and carefully soldered the exposed wires to the cap. Checking each one was secure, he bound the cable with tape. The cables he measured to approximately half an arm's length, snipped them in half, drawing the protective rubber sheaf off the cable, exposing about an inch at the end. Picking up a small plastic box about the size of a cigarette packet, he carefully placed first one wire through a hole in the bottom and then the second wire in the hole next to the first. With the box in his left hand, he drew the wires into the box and taped them down. Adjusting them slightly, he connected them to the small metal brackets. Soldering them securely into place, he inspected his work, testing the strength of each wire, pulling it taut and retaping, making sure both now were firmly in place.

Stretching across the table, he picked up a cylindrical

plastic tube. Taking some more wire, again with the process of stripping each as before, he unscrewed the buttoned screwcap on the tube, threaded the wires up and through the top. Holding the screwcap and positioning the wires on the top of two connectors, he soldered them on. No tape this time, pulling them gently and then drawing the wires back down the tube, the button screwed into the top of the tube. Uncoiling the remainder of the wire from the tube, he gave himself a full arm's length and cut. Stripping these ends, he picked up a small battery assemble, which he had connected to a light bulb earlier that day, and connected the battery to the exposed wires from the tube and pressed the button. The light glowed. Satisfied that the connection was good, he taped the wires to the bottom of the trigger tube and then returned to the small plastic box, which contained his first connections, this time at the top of the box, and he slid the two wires into it which he then soldered to the connectors in the bottom.

Carefully inspecting his work, he placed the now assembled detonator system onto the bench. The only remaining component would be to insert a battery between the two separate connectors and clip the lid onto the top of the box. Once the small red button was pressed, the electrical current would be sufficient enough to detonate the detonator, which, once assembled, would be inserted into the Semtex. The bomb was then live, and it only required a simple push of the button. Over the course of the next few hours, he fashioned two more detonator systems exactly as the first. On completion, he turned his attention to the rucksacks that would be used to hold the devices. Putting one of the bags on his back, he adjusted the straps so the bag would be held firmly into the back of the body. Accomplishing this with all three, he picked the first one up and with a pair of scissors cut a hole into the right-hand side of each bag. Through this, Abbas threaded the long wire attached to the trigger, which would allow the wearer to press the button and detonate the bomb as they needed to. Pulling a large box from under the table, Abbas opened it up and began filling each rucksack with an assortment of nuts, bolts and screws. A good layer was put into each one. When the time came, he would put the Semtex taped securely to the plastic box with the battery in it and then cover this with more nuts and screws, filling the bag to about three-quarters full. The weight would be around 25 lb, enough for each man to carry comfortably. The trigger wire would be threaded through, coiled up and taped to the side of the bag; it would be up to the three men to loosen this when they got close to their target.

Satisfied, Abbas went into the front room of his basement. He would join the others for late prayers later tonight. For now, though, kneeling on the mat, he raised his right index fingers briefly to proclaim his devotion then in the prayers asked Allah for forgiveness and mercy.

Arli had introduced them to Abbas after prayers. Speaking to each one in turn, Nadir and Hakim, they spoke of their destiny and both, he saw, were committed to the cause. The third man, Gilad, was mainly there for support and to assist Arli. He would accompany Hakim, if he needed him to, when the time came. Hakim had been in Iraq working in the accountant's office when the American bombs had struck. Everyone knew that the Americans were coming, even though Saddam had put a blanket across the country, so news was thin and far between. He had hurt his foot when, as a kid, he'd been playing football and had suffered a broken leg, so when it came to serving his country and signing up to attack Kuwait, he had been given a medical certificate stopping him from joining, much to the delight of his mother. On the day, he was in the office. The bombing had startled everyone. Rushing home, the apartment block he lived in with his parents had been demolished. It was several days before they had found the body of his mother and father. Grief had overwhelmed him, and on that day, he swore to his family that one day he would avenge their death.

'Whoever dies in a battle in the cause of Allah or dies of his wounds is the real martyr. Remember that your soul will return to your body; two angels will arrive and sit you up for questioning, they will ask, "Who is your lord, what is your religion, who is your prophet?" When you answer Allah, Islam and Muhammad, respectively, you will be granted paradise,'

Arli continued, and the others followed in answer. It had been going on for weeks now. They knew the time was coming for them to avenge their dead brothers, Nadir, fervent in his mind and words, Hakim speaking heavily but feeling the weight being lifted from his shoulders. Both men were committed to the task ahead, both devoted to and firm in their belief of Allah.

There was a knock on the side of the van. Barry had approached from the end of the road nearest the van and Tony hadn't spotted him, concentrating forwards on his target area. Unlocking the door, Barry climbed in and went into the back.

'Any movement?'

'None, Nadir and the other two came at three, as usual, Nadir and one of the other guys. They stayed longer than normal and left about 15 minutes ago. Got to assume they were planning. What does Leonard want to do?'

'Leonard's out of the country. We got a message to him but no reply as yet.'

'Where is he?'

'Yanksville. He was boarding his plane, so he'll be back tomorrow, late afternoon.'

'Bloody hell,' said Tony. 'Surely we can't wait that long?'

'We'll have to. It's highly unlikely that they will go today, or even tomorrow, if, of course, that is the bombmaker and the owner of the house. We also don't know if they have the stuff to make the bombs either, so we do have time.'

'What about the police?'

'Not down to me to inform them, plus it will take them a few days to arrange a raid. They've got to be semi sure they know what they are getting themselves into. You can't just turn up and bash down a door with big unknowns behind it.'

'Suppose not,' said Tony.

'Sit, wait, take photos, patience.'

Tony nodded.

'I'll get Mike to relieve you on Monday morning, OK? Take it easy. I can't see anything happening for the next 24 or maybe even 48 hours, they, like us, need to prepare. If we are dealing with a couple of maniacs intent on blowing themselves up then even they have to plan when they are going to do it, and a lot of that will rest with the bombmaker, because I can tell you now he won't be rushing anything, not if he wants to live anyway.'

Patting Tony on the shoulder, he continued,

'Well done. Take it easy, and I'll catch you later.'

Barry let himself out; Tony watched him disappear.

Chapter 18

Tony pondered. He had been that unlucky that every time he had been sat taking photos of the house, passers-by and neighbours he had missed the man with the key. He thought back, trying to remember each time he'd been here, his walk pasts, the visits from Nadir and the other three, when the three had become two a few weeks ago and now Mr Suitcase, aka, thought Tony, the bombmaker. He picked up the file next to him and scanned through it: there were dozens of photos. Looking at each one carefully, with one eye on the house as he did so, nothing. Scanning them again, sighing, nothing. I don't believe it, he thought, looking at the house. It was a standard terraced townhouse, fourth one in and no different than the rest. It had a basement, which was obviously part of the house, whereas in some of the houses in the row the basement was a separate flat. On bin day, plastic waste bags were distributed along the edge of the pavement. He had thought it too risky to grab one near the house and have a look through. Then one day he had watched as one of the men, after their nightly meeting, had come out and chucked it next to a pile of others. So that day he still hadn't spotted the owner.

*

Placing the file by his side, he peered through the curtains separating the back of the van and the driving seat and looked up the road, into the mirrors and watched for anyone walking. There was no one about, so he slipped through the seats, opened the driver's door and got out. Locking it behind him, with another quick check up the road, he walked towards the opposite end of the street, away from the high-street end. Lighting a cigarette as he did, he looked at all the houses. Could he make his way across through the attics, he thought as he looked up. The houses, he knew were all occupied, and he guessed that that was probably not an option. Walking to the corner, turning left, he walked alongside the end terrace. The back of the house had a small yard, which was fenced but had no rear exit. The yard backed onto another yard, and then, as he turned the corner into the road parallel with his house, the street looked identical: a row of terraced townhouses and each, as far as he could see, looking over the first fence, had a small yard but no rear exit. When he had first arrived, he had driven up the street to see if there were any back entrances to the houses on his street. He hadn't seen any. Glancing at his watch and noting that he had plenty of time, he crossed over and walked slowly along looking at each mirror image house as he went. About halfway down he paused, lit another cigarette and swore. Opposite, the terrace had stopped, and a very small passage was visible between two of the houses. The houses, as he looked closer, carried on as a terrace but were slightly differ-ent in design. Crossing over, the passage, he saw, was just big enough for a person to walk between. Looking up and down the road, there was nobody around, so he walked carefully down the alley at the end of the houses. Both had fenced backyards, but the gap extended slightly and ran along the back of all the houses. Turning left and then right, he saw you could access just about every house on either side via the back. *Bastard,* he thought, *no wonder I missed the little shit.*

Backing out, he walked back to the van, climbed in and poured himself a tea from the flask. *So that's how he goes in and out, must be,* thought Tony. Looking at his watch, it was almost time for the ritual nightly visits. Picking up the camera, Tony waited, and within a few minutes Nadir arrived followed quickly by the other two. Taking off their shoes, they entered the house with Tony clicking away, capturing their every move.

Sunday turned into Monday, and with a few breaks buying sandwiches and replacing his tea with cold drinks, Tony sat and watched. Tuesday morning there was a knock on the side of the van. Tony released the catch and Barry got in. Pushing through the curtain, Barry sat opposite Tony.

'Right, Leonard's back, and they have decided to raid the place. Leonard is liaising with the tactical team today. Someone will be over later, or tomorrow, to have a look at the place, assuming the home secretary gives the go ahead and they get a warrant. The plan will be to go in on Saturday morning at 7:15 just as they start their prayers.'

'Found a way into the back of the house, alleyway, halfway up the street, leads behind all the houses to their back yard.'

'OK, I'll pass that on. Focus on taking photos of the house. You will see one or two people, probably walking up and down or a car or van that you've not spotted before. Don't photograph them, OK?'

'Yeah, sure,' smiled Tony. 'Do they know I'm here?'

'They will do but they won't approach. In fact, no one will speak or acknowledge anyone in the street from lunchtime onwards today, hopefully, if all goes well with Leonard.'

Tony nodded.

'Also, Mike will take over from you on Friday morning. We need the van out of here, once the raid is done this place will be swarming with the locals and press, so I know. . .' said Barry raising his hand slightly, 'you want to be here having a butchers, but it's too risky, and if they nab the buggers then it's a job well done anyway.'

'Fucking typical,' said Tony.

'Nah, don't worry about it,' said Barry patting his arm. 'You know the score.'

'Here's a radio; it's tuned to 4970 so we can talk to each other; press this button to speak,' he said showing Tony the radio. 'And this one if you want handsfree, but stick this in your ear,' he said passing him an earpiece. 'Clip the radio to your belt, and put this round your neck,' indicating a throat mic.

'We all have one. I'm not expecting we'll need it, but Leonard has now decided that we need better comms with each other when we are out and about. Keep it in your car when you are at work, and of course,' said Barry, 'don't take it indoors with you when you go home.'

Tony looked. 'Not likely, is it?'

'I gotta tell you.'

Tony nodded.

'What about Mike?'

'Mike will be here about 6:30, I think, but don't wait for him, you might as well shoot off Thursday night after. . .' nodding at the house, 'late prayers.' Mike will be on his bike so can whizz in and out as needed.'

Tony nodded. 'OK.' Hitting a button on the camera, he handed Barry the latest batch of photos.

'Nothing much on these. No real change, same as before.'

'Thanks. Oh, by the way. . .'

Tony looked up.

'Leonard's got £35 grand for you.'

'Nice one.' Tony smiled

'Right, catch you later. If anything gives, I'll get back to you, if not, shoot off Thursday and meet up next Sunday morning, OK?' said Barry getting up, nearly banging his head on the van roof, climbing through to the front seats.

'All clear?'

'All clear,' called Tony.

The door shut, and Tony watched as Barry walked up the road and disappeared.

The next couple of days dragged. Tony spent most of his time trying to spot the odd one or two people that he thought might be doing a recon of the place. He thought he saw a few but wasn't convinced. A car had parked up for about an hour or so on Wednesday afternoon, which was Tony's only and best guess of someone doing some spotting. A couple of drivebys early on Thursday and regular as clockwork visits to the house by the faithful, that was it. He saw Nadir this week was on lates for work as he had been coming to the house for the early prayers, but apart from that there was no change in any routines.

Checking his watch, it was 11:45 pm. The road was quiet. The men had left the house, which was now in darkness. Tony had a quick look at the basement as he had made one final walk past; this too was in darkness. Climbing into the van, he set off out of Uxbridge to the underground garage just by Hanger Lane. The barrier lifted and he drove down into the bowels of the parking area. Locking the van and placing the keys in the exhaust pipe, he walked out onto the street, which at this time of night was more or less empty. Spying a cab, he shouted and raised his hand. The cabbie did a U turn, pulled up beside him and Tony got in.

'Russell Street, please, mate.'

Rising early, as was his habit, he dressed, picked the keys up for his car, slid the radio into his waistband, adjusted his jacket, grabbed his bag and left the hotel. His Cavalier was parked about 100 yards away, and as he got in, he placed the radio on the passenger seat checking to make sure it was switched on.

He wanted to get to Bristol and should make it by nine. Traffic would hopefully be in his favour, he thought, heading out of London most were heading in so he could make decent time.

'On site, all quiet,' crackled the radio.

Tony instinctively looked at his watch. *Bit late*, he thought; it was 7:10.

'Copy that, M, anything changes let us know.'

'Will do.' The reception wasn't brilliant. He could make out it was Mike and was pretty sure it was Barry, but it was not easy to tell. *Maybe later*, he thought, *once I get used to them talking.*

Pulling up at the lights and indicating left, the radio crackled again.

'Mo. . . sack. . .'

What? thought Tony.

'Say again,' came the reply.

'Movement. . . house. . . which carrying. . . instructions.'

For fuck's sake, thought Tony, *so much for this keeping in touch bollocks.*

'Say again. . . say again.'

Tony swung round the corner and pulled up sharply and grabbed the radio, sticking his fingers up to the car who was blaring his horn at him.

Pressing the button, 'What did he say, Barry? What did he say?'

'Get off, and don't use names, initials only. We talked about this.'

Twat, thought Tony.

'Say again, M.'

This time the signal was clearer.

'Two males leaving the house, both carrying rucksacks. Who should I follow? Instructions please.'

There was a pause.

'They are splitting up. I'm going off bike following high

200

street male. Lost contact with one target. Repeat, I have lost one, going into high street.'

Mike jumped off his bike, put his helmet swiftly onto the bars and switched the radio mic on to hands free and pushed one earphone into his right ear. As the one male rounded the corner, he quickly made his way up the road, speaking into the radio as he did so. Having no option to follow both, he selected the man heading towards the high street. The other, he saw as he glimpsed his man, had crossed over the road and was now out walking out of sight. Jogging to the end of the street, he looked left and right at the junction, spotted his man and crossed over. The street was busy, dozens heading, it seemed to Mike, mostly in the same direction as his guy.

'Target heading left on High Street, left on High Street,' he reported, now catching him up, just a few people between him.

'Description, M.'

'Target approx. 5,8, male, jeans, coat, carrying rucksack on right shoulder. Normal walking pace, recognise from photos. It's Hakim, Nadir was other man.'

Tony slammed the car into gear and shot off, barging his way into traffic. He was about 10 minutes from Nadir's house in Uxbridge. The lights fell into his favour as he sped along the road, switching from lane to lane, undercutting some flashing his lights at others, as he belted down the road now just a few minutes away.

'Target 100 yards from Tube.'

Tony listened as he swerved right across the traffic into

the road heading down towards Nadir's house; neither man was now very far apart. Grabbing the radio,

'I'm near Nadir's house. Do you want me to go there or help M? I'm minutes away,' he said quickly into radio.

The response was immediate.

'Go to Nadir, find him. Make up something.'

'Will do,' he replied chucking the radio back onto the seat.

'M, you have to stop Hakim. Repeat, immediate stop, do not let him on the Underground. Do not let him enter Tube. Authorised force if necessary.'

Tony caught his breath. *Fuck me!* he thought.

Mike hit the button on his mic, knowing now that everything could be heard and, importantly, it would be recorded for later use if required in court.

Unzipping his jacket, he pulled out his 9 mm automatic, sliding an arm band on with the words 'POLICE' emblazoned on it.

Running forward, he shouted.

'ARMED POLICE! ARMED POLICE OFFICER! HAKIM, STAND STILL!'

The people around him turned looking in disbelief as Mike ran forward.

'MOVE! MOVE! ARMED POLICE OFFICER! HAKIM! HAKIM! STOP! STAND STILL!'

People scattered; seconds later there were just the two of them on the street. Hakim had turned.

Mike raised his weapon, pointing directly at him.

'Hakim, I'm an armed police officer. I will shoot you if you don't do as I say. STAND STILL! Put the bag down!'

Hakim just stared at him.

'Put the fucking bag down, mate. Put it down, NOW! Slowly, put the bag down!' Stepping forward a pace or two, Mike was now within 10 feet of Hakim.

'Put the bag down! Don't be stupid, nothing's going to happen to you. Put the bag down!' Mike waved his left hand slowly, indication he should put the bag onto the floor.

Hakim took the bag off his shoulder.

Mike took a breath.

'Slowly,' he said, making direct eye contact with Hakim.

The whole area had come to a standstill. A hush had descended on the high street. A bus had stopped further up, blocking the road. People had gathered on the opposite side, and some had come out of the shops and were just watching the events unfold. Then the faint unmistakable sounds of sirens began to fill the air.

'Thank you, Hakim. Put the bag down and step away, slowly.'

Hakim held the rucksack in his left hand, looked directly at Mike and said,

'Allahu Akbar,' and pressed the small red button.

Chapter 19

The blast was heard up to a mile away when the bomb detonated, blowing Hakim clean off his feet, the power of the Semtex gorging a cavern in the side of his body. He died instantly. The shrapnel tore through the rucksack at a hundred miles an hour, the metal bolts and screws screeching in all directions, slashing through flesh, severing bone, smashing shop windows, embedding themselves into every conceivable hard and soft material within a 40-yard radius. Behind Hakim, some feet away, a young girl had been admiring her new engagement ring. Now, as she lay sprawled on the pavement, her dress in tatters, she stared at where her hand had been. Torn off like a wrapper from a bar of chocolate, her fingers shredded to the bone, skin hanging like curtains blowing in the wind, the ring and the delicate finger it was on, gone. A rain of metal cut through the people on the other side of the road who had been watching. Car windows were blown in from the force of the blast. The bus shuddered from the impact of the bomb; just about every window exploded into a thousand pieces, the driver too late to cover his face from the windshield as it wrapped itself around him, scarring him for life.

*

The sound was deafening, shattering the eardrums of an old man who was crossing the road. The grandmother in the shop, she had seen Hakim in front of the doors as she was about to leave and wondered why he was standing there, then in an instant a bright light blinded her. The explosion obliterated the glass door as she went to pull it open, and shards of glass slashed into her hand, head and heart killing her before the wave took her off her feet and threw her fragile body across the floor like a ragdoll. A young mother coming out of the pharmacy on the other side of the road pushing her four-month-old baby girl was caught as several nuts and screws penetrated mum's left leg. Screaming, she fell to the ground, the flesh blown away, leaving a gaping wound, broken bones and blood pouring from where her knee had been. The metallic projectiles had no feelings, they were indiscriminate, unforgiving about who and what they maimed; a bolt cut through the top of the pram cover headed for the young child's face caught on the metal chain holding the brightly coloured mobile toy and was deflected, passing the little girl's head by an inch, tearing a hole in the pillow and out the back of the pram.

Mike had taken the full brutal explosion head on. With no time to react, he was thrown backwards, careering into a young man who had come up behind him. Mike's body had shielded the man for an instant. The paroxysm knocking them both off their feet, they landed with a crash, the young man smacking his head hard against the concrete immediately rendering him unconscious. The nuts and screws had drilled into Mike's torso with the speed of bullets from a machine gun, cutting him down dead before he could blink. Mike's dishevelled body now lay crumpled on the floor, his hand still gripping his gun, not having had time to fire at the man who had killed him. The hand now several feet from his arm lay blood soaked in the gutter. The hot metal from the lethal device had ripped straight through Mike and into the young man, whose spleen was falling loosely onto the liquid red pavement from a yawning hole in his stomach.

The pain of death and mutilation came to men and women, young and old. The carnage was everywhere, total, devastating, and in that split-second, dreams were shattered, hopes destroyed and lives changed forever.

Leonard slammed down the phone, rising to his feet at the same time.

'Jennifer!' shouted Leonard grabbing his jacket, almost running around his desk. By the time he got to the door, Jennifer was stepping through.

'Yes, sir.'

'Get the home secretary, patch him through to the car.' Julian, who had been listening in, put down the extended earpiece attached to the phone and dialled downstairs for Leonard's car.

'Let's go,' said Leonard to Julian. The two men ran down the corridor with Jennifer in tow, relaying instructions to her as he went. Hitting the stair door, he paused, turned and said,

'Get Rob and Mark down here now as well.'

The two men bounded down the stairs; it was quicker than waiting for the lift. The stairs to the four floors disappeared in a blur, barging through onto the ground floor foyer, the doorman, already aware of the emergence of the two men, opened the large wooden door, which fronted one of the many buildings near the prime minister's office in central London. The car had drawn up outside and Leonard's protection officer was holding the door open for him. Leonard got in and Julian slid in beside him, pushing an earpiece attached to the radio into his ear as he did so.

The cars, blue lights hidden in the grill and on the dash, with sirens blazing, took off into the city traffic. Derek, Leonard's driver, responding to messages relayed to him through his own earpiece was being given traffic information to Uxbridge gathered in real time through the myriad of cameras that now watched over London. Picking up Marylebone Road, Derek caught sight of an ARV in his rear-view mirror. Receiving instructions, he pulled over at speed. Briefly, the car swept past Derek, dropped in behind the powerful fully emblazoned 3L Senator, the distinctive yellow dots visible from any angle on the car marking it as an active ARV. They would lead through to Uxbridge and deploy on site; the journey would now be a lot quicker.

'Update,' said Leonard to Julian.

Julian had been sat with Leonard listening to the running

commentary from both Barry and Mike as the events played out on the high street. They both had heard the noise, and with repeated requests from Barry to Mike it was but a few seconds when they had realised the worst.

'Still no contact; Barry has assumed fatal. First emergency services arriving on scene reporting several fatalities, many injured, precise numbers unknown.'

Arthur leaned between the seats, car phone in hand.

'Home Secretary for you, sir.'

Grabbing the phone, 'Mr Home Secretary, numbers unknown at present, several dead, lot of destruction. It appears Hakim set the bomb off as our man approached him.'

Pausing for a moment, listening.

'Yes, sir. We fear the worst, sir. We need the go ahead to bring the raid forward. Another one of the group I briefed you about, Nadir Al Najaf, was also seen leaving the house carrying a rucksack, whereabouts unknown at the moment.' Again listening, with a pensive look on his face,

'Yes, sir.'

Giving the receiver back to Arthur and looking at Julian, he said, 'They will contact the commander and the raid will go ahead today. What's the news from Barry?' He had heard Julian talking to Barry while he had been on the phone.

'Yes, sir. Tony is at or near Nadir's home, just waiting for an update.'

Leonard nodded. 'He cannot approach him, understood.'

'Yes, sir.' Julian got back on the radio immediately and relayed his conversation to Barry. 'I repeat, absolutely no contact, follow or stay put only.'

'More details coming in, sir,' said Arthur turning to Leonard.

'Go on.'

Tony had chosen a couple of back routes to get to Nadir's house. He had heard the noise on the radio and suspected that the high street would be blocked if Mike had shot Hakim, so steering clear he had a couple of streets to go. Pulling left then right he got into Nadir's road, slowed and started to look for Nadir. Knowing he would have come up the road towards him, keeping his head low he was keen not to be spotted. About 50 yards from Nadir's house, a red Peugeot pulled out in front of him and headed towards the junction.

Fuck, is that Nadir? Speeding up a little he got close enough to read the number.

'It fucking is!' he said out loud.

The car turned right onto the A40. Tony fell in behind him racking his brains to make sure it was the same plate. Grabbing the radio, he said,

'Nadir is in his car on the A40 heading for the M25. What shall I do?'

The response was immediate.

'Are you sure? Repeat, are you sure?'

'Yes, definitely his car. Red Peugeot. . .' he continued, reading the number plate out for Barry.

'Stay behind. Follow only, repeat, follow only, do not approach. Instructions to follow.'

'Understood.'

Barry quickly typed the number plate into his computer. A second or so later the information burst onto his screen: 1984 red Peugeot, owner registered as Nadir Al Najaf.

Barry picked up the radio.

'Julian, put me through to Leonard.'

'B, passed over M25 on M40 heading towards Oxford,' said Tony. 'Any news on Mike?'

'No, not yet, still waiting for an update. Stay behind Nadir; do not lose him. Help is coming,' came back the reply over the radio.

Tony lit a cigarette; the speed was constant. He wondered what had happened on the high street. Although he was not sure, it seemed like a gunshot, but he hadn't really been listening too closely as he had been belting down to Nadir's. No word from Mike though, he thought, maybe they had to turn the radio signals off in the area. Someone had said before that people listen to the police radio, so they change channel in emergencies, making it difficult for eavesdroppers.

'Passing High Wycombe, steady speed.'

'Thank you, T. Keep us posted,' came the reply.

PC Dave Black and PC Sarah Jones had just come onto the M25 from the M11 when they got the call. Sarah was driving, loving the power of their new Senator. She'd heard this was the last one they would get before changing make; she didn't mind, the car was a beaut to handle.

They both had heard the news a few minutes ago about

Uxbridge and were waiting for further details to see if they would be needed. They were quite a way out but could cover the distance nicely so were surprised by their instructions

Dave turned to Sarah. 'Step on it then,' he said hitting the buttons for the blues and twos. The impressive 3L engine roared, hitting the outside lane at nearly 100 mph, Dave taking details as she went.

'M40, red Peugeot heading towards Oxford, possible RAF Brize Norton. Has suspected explosive device on board.'

Sarah glanced at Dave, raising her eyebrows. 'That's a new one,' she said. The car was now clocking 120 mph, slowing occasionally for the traffic that hadn't seen them coming.

'Come on, get out of the way! Look in your mirror!'

Dave ticked off in his head the equipment they had on board. The armed response vehicle had a selection of kit for all types of emergencies: first aid, bollards, shovels, rope, light-weight aluminium blankets and importantly, two Heckler and Koch carbines along with the Glock handguns that were strapped to their belts. As and when needed, he would unlock the compartment between the seats, ready his Heckler and give Sarah hers. Speed was of the essence; they had practiced the manoeuvre many times and had deployed it on several occasions in the field. It was tried and tested and had become second nature to the pair. The moment the car came to a halt the pair would be out, gun in hand, assessing the situation.

'They have someone tailing the Peugeot,' said Dave to Sarah. 'Just passed High Wycombe. When we get close, they are going to patch us through to the guy.'

'Hope he's a bit savvy, don't want him fucking it up.'

Dave nodded. 'Are we getting help?' said Sarah.

Dave hit the talk button and relayed the question, along with several others he had, to the control centre in central London.

Sarah, concentrating on the driving, passed Watford and was a few miles now from the M40 junction, still 40 minutes from the suspect car but making good progress. Fortunately, at that time of the day it wasn't commuter traffic, so whilst busy it was navigable.

The radio clicked; Dave listened intently.

'Understood. TA51 out.'

'We've got TA90 and 91 coming out; 90 is on the M4 heading from Heathrow; 91 should be with us by the time we get to the M40. We have to stop it before it gets to the base at Brize Norton. Threat level severe, we cannot let it get in. Bomb squad have been despatched as well. OK, so let's get a wiggle on.'

Pressing the accelerator harder, Sarah gave Dave a quick look.

'So, what we looking at then, two bombers, this guy and Uxbridge?'

Dave shook his head. 'I have no idea, but if they are related there could be more, I suppose.'

'Who's the guy tailing?'

'Don't know, they've just said he's on 4970 MHz, so when we get a bit closer, they will patch him in first.'

'Coming off M40 heading towards Oxford,' said Tony on the radio. There had been no erratic driving by Nadir, so

Tony suspected that he had not been noticed following him. He had maintained a steady speed throughout and now, as Nadir had started to indicate, Tony began to wonder what was going to happen next. He hadn't seen any police cars nor heard much from Barry apart from a few conversations as updates; he didn't know what help was coming.

'Any news on Mike and what help is coming?'

'No news yet, there's a blackout in the area. Sorry, T, soon as I know I'll give you an update. A couple of police cars are on route and will be with you soon. When they get close, we will patch you through to them so they can talk you through what you need to do, OK?'

'OK.' Grabbing a cigarette, he slowed down as they approached the first set of lights on the outskirts of Oxford's ring road.

Screaming past High Wycombe, Sarah had been joined by TA90. Another ARV, their beat was mostly stationed at Heathrow Airport, circling the airport, and every two weeks, Paul and Gary, the firearms team, would swap and do a week's walkabout in the airport itself. Long serving members of the Met, they all knew each other and had been on many training exercises together, one of which was stopping a speeding car safely.

'TA90 on your tail, TA51.'

'We see you.'

The two powerful vehicles made short work of the M40, and by the time Tony had followed the A40 round Oxford and was just getting onto the main Cheltenham road, TA91 had caught up and the three were now blasting around the ring road in hot pursuit.

'T, patching you through to police vehicle TA51, who's close by,' came over the radio to Tony.

'This is TA51, repeat TA51. Where are you, T?'

'Oh, hi, I'm about one mile out of Oxford, couple of miles from Witney.'

'OK, T. Do you still have Peugeot in sight?'

'Yes, couple hundred yards in front of me.'

Sarah hit the dual carriageway heading for Witney at just over 110 mph. With the two other cars attached to her rear, they hurtled down the road, the speed camera situated at the start of the dual carriageway flashing in a paparazzi frenzy. Dave leant forward, switching off the sirens and lights, not wanting to alert Nadir.

'I'm passing Witney now, about three miles to turn off for Brize Norton, I'm in a blue Cavalier.'

'We will be with you any minute now. When you see us, stay at your speed, we will pass you. When we pass you, slow down, do not stop, understood?'

'Understood.' Tony looked at Nadir's car. Two miles before the turnoff, he looked in his mirror. 'Where the fuck are they?' he said out loud. Looking again at Nadir and then in his rear-view mirror he saw them.

They closed in behind Tony's car waiting, then after a few hundred yards came the deafening noise of three sets of sirens as the cars shot past him blue lights blazing. Nadir had indicated to pull down the slip road to Brize Norton, and as he did so TA51 passed him, startling him for a second. He looked, a second car was next to him, and glancing in his mirror he saw a third directly behind him. The car in front was slowing; Nadir had no choice but to slow down. The T junction at the end of the slip road came into sight, and as the first car stopped, Nadir slammed on his brakes.

In unison, Dave and Sarah, along with Paul and Gary, were out, locking their weaponry into their shoulders.

'ARMED POLICE! DO NOT MOVE!'

Nadir was shocked; what was going on? Before he could think, the door was pulled open, a hand came in, grabbed him by the collar and yanked him unceremoniously out of the car. He sprawled across the tarmac. He could hear people shouting at him, but his mind was cloudy, and he couldn't think properly. More shouting and he was rolled over. A man put a gun to his head, and he could feel hands roughly feeling his clothes, body, legs. He was rolled over, again a knee in the back, and both arms were pulled behind him and he could feel the handcuffs tight, hard, cold on his wrists.

Dave had taken the decision to whip Nadir out of the car as quickly as possible, deciding that the rucksack he had been told about would either be in the footwell or on the back seat. Immobilising Nadir as fast as they could, he hoped, would prevent Nadir from detonating the bomb. Shock tactics sometimes worked best, and in this instance, it did. With Nadir secure, Dave looked up: the base entrance was 200 yards away.

Chapter 20

Speed and surprise were of the essence. The first two vehicles swept into the road, came to a halt, and as they did so a six-man team from each vehicle leapt out. The first group ran up the few steps to the door. The lead man, battering ram in hand, struck the door inches above the handle; the door gave way immediately. Old and in need of repair, the wooden door and lock had seen better days; a sturdy blow splintered the wood and the door crashed open. The man stepped back; his colleagues burst through into the hallway.

'ARMED POLICE! ARMED POLICE!' came the shout.

Two more vehicles appeared in quick succession, pulled up, and several more heavily armed and wearing bullet proof vests SFOs from SO19 joined their teammates as they surged forward, some up to the house, others to the basement. Leaving nothing to chance, the commander had sent more men to enter the back of the house at the same time. They couldn't afford to creep up to the house in broad daylight, and in the middle of the day it had to be a fast, coordinated and furious entry into the building.

Running upstairs, kicking in the doors, the police barged into each room. The group downstairs hurtled into the sitting room and then met the attack team coming through the kitchen. The basement team again easily smashed open the small wooden basement door, moving swiftly into the rooms, flashlights illuminating the scene.

'All clear, first floor.'

'All clear, basement.'

'All clear, bottom floor.'

The road was blocked at both ends, and people were beginning to come out of their houses to see what all the noise was about. Several local police officers had now been deployed and were working themselves along the street.

'Don't worry, nothing to worry about. If you could please go back inside, just for now.'

'What's going on, mate?' said a man coming out of his house, half dressed.

'Nothing to worry about, sir. Could you go back inside? It'll be all over soon.'

Derek approached the police car blocking the road. He lent out of the window and flashed his badge; the car reversed, allowing Derek to enter the street where the raid on Arli's house was happening.

As he came to a halt, Arthur got out, went over and spoke to an inspector, who was talking to several of the SO19 team. Showing him his badge, a quick word and then he came back.

'Empty, sir, no one is present.'

'Let's go,' said Leonard getting out of the car. The three men went into the house, first the sitting room; Julian had gone upstairs.

'Nothing upstairs, sir. Detailed search later but nothing obvious.'

'These lead to the basement,' said Arthur holding a door open in the hallway.

Switching the stairs light on, they all went down and into the room where Abbas had constructed the bombs. Leonard walked over to the table, surveying the left-over cables, packages and noticing a handful of nuts and bolts in one of the boxes on the floor.

He had said his prayers early. He had demonstrated to the men the night before on how to detonate the bombs so had no reason to stay at the house any longer. He packed his bag, leaving the house that morning at about 6:45. Abbas, with his small suitcase, made his way back to the Tube on the high street. Jumping on the first train on the Metropolitan line, it took him to Bakerloo, and after a short delay he connected through to Paddington arriving at around 7:40. Purchasing a ticket on the newly opened Heathrow Express, he picked his seat and waited. His airline ticket had been bought in advance, so at Heathrow, Abbas walked across the concourse and checked onto BA487 to New York. The lady smiled at him as he handed her his Saudi passport, confirming his seat and departure time. Abbas went through security, over to the large seating area, sat and waited: his flight was at 1:15 pm. His job was done, for the moment, in this country.

The dual carriageway from Witney to the Burford Road roundabout was closed in both directions. All traffic detoured to Witney on the Burford Road and anything coming from Oxford was diverted into and either around Witney or via Bampton, Farringdon and then up to Lechlade before getting back onto the A40 heading towards Cheltenham. Nadir was being held in the back seat of Dave's car. After being thoroughly searched he was arrested and informed of his rights. Protesting that he didn't know what was going on he now waited in silence. The three police vehicles had pulled away from Nadir's car and were now several hundred yards to the right of the base. The base had been informed by command at the Met and was now effectively shut down to entry. They could see from where they were several Land Rovers had blocked the entrance and had the American equivalent to military police on guard outside. Cars that approached were being turned around and sent back down towards either Bampton or Lechlade.

Several local police cars were in strategic locations around the area and the bomb squad had arrived. The area sealed off, the captain of the bomb squad was now in charge. His team were now donning specialist bomb blast Kevlar vests and suits. One man was steering the bomb squad robot arm out of the modified Land Rover. The clever unit would approach the vehicle and allow the tram to view the rucksack in greater detail, then deciding on the best way to dispose of the bomb itself.

'Are we taking him back to ours?' said Sarah.

'No word as yet,' said Dave. He watched as Gary and Paul were taking it in turns to stand by Nadir. Dave sat by the radio in the third car and waited for instructions.

He didn't have to wait long; the radio crackled.

'TA51, this is Chief Inspector Hargreaves, repeat Chief Inspector Hargreaves.'

'TA51, sir, PC Dave Black and PC Sarah Jones.'

'Patching you through to Leonard Hewes-Smith. You have my permission to act on his instructions.'

'Yes, sir.'

A short break in the line and then he heard Leonard.

'PC Black, Leonard Hewes-Smith.'

'Yes, sir.'

'We've met, a short while ago you assisted at Tilbury.'

'Yes, sir,' Dave raised his eyebrows; Sarah nodded.

'I remember, sir, what do you want us to do with the suspect?'

'We need him at a location not far from you. Absolute discretion is needed. You will be met; please do not attract attention on your journey.'

'Yes, sir.'

The radio went dead then opened again. Leonard gave him the address of the location he wanted Nadir to be taken to.

Putting down the radio, 'Let's go,' he said to Sarah.

'See you later, guys,' he said to Gary, and with a wave and a nod he took the driving seat. Sarah climbed in beside him and opened up the map in front of her. With Nadir secure in the back, they reversed and set off up to the A40, left and on towards Burford.

Burford, they turned left heading down towards Lechlade then through Fairford and onto the outskirts of Cirencester. Circling Cirencester towards South Cerney, the house they were looking for was set back slightly, gated and next to the Duke of Gloucester Barracks. Not part of the barracks, it was a private five bedroomed house which had served as a safe house for the intelligent services for some years. The house was relatively easy to spot from the main road, which gave Dave plenty of time to slow and indicate before turning into the driveway. A man was waiting and had opened the half height wooden gates for them. Crunching up the drive, they arrived at the door where another man was waiting for them. Sarah looked around; the only noticeable thing, which was slightly unusual for a house, were the cameras on each of the corners of the building, but other than that it just seemed like a normal 1930s detached small country house. Underlying the obvious camera security, there were sensors covering the entire garden and several more cameras placed strategically in the overhanging trees along the drive and at the back of the property. Anyone climbing over the fence would immediately trip a sensor activating an alarm inside.

Sarah got out as the man approached.

'All yours, mate,' she said opening the back door.

'Thanks, you can loosen the handcuffs.'

'No problem,' said Sarah turning Nadir around and releasing the cuffs. Pushing him forward, the man took his arm, nodded at Dave and Sarah and walked Nadir into the house.

'Why am I here?' said Nadir struggling a little to get his arm free. Another man appeared from the front room, crossed the hallway and clipped more handcuffs on Nadir.

'Down here,' he said as the men walked to a door leading to the basement.

'Why am I here? Who are you? What's going on?' His questions unanswered, they went down to the basement. A door unlocked, swung open, and as Nadir went in the first man uncuffed him.

'Sit here,' the man said manoeuvring Nadir to a chair behind a table with his hand on his shoulder. Nadir was positioned in the chair; his right hand was attached to a chain on the desk, and before he could do anything his left hand was also attached. The chain went through a ring on the desk; he was able to move his hands left and right but was firmly shackled in place.

'What the fuck are you doing? Why am I here? Who are you?' The questions kept coming.

'Do you want a drink? Anything to eat?'

'Fuck you, what the fuck is going on?'

'OK,' said the man, turning. The two left the room, Nadir hearing the distinct click of a lock as they went.

'Come back. What the fuck are you doing? Where am I?' he shouted, pulling at the chain, trying to stand. 'Bastards, come back,' fell on deaf ears.

After a while Nadir settled down and looked around: a single table, which he was chained to with what looked like two microphones embedded in it, a phone, which he couldn't reach – he'd pushed the table, but it was anchored to the ground. There was his chair and one other, two cameras, one in either top corner, facing him, and a solitary button next to the door, but other than that the room was empty, lit by a soft bulb, all he could do was sit and wait.

Brushing her hair back and tying it with a bobble she looked in the mirror: smart, not overly, some make up but not too much, the red lipstick a favourite. She smoothed her skirt, pulled at the blouse and slipped on her jacket. She would be in court for several hours and wanted to make sure she was comfortable. Heaven knows how long she would have to wait for them to call her, but she'd gone through her notes again last night, looked at the file and the photographs, confident that any questions she could answer without hesitation. The trial was one of many. This one was of a Yardie they had pulled in several months ago on a stop and search. He had been in the wrong area and had sped off when approached. He had been cornered and on searching the vehicle they had found a firearm and a small amount of cocaine. He wouldn't get much for the cocaine but was looking at several years for the handgun. Pleading not guilty was a bit futile, but they all did to begin with. This gun had his prints all over it, and when they had raided his flat, they found several boxes of ammunition tying the gun to him.

The court hearing had gone well. Izzy had given evidence by midday, which was lucky, she thought. Coming out of the court, on the way back to the office there were updates both from control and from the local radio station; the chatter was all about the explosion in Uxbridge. Devastating news, it had been some time since London had suffered an attack. The news gave some details, but reporters were still scrambling around for eyewitness reports and definitive information from the Met.

Parking up, she bounded up the stairs and into the office; everyone was there. The hush over the room was palpable as she entered. The TVs were on, each on a different news channel, people standing and watching as more and more details emerged.

'You seen this?' said Bill.

'Caught some of it on the way back, unbelievable,' she said.

'I cannot believe someone would do this.'

'I know, thought those days were over.'

'Yes, terrorist on his own, lone bomber, for fuck's sake.'

Izzy's phone rang; putting her bag down she picked up. 'DI Taylor.'

Izzy started to listen, sat down and grabbed a pen; scribbling furiously she put the phone back down.

'OK, everyone listen up,' she said standing.

The team stopped what they were doing. Izzy came from around her desk and stood in the middle of the office.

'We've all heard the news, a desperate situation. Unfortunately, we believe that one of our own has been taken down. Not sure who or why he was there, but the DCI has confirmed the fatality.'

Startled looks and mumblings came from the group.

She looked around: some had been close to one or two IRA bombs in the past and could remember the chaos caused by such a blast. The team had swelled in numbers now as the information was pouring in about Rinori and his gang. Surveillance was going well. His gang had also grown in numbers, and they knew it wouldn't be long before he took a delivery.

'I have some names for you: Nadir Al Najaf, Arli Jassam and Hakim Al-Fasih. Hakim set the bomb off in Uxbridge. These. . .' she said putting two pieces of paper onto the table, 'are the addresses we have, one of which is a mosque. We are not involved in the case, but the DSUP wants everyone to search their records from at least the last year, files, witness statements, notebooks, everything for that matter that might contain these names and addresses. It's a needle, I know, but the thoughts are that they got the explosive from somewhere, where better than the scroats that we deal with. OK, get to it, fast as possible, please.'

Not alone in the request, dozens of departments and officers across the Met were now searching new and old records, anything that could throw up the slightest bit of information about the group and of course, very much a needle in a haystack, the actual bombmaker himself. *Slim chance*, thought Izzy, *but we gotta try.*

Chapter 21

Tony sat at the table, stunned.

'Fucking hell, that's just. . ..' the words trailed off.

'I know,' said Barry shaking his head.

'Why didn't you tell me?'

'We couldn't over the radio. Never know who's listening, and we needed you to focus on what you were doing.'

Tony nodded, 'Yeah, but even so.'

Lighting a cigarette, he offered one to Mark, who lit up. No one was in the mood for talking.

'Leonard will be here shortly,' said Barry.

Sitting in silence, Tony thought about the time he had spent with Mike, on his bike, his new baby. *God knows what his wife will do,*' he thought.

As if telepathic, Barry said, 'His wife and baby will be looked after. . .' pausing and then adding, 'for the rest of their lives.'

'Good,' said Rob.

The door opened; Leonard, looking aged, pulled up a chair and sat down.

'Business, I know it's hard, but we can cry later. For now, we need answers, and fucking quick.'

Looking from one to the other, he continued,

'We have Nadir, and I believe he can give us the informa-tion we need. We don't have much time. If, as previously agreed, there are three bombs then one is missing and needs to be found. The house is empty; Arli and the bombmaker have gone. Searching has revealed nothing, so Nadir is our main target. He needs to talk, suggestions?'

The conversation continued: what was the best way to get him to talk?

'OK, Tony, you and Barry get to Nadir. Rob, Mark, stay in London.'

The journey up to Cirencester was mostly in silence. Tony knew Barry knew Mike far better than he did, so he guessed his thoughts were on their time together. He didn't know how long they'd known each other, but the team had been created a while before Tony had joined. It had been decided that Tony would do the interview, firstly, because his relationship with Mike was not as close as the others and therefore, he was less prone to doing Nadir any serious harm and secondly, it was hoped to throw Nadir off balance seeing Tony. It was dark by the time they pulled into the driveway. Expected, the gates had been opened and a man was waiting for them as they got out of the car.

'Hi, Keith,' said Barry.

'Hello, mate, sad news, yes?'

Barry nodded. 'This is Tony.'

'Hi.'

'Hi.'

'Where is he?' said Barry.

'Downstairs.'

'Has he had anything to eat and drink?'

'Yes, an hour or so ago, keeps moaning about his rights, as you can imagine.'

'Comms up and running.'

'Yes, all ready to go,' replied Keith as he led them down to the basement and pointed to a door.

'We're in here,' he said opening up and letting them both go in.

The room had a couple of desks, several monitors, various telephones and a bank of switches.

'Here,' said Keith to Barry, indicating a seat. 'Who's doing the interview?'

'Tony.'

'OK. Tone, next door. Whenever you are ready; we'll be watching and listening,' he said pointing to the monitors. Tony looked at the one nearest to him: it had a close up of Nadir chained to the table.

'Don't worry, he can't get at you, and the table is secure.'

'As we planned, Tony, OK?'

Tony nodded, put the folder under his arm. The interview had been sketched out. It would be fluid, depending on the answers he got, but they needed a lot of information, and it could take some time. Short of beating the answers out of him, which wouldn't play well on the monitors, it would be down to tactics.

Tony opened the door and looked at Nadir.

Nadir's startled eyes widened. 'What the fuck!'

'Evening, Nadir, you remember me, obviously, Tony.' Walking towards Nadir, he put the folder on the table and sat down.

'Do you need anything before we chat?'

'What the fuck you doing here? Who the fuck are you?'

'They tell me you've eaten and had something to drink, so I have a couple of questions for you.'

'Go fuck yourself. Why am I here? Who are you people? I have rights.'

Opening the folder, Tony made a display of pulling out a piece of paper and taking a moment to read it.

'Nadir Al Najaf, 32 years old, married. Iraqi, married to Bahi Al Najaf, two children, a newborn girl by the name of Polla and an elder daughter Kala, Polla born in the UK, Kala was born in India. You and your wife studied at the University in Mumbai where you were sponsored by Professor Dougan to acquire a post at RAF Brize Norton, the American run airbase. Does your wife know what you had planned?'

'You're a liar, you tried to set me up. Who do you work for?'

'What was your plan, Nadir?'

Returning to the folder, Tony took out several pictures and pushed them towards Nadir.

'We've been watching you for a while. Who's this man next to you?' he asked, pointing to Hakim.

Nadir sat back and ignored the picture.

'I have another one,' said Tony pulling out more.

'Who's this? This is you, and you are with him. You must know who he is, Nadir.'

Again silence.

'Who did you meet in the house?'

'Who owns the house?'

'What did you do in the house, Nadir?'

Silence.

'You might as well tell me. What happened to this man, Nadir?' he asked pointing at an early picture of Gilad. 'Not seen him for a while, what happened to him?'

'I have rights. I want to make a phone call to my wife.'

'Rights, oh, OK, well in here you are in no man's land, no one knows you are here. I expect your wife, over the next day or so, will wonder where you are, make a few phone calls, but there will be no trace of you. That is until you start talking.'

'You can't do that, that's against the law. You must let me speak to a solicitor.'

'Who's this man? What did you do in the house, Nadir?'

'I'M NOT SAYING ANYTHING! I HAVE RIGHTS!' screamed Nadir.

'Not in here you don't. You are in limbo, and until you start answering my questions this is where you are staying.'

'FUCK YOU!'

'Who made the bomb, Nadir? What is his name?'

'Where's Arli, Nadir? Where's the bombmaker?'

Nadir spat on the photographs.

'I know you are not the bombmaker. What's his name? Where is he?'

The questions continued, each picture, more questions, more silence.

'Why did you want to bomb your workmates?'

Nadir glared at him. 'They're not my workmates, they are terrorists who deserve to die.'

'Why?'

'Fuck you!'

'Tell me, why do they need to die, Nadir?'

Nadir looked at him, rage in his eyes. 'They killed my brothers. You, them, they all need to die.'

'And you are willing to kill yourself in the process?'

'Allah is great, Allah will look after me.'

'Maybe, but what about your family, Nadir? What about your daughters, your wife, are they to suffer as well?'

'You don't know what pain feels like. Cosseted in this country, living an easy life, you don't understand the struggle we've gone through, the deaths our families have had at the hands of our aggressors.'

Tony looked at him. *Pain, suffering, death,* he thought, *we've been on the receiving end of terrorists for years. The IRA indiscriminately bombing, killing women, children, men and some of my friends.* Tony swallowed and chose not to retort.

'Where's the bombmaker and Arli, Nadir, that's all I want to know?'

Silence.

'OK, we'll leave it for now,' said Tony looking at his watch. 'You sound agitated, need some rest. We'll pick it up again in the morning.' Gathering the pictures, sliding them back into the folder, he stood, walked to the door and pressed the button. A click and the door swung open. Tony stepped out, and the door closed.

'What do you think?' said Tony to Barry in the next room.

'Well, at least he's sort of talking and has admitted he was going to use the bomb at work.'

'Tomorrow then.'

Tony rose early, looked at his watch, showered, put on some clean clothes and went downstairs. He could smell the breakfast and walked into the dining room. Pouring himself a coffee, Barry joined him. 'Ready?'

'Yes, let's go.'

Nadir had been locked into place. Tony nodded to Keith as he left the room. Sitting down, he looked at Nadir.

'Sleep well?' he enquired.

'OK, where is Arli and the bombmaker, Nadir? I am running out of patience now, so if you want to get out of here you need to tell me.'

Silence.

Pulling a photo from his folder, he pushed it towards Nadir.

Nadir's eyes widened.

'Your wife and baby.' Tony had taken the photo a while ago when he had spotted Nadir's wife pushing the pram home one day.

'Oh, and this. . .' he said taking another one out, 'is your daughter Kala. Pretty girl, she seems to have settled in well.'

'So?'

'I need to know where they are, Nadir, Arli and the bombmaker, what's his name?'

Silence.

'I don't have any more time for this, Nadir,' said Tony slamming his hand down hard on the table. 'Tell me where they are. . .NOW!' shouted Tony.

Nadir jumped. 'I don't know, I don't know anything.'

'Liar, you do, and you are going to tell me.'

Nadir just looked at him.

'Do you love your wife and children?' said Tony pointing at the photos.

'I think you do. I'll give you one more chance to tell me what I want to know. Where are they and what's his name?' the tone had changed, menacing, aggressive.

Silence. Nadir spat on the floor.

'Fuck you!'

Tony picked the receiver up on the phone, dialled a number and flicked a switch. The loudspeaker burst into life; the ringing tone sounded out.

'Hello.'

'It's Tony. Nadir wants to speak to his wife to tell her he loves her.'

Nadir looked at Tony, startled. 'You're in my house?'

'Nadir, Nadir, where are you? What's happening? Men are in the house.' Her voice cracked. He could hear the tears and then he heard his daughter crying in the background.

'Bahi, Bahi, don't be afraid. Everything will be OK.'

He heard a scream as the phone was ripped out of her hand.

'Bahi, Bahi.'

'I need to know where they are, Nadir.'

'Bahi, Bahi,' screaming at the phone.

'Where are they, Nadir?'

'I don't know. I don't know. I want to speak to Bahi.'

'She's holding your baby,' said Rob over the phone.

Nadir could hear his wife and Kala, his elder daughter, crying in the background.

'Where are they, Nadir?'

'I don't know. You can't hurt my family, the police don't do that,' cried Nadir. 'Let them go, they've done nothing. . .'

'I'll ask you one more time, Nadir, where are they, oh, and we're not the police.'

'I don't know anything. Let my family go,' he said, straining now at the handcuffs.

Tony looked at him and picked up a photo.

'Do you have a favourite child, Nadir? I know most people say they love all their children the same but secretly they have a favourite. Do you have a favourite?'

The crying over the speaker was getting louder.

Nadir's scared eyes looked at him. His mouth open, he sat forward quickly, anger flaring in his eyes.

'Let me pick one. . .how about Polla?'

Nadir gasped in disbelief.

'Last chance, Nadir, where are they?'

'Nadir raised his hands pointing at Tony the best he could. 'I don't know, I don't. . .'

'Rob,' said Tony into the microphone.

'Yes.'

'Tell Mark to kill Polla.'

'OK.'

'NO! NO!'

The shriek was loud and ear piercing as Rob held Bahi while Mark pulled the little baby from her arms.

Screaming, Nadir's tears were beginning to well in his eyes.

'Five seconds, Nadir, where are they?'

NO! NO! NO! You won't, you won't, I know you won't,' he screamed at Tony.

'Three seconds.'

'Two seconds.'

Tony looked at Nadir. 'Where are they?' The atmosphere dropped, and Nadir started to panic. Tony's voice was steady, calm, but now every word was menacing.

'NO!' yelled Nadir.

'One second.'

'NO, I don't know.'

The gunshot was loud; the scream that followed would last in Nadir's head for the rest of his life.

Nadir howled, rose and tore at the chain, trying to free himself to get to Tony, the chair flying backwards, yanking with all his might at the metal tying his wrist together, the cuffs, they held firm, the table, rock solid.

'You fucking bastard. I'll kill you,' bawled Nadir.

Tony switched the receiver off, cutting off the screams from Nadir's house. He sat back, pulled a packet of cigarettes from his pocket and lit one up.

'You don't mind if I smoke, do you?' he said lightly.

Words hung in the air; Nadir just looked at him, tears flowing uncontrollably down his face onto the table. He put his head in his hands and started wailing.

Tony smoked. Halfway through he flicked the fag on the floor and squashed it.

'That's enough. For fuck's sake, you've still got another daughter.'

Nadir opened his mouth to say something, but the words didn't come out.

A few minutes passed as the reality sank into Nadir, wiping the constant stream of tears from his face, blubbering and dribbling from his mouth, kneeling now.

'Where are they, Nadir?' asked Tony.

'I don't know, I don't know,' whimpered Nadir.

'I think you do. What's your other girl called?' he said picking up the photo.

'Ah, yes, Kala. Do you love her too?' he said looking up at Nadir.

Nadir was breathless. 'You wouldn't, you can't, she's my little girl.'

'I can and I will. Last chance, where are they?'

Nadir shook his head.

'Oh, I'm not going to kill her. Mark will chop her hand off, right one probably. Is she right-handed?' said Tony casually.

Nadir just looked at him incredulously, more tears beginning to flow, his mouth opening and shutting, no words coming out.

'You will go to jail, Nadir, and every time your daughter comes to visit you will see how you ruined her life, unmarried, destined to be a spinster, because of you, hating you for the rest of your life, can you live with that?'

Tony picked up the receiver and began to dial.

'He's in Brighton,' sobbed Nadir.

Tony paused, 'Who?'

Nadir looked at him.

'Who?' continuing to dial.

'Arli, I don't know the bombmaker, he came a week ago. He walks with a limp. I think his name is Abbas, but I'm not sure, but he's gone. I think he's left the country.' The words were now spilling from his mouth.

'What's Arli doing in Brighton?'

Nadir took a deep breath, wiping the wetness from his face.

'Don't stop now.'

'He's going to blow himself up at a Brighton hotel, I think.'

'Which one?'

'I don't know, honestly. . .' shuddered Nadir, 'don't know,' he continued, shaking and putting his head in his hands.

Tony looked at him, paused then put the phone down, picked up the photos and rose and walked to the door.

'You killed my daughter, you bastard. Allah will never forgive you,' Nadir screamed at him as Tony put his hand on the door handle.

'Don't be stupid,' said Tony opening the door, turning to look at him for one last time, 'of course she's not dead.'

Nadir's eyes widened in disbelief.

Tony looked at him in disgust.

'We don't kill kids. It's not her fault that you're a cunt.'

Chapter 22

'Get that?' said Tony to Barry as he went into the room next door.

'Yes, on tape,' said Barry.

'What now?'

'Leonard was watching, and you need to get to Brighton as soon as.'

'Couple of hours from here.'

'No, Keith will drop you next door. There is a lift waiting for you,' said Barry, rising. 'I'm going back to London.'

'So, what do you want me to do?'

Handing Tony a camera and radio set, he replied, 'If you get the chance, photograph Arli, but don't go near him. Understand?'

'OK, sure, but what if he is carrying another rucksack?'

'You'll be met when you get there. If you spot him let us know. Keep him in view if you can. Some guys are on their way down there now. Also, the local and special ops squad will be available as well. There will be a lot of people around who will deal with him. If you spot him, and I repeat, Tony, Leonard has expressly said you are not to go near him. You gotta stay out of the way, understood?' said Barry strongly.

'OK, fair enough. Why do you think Brighton? What's going on down there?'

'We are checking now, not sure at the moment. Right, go.'

'This way,' said Keith.

The two men walked quickly out of the house and into a waiting car. The journey wasn't far; onto the main road, Keith turned right and drove a couple of hundred yards into the base. Flashing a badge at the sentry, the gate was lifted, and Keith drove round the first set of buildings and headed towards the airfield.

'You've been here before then?' said Tony.

'Yeah, many times. Right,' he said pulling up, 'that's your lift over there. They're waiting for you,' pointing.

'What, on that?' said Tony with surprise.

'Just for you.'

'Fuck me,' said Tony out loud. Keith put his hand on Tony's arm. 'When you get out, keep your head low, and I mean low, OK. See that guy there, he'll take you on,' he said, pointing to an airman decked in green overalls with a helmet standing next to the chopper.

Grabbing the camera, Tony, head down, walked quickly over the grass. The noise was deafening; the motors had been fired up and the blades began to turn faster the closer he got. The man grabbed his arm and helped him up the tailgate into the bowls of an enormous Chinook.

Unable to hear anything, the crewman guided Tony to a seat, helped him with the seatbelt, strapping it tightly, then put a pair of headphones on him and adjusted the mic. Finally, he made a gesture of thumbs up, stay put. The air crewman walked back to the doors, attached his headphone cord into the side panel, hit a button and the tailgate began to rise. Once firmly in place, he sat, belted himself in and waited. Tony looked around in awe: it was huge, empty. Apart from him, there were some crates near the front and the crewman at the back. The noise from the engines had been dampened by the headset he was wearing, which Tony was grateful for, wondering just how noisy it would be if he didn't have them on. Never having been on a helicopter before, he was surprised at the force he felt as it left the ground.

After a few minutes of being air bound, the crewman unclipped himself and came over and sat next to Tony. Leaning forward, he flicked a switch on Tony's headset.

'Can you hear me?'

It came through loud and clear.

'Yes, I can.'

'OK, talk normally. My name's Bernie. Don't get out of your seat. Don't take the headset off, and don't smoke, OK? I'll look after you while you're on board.'

'Yeah, sure. How long will we be up here?'

'About 45 mins, OK. I'll come back when we get close.' Uncoupling himself, he went off towards the front of the helicopter, leaving Tony with his thoughts.

Even with the headphones on, the noise from the two engines came through, and as he looked around, he tried to imagine how much equipment they could get into one of these things. Quite a bit, he decided. Passing that off, he began to think about the interview with Nadir and then Brighton. Why Brighton? Why a hotel, not a festival? Holiday crowd? Deciding that as there were hundreds of far more famous and concentrated attractions for holiday-makers to go to that could be targets, he dismissed that thought. As the minutes flew past, concentrating on questions and possible answers, Tony didn't see the airman come back, and only when he stood in front of him did he look up. He flicked the switch to hear him.

'Put this on,' he said passing him some clothes. 'And put yours in this bag. Make sure you tighten it up, OK?'

'What's this?'

'Wetsuit. You worn one before?'

'No, what do I want a wetsuit for? We're not landing in the sea, are we?'

Bernie laughed. 'No, mate. When we get close,' pointing to the tailgate, 'I'll drop that, and you jump out. It's not far, and we will only be about 50, 100 yards from the beach.'

Tony looked at him, then at the tailgate, then back at Bernie.

'What?' he said incredulously.

'It goes down, you jump out, swim to the beach, piece of piss.'

'I'm sorry, jump out. . . why are you not landing on the ground or at an airport or something?' A faint sense of panic was appearing in his voice.

'We're practising. We do this all the time with the Marine boys. We fly high, come in hot, tail goes down, those guys jump 10 feet or so, we fly away, all done in less than a minute. Put this on,' he continued, pushing the wetsuit at Tony. 'Keep you dry. You can swim, right?'

Tony swallowed, looked at the door then back at Bernie. 'You can fuck right off!'

'Sorry, mate, orders. Don't worry about it, you'll be fine. Ten minutes, OK?' said Bernie patting him on the shoulder, walking away.

Tony, his throat dry, his palms damp, licked his lips. *Fucking hell*, he thought. *I knew I would die one day, but I didn't think it would be like this.* He wiped away a bead of sweat that had appeared on his forehead.

The journey went quicker than he would have liked, and with a trace of anxiety he saw Bernie beckon him. Unclipping the cord to the headset, he stepped forward. Bernie checked his wetsuit, made sure his bag was strapped to his ankle and patted him on the shoulder. 'Piece of piss!' he shouted at Tony as he took his headset off. Tony could feel his stomach turn as the helicopter dropped from the sky. Bernie hit a button and the tailgate began to lower; the wind blew in and Tony braced himself. With the huge steel door now open completely, he could see the whole of Brighton seafront. Bernie helped him onto the tailgate towards the edge. Tony looked down as the pilot expertly lowered the Chinook closer and closer to the sea. On the tip now, Tony waited, watching Bernie, who was talking into his headset as the sea approached. The Chinook hovered; Bernie gave the thumbs up to Tony. He breathed hard, closed his eyes, sucked in his breath, clasped his arms to his chest, as

Bernie had shown him, stepped forward and with his heart pounding looked at the sea and in one motion walked off the platform and dropped down.

His bag followed him; he hit the sea before his bag had barely left the chopper. The pilot had done a brilliant hover; his fall was only about eight feet, and as he sank into the sea, Tony kicked his legs hard and broke the surface. Looking in the direction of the beach, he began to swim. The helicopter, he could hear, was getting dimmer and dimmer as it climbed and headed away in the bright blue sky.

They had planned well; his drop was in deep water, but this gave way very quickly to sand, and as Tony felt his feet, he breathed a huge sigh of relief. Grabbing his bag now, he waded towards shore. There was a man waving at him on the beach, and within a few minutes Tony was out of the water and pulling his wetsuit cap off his head.

'Hi, Tony, well done. This way. I'm Wayne,' he said grabbing Tony's bag for him. 'Got a car just over there where you can change.'

Tony nodded.

'You OK?'

'Yeah sure, piece of piss.'

'Come on then.'

Tony had come ashore on the small beach at Rottingdean. The area was quiet where they were, and Tony quickly got out of the wetsuit into his own clothes, and they headed towards the town.

Checking the radio, Wayne clicked his radio button. 'I'll be close by most of the time. Couple of guys are on their way in and will meet up with us. We should also be in contact with Barry on the radio. He's still in transit, but everyone can hear what we are saying, OK?'

Tony didn't bother to ask who 'everyone' was, he just nodded. 'Do we know what a potential target is?'

'Could be a couple of hotels or the conference centre. There's stuff happening today and over the weekend. We've been trying to get people to each location, but there are loads to cover. The local bill have been informed, so hopefully, we can get to him before he does anything, that's, of course, if it's the town what he's after and, of course, if we spot him.'

Tony nodded. 'OK, let me out here,' he said. 'I'll start walking on the prom.'

'OK, I'll get parked,' Wayne said, holding the radio. 'I know Brighton well, so let me know where you are or what you are passing, alright, and I'll get the guys to hook up with you.'

'OK.' Getting out of the car, Tony looked around. This was not going to be easy, he thought as he joined dozens of holiday makers wandering along. He was at the marina. *Not worth wasting time in here*, he thought, *hardly a target, nice boats but not superyachts*. A myriad of small hotels was overlooking the sea as he walked on the upper promenade towards the pier. Keeping to Marine Parade, it overlooked the small parallel road beneath the railway line. Not rushing, trying to look at everyone he came close to and keeping an eye on the opposite side of the road, the hotels and houses were getting bigger the closer he got to the pier.

'Hi, it's T. I'm at the pier,' he said into the radio mic.

'Copy, hold tight, T, it's B here. You'll be joined any minute now.'

Tony looked along the pier: holidaymakers everywhere, kids with ice creams, mums with pushchairs and old people wandering around. The day was warm, a light breeze coming off the sea, blue sky, and as Tony looked over the railings the beach was filling up. A lovely summer's day.

'Tony?'

Tony looked round; two men had approached him, and the first held out his hand.

'Hiya, mate, I'm Buster. Barry sent us. Wayne pointed you out to us,' he explained, indicating to the car at the kerb. Wayne waved and drove off. Tony took his hand, 'Hi, any plan?'

'No, you just walk, we'll follow your lead. I'll be with you; Harry will be further up, OK? Take as much time as you need.'

Tony nodded.

Tony lit a cigarette, turned and entered the pier, stood by the entrance and looked at the people as far as he could see up to the end where the arcades and café were.

Shaking his head, the men began a slow walk along the paved concourse. Stopping occasionally to look over the railings at the people below where the bars were and at some fairground attractions, he looked at everyone in turn, trying to remember exactly what Arli looked like.

He looked at his watch; he'd been here two hours, and he had not seen anyone even close to looking like Arli.

'Let's try across the town.'

Crossing the road, they passed the Brighton Grand, turned left into West Street, passing bars and restaurants, Tony looking at everyone who passed them. At the junction of Queen's Street, they turned right onto North Street: more shops, more tourists. Many of the single men he saw carried bags, others with suitcases and backpacks. The street was busy, the pavement crowded.

Could he go for the Pavilion? Tony thought as they came across the impressive building, a former residence of the royal family and a great favourite of George IV. Walking up through the ornate Indian gate into the grounds, he passed in front of the building. Stepping onto the grass, Tony looked around: it was busy, the bars to the entrance were full, some people were picnicking on the grass, kids playing ball games, enjoying their time in the sun.

Turning full circle, he lit up a cigarette, shook his head and set off again slowly out the other side through North Gate and past the statue of George IV. Deciding not to cross the busy road to Victoria Gardens, the three men headed round and down back towards the seafront with Harry on the opposite side of the road.

Tony stopped abruptly and grabbed Buster's arm.

'There,' he said pointing to a man, losing sight of him as he rounded the bend of the road.

Tony started to run down the street, Buster on his shoulder. Harry, on the other side, started off on a trot to keep pace.

'Slow down,' said Buster holding Tony's arm.

As they rounded the bend, cars coming towards them, Tony spotted him crossing over the two-lane road into the centre.

'I'm sure it's Arli.'

Getting closer, he could see his back: the man was wearing a rucksack, a heavy coat, and as Tony got closer and closer to him the man stopped, turned, looked left at traffic coming towards him before crossing over, and at that split-second Tony saw his face.

'It's Arli.'

'You sure?'

'Absolutely.'

Buster looked at him, 'Positive?'

Tony thought for a second.

'Yes, positive.'

'Stay here, and I mean stay here. Stay out of the way, Tony,' said Buster quickly, setting off, leaving Tony. He watched as Buster began speaking into his throat mic as he started to jog down the road. Out of the corner of his eye he saw Harry was also at a pace following Buster's lead. Arli had kept on walking, but something must have spooked him because he turned and looked directly at Harry, who was closing in on him. Then spotting Buster as well he saw the two men were running towards him. Arli panicked, ran straight across the traffic and into Old Steine Gardens with Harry and Buster on his tail, gaining ground every second. Now out of his eyeline, Tony stopped walking and waited, not wanting to get too close. Within a few seconds, he heard shouting and then some loud bangs and then quiet.

The peace didn't last long as moments later people burst out of the gardens and onto the road, the cars braking sharply, some blasting their horns; people were screaming. Tony's hands went cold, he knew what had happened, and in those few seconds where time stood still, he replayed the picture of Arli as he had turned to cross the road, praying that he hadn't made a mistake in identifying him.

Chapter 23

The room was full; about 20 people, male and female, were gathered. Most were sat, some at the table, others leaning against the wall; quiet chatter filled the room. The blinds were drawn and one of the fluorescent tube lights flickered occasionally. It was turning dull at either end, a sure sign that at some time in the near future it would extinguish itself. The table was filled with ashtrays and coffee cups, some still steaming from the hastily gathered machine that everyone had to pass in the corridor on the way to the room. Someone had opened a window slightly to let the stream of smoke filter away. DC Simon Carrs looked at his watch: five to. They waited. The meeting was set for eight, and no one was going to be late. At precisely 8:00 am the door opened and DCI Paul Jackson, with his assistant, came in; the room immediately went quiet.

'Morning, everyone.' Not waiting for replies, he stood at the head of the table.

'The death of our colleague at the hands of one of the terrorists, Hakim Al-Fasih, two days ago has been confirmed. The second terrorist, Arli Jassam, was killed when officers tried to restrain him in Brighton. The third terrorist, Nadir

Al Najaf, has been arrested. You still need to examine past records for any mention of these men, the mosque they attended and any, and I mean any, slight reference to or indication of any bomb making or explosive material.'

The group nodded.

'Do we know what the target of Jassam was?' A question was raised by one of the men.

'Not at this time, no, investigations are continuing. Now. . .' turning to the whiteboard behind him, 'the Kodra setup. This. . .' he said pointing to photographs on the whiteboard, 'is the main house, we have identified, which may be the lab. It's in a cul de sac on the edge of this farmland. Not overlooked other than the houses that are in the same enclave, one way in, one way out. If it is the lab, then this will be the focus of one of the raids as and when we get confirmation.'

'He can smell a photo opp coming up,' said Bill quietly in Izzy's ear.

'Unless it goes tits up then it's my bag,' replied Izzy.

The meeting went on, covering the surveillance in place, members of the gang, cars that were being used and of course, the warehouse factory unit.

'Deliveries are constant. We have checked the cargo manifest, and it all appears legitimate: food stuff from suppliers, mostly in Italy. It comes into the warehouse, and then the small delivery vans, every couple of days supply the restaurants throughout the UK. On the surface it's a straightforward distribution chain. It would not normally attract any attention. If the heroin is coming into this place, then we need to ascertain what shipments and how often.'

Jackson's assistant leaned forward and whispered something into his ear; Paul nodded.

'OK, everyone, lot of work still to do. Izzy has a rota for you.' And with that he turned and left the room.

Izzy got to her feet. 'Wait a minute,' she said as a few started towards the door.

'I need. . .' she began, reading off a list of jobs for most in the room.

'That's it,' she said indicating the meeting was finished. 'Thanks, everyone.' Looking over the table, 'Bill, can you grab the others.'

The room emptied out. Izzy took a sip of her coffee, opened the folder as her close team sat down.

'We know that traditionally the Albanians are coke dealers. My guess is that Lorenc was left behind here to take over from Tariq after he died, which means that the Italian deal was not part of the original plan.'

'Do you think the house then must be for the cocaine?' asked Wayne.

'I do. Rinori has enough people on the ground now, or near enough, to distribute it, and if the information we have is correct, that the Italians have done a deal to offload the heroin, then Rinori is going to try and corner both markets, or at the very least become a seriously big player alongside the Yardis and Pakistanis. We need to know how he's getting both delivered into the country. I can't see that it's on the same transport; it has to be different.'

'Unless he drops the coke in favour of the Italians,' said Claire.

'Possibly, but then he would have offloaded that house. How we doing with coverage on it, Bill?'

Picking up the latest report, he answered, 'Little or no activity, members of the gang have visited a few times, but we can't get close enough for photos. We are at the bottom of the road leading to the house. It's too obvious, as you know, to be in the cul de sac itself, and walkbys would arouse suspicion, so we are reliant on spotting them as they drive past, or if one of the guys is on a follow, then radioing us to give us the heads up. I've been round the back in the field; there's no cover in it to get close enough to see through the windows or get any photos,' he said handing the report to Izzy.

'What about the warehouse/factory? It says that we are monitoring eight to six but not at the weekends or evenings.'

'The DCI hasn't signed off on any overtime,' said Bill, 'so surveillance is limited to normal working hours for his crew, apart from the factory, which we are covering 6:00 am till 8:00 pm. If we are going to nail this crowd, then we need far more hours and more people to cover night shifts etc.'

Izzy shook her head. 'Too much to ask for, the bad guys to work Monday to Friday nine to five, I suppose. OK, I'll take it up with the DCI.'

A standard 40 ft air-controlled container lorry left Southampton docks. With over 30 million tons of goods coming into the port each year, it is impossible for the port authorities to check each vehicle. The odds are stacked against them finding any contraband on the lorries, unless they receive a tip off or the papers that the drivers carried were incorrect. This lorry had all the correct paperwork and sailed through customs and out onto the open road. For the lorry, the journey would take about three hours, up the M3 clockwise, around the M25, down the M11 and pulling off at Redbridge, turning left to Gants Hill and then the short run up to the industrial estate on the Southend Road. The distribution warehouse, the driver knew well, was Stafford and Sons, a major fruit and vegetable wholesaler. Arriving just after midnight, he backed the trailer into the bay. Grabbing his paperwork, he jumped out of the cab.

The back doors were unlocked, and a forklift began the process of offloading the pallets of fresh bananas. Putting them into the warehouse, most of them would be reloaded within the next hour or so onto smaller lorries, which would arrive at the New Spitalfields market by 4:00 am that morning. Fresh as they could be, having been picked in Ecuador three weeks earlier, they arrived in a temperature-controlled container into Durres, Albania. The bananas were then both custom and quality checked before shipping onto Southampton. The journey was from Durres and across the sea to Bari in Italy, where the lorry went through Italy into France embarking on the ro-ro at Le Havre. It was a trip that the driver made once a week. The appetite for bananas in the UK was constant, and there was never any relaxing in demand for this bent, yellow, sweet fruit. Jake Stafford had taken over the firm from his father in the early eighties, and it had now grown into one of the major importers of fruit and veg from around the world. He sold most of his produce at Spitalfields. His father had developed good relationships with his customers, who came from hotels, restaurants and over the recent years, large event companies. The tonnage of fruit and veg that passed through his business now accounted for some eight million in turnover for the company.

There was a constant stream of lorries delivering goods throughout the night, and then from 3:00 am onwards a myriad of smaller lorries, trucks and vans arrived, either to distribute to other markets around the UK that day or to customers who bought in bulk and provided their own transport. Karim and Grail were two of these. Backing their vans up to the loading bay, the warehouse supervisor waved, and the forklift selected first a pallet for the one vehicle and then another for the second. With paperwork in order, both vans set off with their cargo of bananas. The vans split up: Karim headed for Chigwell Heath, a short journey, and Grail went south towards Woolwich. Passing London City Airport, he drove through to the pier entrance and waited for the ferry. Once over the Thames, he carried on down past Woolwich Common and picked up the A2, swung a right and after a couple of hundred yards dropped off left into Kidbrooke. Taking the first left halfway down the road, he entered the small industrial estate. As he looked around, a lot of the units had been knocked down in favour of office blocks, and it wouldn't be long, he thought, before the unit he was heading for would also fall under the redevelopment hammer.

*

Spotting his unit with the 'Shaw and Sons Sewage Cleaners' sign across the front, he backed the vehicle up to the roller doors, jumped out, unpadlocked the door, walked into the outer office, unlocked the second door and then went through the small corridor into the warehouse and pulled on the chain to roll up the floor to ceiling metal door. Locking the chain down, he reversed in. Unhooking the chain, he closed the door and opened the back of the van. In the unit an Audi Quattro sat next to a large waste container; there were several tables along the side wall near the office and an assortment of holdalls. At the end of the tables was a pile of unfolded cardboard boxes on a pallet. In the centre of the unit was an oblong pit; it had been used by mechanics in the past to inspect the underside of cars that they were maintaining, and it now had boards slotted in to provide a complete floor.

Climbing into his own forklift truck, he carefully manoeuvred the prongs under the pallet and pulled it out and placed it on the floor close to the tables. Unwrapping the polythene that had been stretched around the contents of the pallet, securing it, it revealed, as with all the pallets from the main lorry, a pile of banana boxes. These, however, were different. There were 16 boxes stacked four on four, and the top four Grail picked off the top and chucked them to one side near the wall. From the next layer, he took a box, which he placed on one of the tables and opened it up. The inside of the box contained an outer circle of bananas enclosing twelve 2 kg bags of cocaine. These he placed on the table, discarding the box and excess bananas with the others. Each of the further eleven boxes were packed exactly the same, yielding in total 288 kg of cocaine, just over a quarter of a tonne. At around £30,000 a kilo, Grail stood back and looked at the pile of dope. He smiled; £8 million, not bad, he thought. With Karim's boxes it made just over half a tonne of cocaine imported with a total haul of around £17 million.

Breaking into his thoughts, he heard the horn sound. Checking through a spy hole in the door, he unhooked the chain and pulled the door up high enough for the two scooters and their passengers to get under. Locking the door down, he turned his attention back to the piles of cocaine.

'Hey, man. All good?' asked Genti, climbing off the pillion of one of the scooters.

'Yep, sweet, all here.'

'OK. Gam, you and Dar move the boards,' he said indicating to the boards covering the oblong pit. Moving the boards, Gam jumped in and waited for the first packets of cocaine. Two thirds of the haul was stashed inside the pit, covered in a tarpaulin, and then Gam and Dar replaced the boards.

'OK, let's bag it up,' said Genti, picking up the first of the holdalls and looking at the remainder on the table.

Genti pulled a notepad out of his pocket, looked at the first page and said, 'Three.'

Over the course of the next 15 minutes all the remaining bags of cocaine were all placed inside the holdalls.

A car horn sounded outside; Genti looked at his watch – 5:00 am – and nodded.

Grail raised the door again and another Audi Quattro reversed into the unit. Getting out, two of their cousins fist pumped the other four. 'Let's do this.'

Opening the boot of both Audis, the assortment of bags and holdalls were stacked inside.

Genti checked his 9 mm: loaded. He clipped it back into his shoulder holster; the other men, checking their own weapons, did the same.

Grail opened the door; the scooters went out first followed by the first Audi. The scooters and the Audi shot off. Genti waited for Grail to lock down the unit and climbed in beside him in the second Audi. With a toot of the horn the scooter led the way out of the industrial estate. The delivery run would take a couple of hours. The procedure was the same each time: the scooter would go first to the drop, scout the area, making sure the buyers were there, report back to the Audi who would then come down to the meet. In less than two minutes the cocaine and money had exchanged hands. The scooter men watched; they had dropped back and were waiting for any sign of trouble. All the men, fully armed, would have no hesitation in protecting their gear.

Two BMWs and two more scooters were waiting for Karim as he too drove into a small industrial estate just outside Chigwell. The process was much the same: into the unit, unloading of the boxes and distributing the 2 kg packets of cocaine between bags and the pit then into the boots of the cars. Locking up the unit, Karim got into the lead BMW with one of his cousins, and both cars set off for first Brixton and then onto Croydon. A few stops along the way, as the cars split up, both had scooters to scout the drops before the money and coke exchanged hands. With both of the cars now stacked with cash, they headed back to the unit where Grail had started from. Genti was already there, the two Audis set apart slightly, parked on the street outside. As they reversed into the unit, Grail locked the door down.

'Hey, man. All good?' said Karim flicking a switch; the boot of one of the BMWs opened.

'Clockwork, any aggro?'

'Nah, sweet. Here we go,' he said lifting a few bags out of the boot and putting them on the table where Genti was counting a pile of money. Once counted, Dar had been folding the flat cardboard into boxes which were then used to store the money. Taped down, each small box was placed inside the pit alongside the cocaine they had stored earlier.

Small talk and smoke filled the air; most would be out tonight drinking and celebrating the success of the first major delivery.

'How much was the camera bloke?' asked Genti.

'Eighteen hundred each,' replied Karim.

'Fucking hell, for just a couple of cameras.'

Karim shrugged his shoulders. 'He said the line BT had put in was OK and it was a system that you can view from your house, which you said you wanted.'

'Fuck's sake.' Genti picked up a wad of twenties and started to count.

'Here's five. Get it done. Also, get a couple of locks for the outside of those,' he said pointing at the roller door.

When's he going to do it?'

'Monday, he said.'

'Both?'

'Yeah.'

'You lot. . .' shouted Genti at the others.

'Clear this up; stick it in the van,' pointing at the pile of empty banana boxes and stray bananas.

Rising from the table, with the last box going into the pit, he watched as the long boards were placed over the hole. The pallet the boxes were on he dragged to the boards, making it look like it had been discarded. It was unlikely that anyone would get in, but if they did, hopefully, they would see the place was just empty.

'OK, right, here we are,' Genti said picking up several wads of cash from the table.

'Six grand each. Don't go fucking mad, alright,' he said, giving each one of the smiling cousins a bundle each.

'This is just the start. Keep it tight. No one fucking knows, OK?'

Poking his head out of the office door, Grail whistled. Karim opened the roller door and the two BMWs and scooters drove out; the Audis and their escort scooters shot off as well. The last to leave was Dar, who had jumped into the van. He waited while Grail locked up and got in beside him. Their first job was to go to the other unit, load up with the empty banana boxes and dump them near Spitalfields market.

Chapter 24

Junk pulled up in front of the block of flats, the large Mercedes purring as he waited for his passengers. Looking at his watch – Femi was notoriously a stickler for punctuality and he had received a beating on more than one occasion for being late – nodding, *Not this time*, he thought. *I'm early.* Up on the fourth floor Femi cast an eye in the mirror: his bright yellow shirt and green blazer were smart and clean; the gold chain around his wrist offset the Rolex and several gold rings. Emblazoned with gold necklaces, he smiled, the gold tooth glistening as he did so. Opening up a small drawer on the dresser, he grabbed a handful of cash. Lighter and cigarettes in his pocket, he left the bedroom.

'Ready?' he said to the men in the room. With nods, the three of them left the apartment, punched the lift and exited the block of flats.

With Femi in the rear seat behind Junk, George got in beside him and Sayo jumped into the front. Junk powered the car, picking up the main road into town. The journey was short, and as they pulled up outside Stringfellows, Cono was already there waiting for them. Letting Junk park the car, the four men went into the club, sailing past the eagerly waiting crowd, who started moaning at the doorman about special treatment for some. Landing on deaf ears, the crowd resumed its line and waited patiently for the next lot to be let in. It was 10:30 and the club was buzzing. Femi and his crew walked through the club towards the back and into the roped section. A table had been reserved for them; spending, on average, £15,000 a night, they were always welcome. The waitress brought them champagne straight away; settling in, the men began to smoke and drink. The club, with its deep red lush carpet, sparkling walls and shiny bright bar with gorgeous looking girls to serve the predominantly male clientele, was absorbing.

Tony had seen Femi and his men come in. Standing at the bar, he had turned away as they passed. Watching them slide into their seats, his attention turned to the young lady who stood next to him. Standing back slightly, she began to dance. With a swirl, she let her arm stroke the face of a man who had been standing next to Tony. Dancing in time to the music, she took his glass of champagne from his hands, took a sip and delicately put it onto the bar. Sliding a leg between his, she rotated her hips seductively and slowly moved her body up and down his. Letting a strap fall from her shoulder, her eyes fixed on her man, she dropped the other strap holding the top of her silk dress. Swaying to the music, she turned and seductively turned her body into his. Slowly gyrating into him, she turned and slipped the dress further down her body. It fell to the ground exposing her pert breasts. Pushing herself against his chest, she kissed his cheek, smiled, picked up his glass of champagne, stepped out of her dress and beckoned him to follow her.

Wonder how much that cost? thought Tony as he took a sip of the most expensive lager he had ever bought.

The club was getting busier and noisier now. The lights had dimmed, and the glitter ball was spinning, flashing light across people's faces, the music getting louder, and as Tony looked around, many were on the dance floor embracing their escorts. Some had chosen to eat, some tables had endless bottles of champagne delivered, so the atmosphere was building nicely. Tony walked around, taking in the size of the club, the smoky atmosphere, strobe lighting, sections that were lit by red neon lights creating a sexy mood, the dancing area, the girls and the extravagance. Placing his drink on a high round table, he lit up a cigarette. A couple of tall well-dressed girls were walking towards him; they stopped and unhooked the rope to a semi-circle table that was on the edge of the dance floor. Sliding in, she too lit a cigarette. Tony looked up to where they had come from and smiled. Peter Stringfellow, with his trademark long curly grey hair, beaming smile and jovial demeanour was shaking a few hands as he made his way down. Sliding in beside both the girls, he was joined by another man; champagne arrived, toasts were made and laughter rang out. Peter's evening was just about to begin.

Finishing his second pint and declining the services of an attractive lady who wondered if he would like her to dance for him, he placed his glass on the table and headed towards

Femi. Clouds of cigar smoke filled the small area where he was sat, and as Tony approached, he could see several empty bottles of champagne and an assortment of cocktail glasses on the table in front of him. He had timed it just as Cono had left the table for the toilet; the seat next to Femi was empty. Tony strode up to the table and in one swift movement unclipped the rope and sat down next to Femi.

Before Femi or his men could react,

'You must be Femi. Tariq said you might be able to help me,' Tony started with a smile.

Femi took the cigar out of his mouth.

'Fuck off, man.'

'Thought we could do some business. As I said, Tariq gave me your name.'

Femi looked at him, shook his head and held his hand up to George, who had stood and was about to grab Tony.

'You got balls, man, but I don't know no Tariq.'

'Yes, you do. He's fucking dead, as you know, and what you gave him came to me, and now I'm fucked. I need a supply. You know what I'm saying?'

Femi grinned and laughed loudly; the stench of his cigar and fuelled alcoholic breath washed over Tony.

'If Tariq's dead, as you say, who's going to vouch for you, botti?'

Ignoring the question, Tony continued. 'We both know what we are talking about. With Tariq gone I reckon you need a new buyer. I can do that.'

'See this magu oh,' said Femi looking at George with a smile.

George leant forward.

'Fuck off, while you still can, tule jare.'

Tony put his hand up. 'Wait!'

Sliding his hand into his jacket pocket, he pulled out an envelope and put it on the table in front of Femi.

'A token of my business to you: thirty-five large. Now you can burn it, chuck it away or spend it, I don't care, alright.'

Standing, Tony looked at Femi.

'It's yours. I'll be back next week.' Turning, he stepped out of the roped area and made his way out of the club.

It was an educated guess. He'd seen Femi with Tariq, and as he ran through that meeting in his mind, he had thought at the time what the two men had in common. It was unlikely to be drugs, thought Tony. Femi would get his own supply, which left women. He'd read the report by the Met officer DI Taylor who had said she had seen several women being offloaded from a bus into the back of Tariq's sister Sihina's brothel. Now, with Tariq dead, Femi would be looking for a new customer, hopefully,' thought Tony.

'Go left, now quick right.' Femi looked over his shoulder through the back window.

'Turn again,' he said quickly.

Cono, next to him, was also looking.

'Stop! Quick, turn the lights off!

The car came to a screeching halt. Sayo killed the lights, and everyone slid down in their seats.

'Anything?' asked Femi.

Sayo and Junk were peering into the wing mirrors.

'Nothing.'

'Nothing.'

'OK, wait a minute,' said Femi.

Cono poked his head above the back of the seat; a minute or so later, he said,

'Can't see anyone.'

'OK, let's go.'

Femi lit a cigar and cracked open the window.

'Hounslow tonight.'

Pulling up outside the flat, Femi and George got out.

'Cono, you come up with us; you two, park up over there,' said Femi pointing.

'Cono will come down in a couple of hours to swap, OK?'

The two men nodded.

Inside the flat, Femi poured him and George a whiskey. Cono had gone into the bedroom to get a couple of hours sleep.

'You think he's legit?'

'We weren't followed, so if he was policeman then he ain't got no bros. How much pepper did he give you, man,' said George slowly.

Femi pulled out the packet from his pocket and counted the money; Tony had given

him £35,000.

'He's not playing around. Don't think the police would give that sort to mess about with; he could be legit.'

Taking a large gulp of the whiskey, Femi tossed the money on the table. *If he was on the level, then it would solve a problem and keep the money coming in. However, what does a white man want with a dozen or so black girls, and what stable is he going to hang them in? Something's not right.* Femi walked over to the table and picked up the bottle. 'Another?' he asked, looking over his shoulder at George.

'Always,' said George. 'So what you going do, man?'

'Get Benj and Abeo down here. We'll use them as backup. Make sure they bring their big autos, OK?'

'So, how do you want to play it?' asked Barry.

'He needs to come up with a figure and then a drop point. If I suggest a drop point, he'll get suspicious. My guess is that he'll bring quite a bit of firepower and some girls. We're not going to get them all unless we can tail Femi and his gang for the next few weeks to see where they come in, and then it's by chance that Femi will actually be at the delivery site. If he's not, then the best we could hope for is a couple of his gang and a few months' disruption.'

'I agree. Take Mark with you to the next meeting. They need to see you have backup and then there won't be any surprises when the meet goes down.'

'What about entrapment? Heard that could be a problem maybe,' enquired Tony.

'No, don't worry about that. The rules are they know they are committing a crime so us enticing them doesn't hold up in court.'

The room in a terraced house on the edge of Lexham Gardens in Kensington was the latest meeting point for the team. When Tony had walked in, he'd sat at the table, lit a cigarette and waited. With the death of Mike, no one was in the mood for any banter. Although Tony wasn't too close to the guys, they held a bond, and with one missing it left a hole. Leonard wasn't at the meeting, and Tony didn't like to ask, so he just waited.

'The funeral is on Thursday,' said Barry. 'I'm sorry, Tony, but you can't come,' and nodding at Rob, 'neither can Rob'. Barry put his hand up as Tony was about to say something.

'It's too dangerous. Not dangerous as in life threatening but dangerous of future recognition. There will be people there, and possibly, and I say possibly, members of the press. Me and Mark can pass off as just military friends, no one would question that, but we can't risk you or Rob being seen, sorry.'

It had started to rain outside. Tony opened the wardrobe door and looked at his range of shirts. He wasn't in the mood for a night out, but this was business. It had been a couple of days since the funeral. Tony had travelled up despite Barry saying he couldn't go. He hadn't gone to the church but had waited behind trees in the cemetery. It was a miserable day, cloudy and with spots of rain, a perfect setting for a sad funeral. Tunstall cemetery is unique as it lies on the eastern slope of Chatterley Valley and is so steep that Tony wondered how the graves manage to cling to the side. Mike had been honourably discharged from the army and was entitled to a full military funeral, and when Tony got there, he'd easily spotted the guard in place by the grave. Sliding behind a tree near the bottom, he watched as the car arrived and the coffin was taken by the pallbearers, some of whom were in uniform. They had carefully placed

267

Mike down next to his grave. There was quite a gathering of people, many in uniform. He had seen at the cemetery gate a lone photographer; keeping an eye on him, he had steered well clear. The ceremony, overseen by a priest, was over quickly and then he'd watched as they slowly lowered Mike into his final resting place. That was enough, thought Tony, as he slowly made his way out of the back of the cemetery with the haunting sound of crying in his ears.

Selecting a mauve shirt and light brown jacket with matching trousers, he grabbed his cigarettes and money and left the room. Hailing a taxi, he looked at his watch: 10:30 pm. *Plenty of time*, he thought.

Walking into the Anchor on the corner of St Martins Lane and Great Newport Street, Tony saw Mark at the bar.

'Hello mate, beer?' said Mark.

'Cheers.'

'How long?'

'Give it an hour or so,' said Tony.

Picking up their beer, they stood at one of the many tall tables. Tony raised his glass.

'Mike.'

'Mike.'

Idle conversation passed the time, mostly centring on the latest football matches of the day. Mark, an avid West Ham fan, said, 'Sinclair scored again.'

'Lucky then, doesn't score many, does he?'

'Better than that dick Lightbourne at Stoke.'

'Fuck off!'

Tony smiled, looked at his watch and nodded.

The club was busy as always. Coming up to midnight, Tony and Mark made their way through to the bar. Femi and his men were already seated in what appeared to be their usual semi-circle alcove behind the red rope. Not bothering with a drink, Tony unhooked the rope and sat down next to Femi, squeezing Cono out of the way.

'Well?' said Tony.

Femi looked at him and smiled, the gold tooth glinting from the strobe light.

'Who's your friend?' he said looking at Mark.

George had stood up and stood in front of Mark. Mark didn't move and stared straight back at George.

'He's mine, and others. We doing this or not?'

'Hey, man, slow down. Let's have a drink,' said Femi leaning forward and picking up two glasses in one hand. He then poured some champagne into them and offered one to Tony.

'Does your man want one?'

'He doesn't drink,' said Tony taking the glass, not taking his eyes off Femi.

'Let's do business.'

Femi kept the glass and chinked it against Tony's. Tony waited for him to drink. Femi swallowed the glass whole; Tony did the same. Femi nodded as if it was some sort of approval.

'Well?'

'How many do you want, Aboki?'

'Fifteen for now, twenty next time. You do that?'

FAMILY!

'No problem, forty-five each.'

Tony looked at him, snorted. 'Fuck off, that's not going to happen, at best thirty-two.'

'Femi shook his head. 'No, man, forty-five each.'

'No, thirty-five tops.'

'Forty-five.'

'No, fuck it, I'll go elsewhere,' said Tony standing.

Leaning to unhook the rope, he looked at Mark. 'We're off.'

Mark took a step back.

'Wait, aboki, wait, sit, sit,' said Femi patting the seat.

Pausing, Tony looked at Mark then at Femi; Tony sat.

'Don't waste my time.'

'Thirty-eight and we have a deal,' said Femi holding his hand out.

Tony looked at him. 'For fifteen, less for twenty.'

'We can talk. Let's do this.'

Tony took his hand.

'When and where?'

Femi looked up at George. 'Hey,' he said, nodding. George put his hand into his pocket. Mark reacted, took a step back and put his hand inside his jacket.

'It's cool,' said Femi, standing quickly.

George took out a piece of paper and handed it across to Mark. With his left hand, Mark took the paper.

'You staying for more drinks, my friend?' said Femi turning to Tony.

'Next time,' said Tony standing, putting his hand out. Femi grinned.

Chapter 25

Getting out of the cab in Grosvenor Street, Tony paid the driver and walked back up the street and turned right into New Bond Street. Crossing over, he walked the short distance to the impressive building and entered through the canopied doorway. Occupying the site since 1917 in the heart of Mayfair, Sotheby's had enjoyed an enviable reputation of offering for sale some of the finest items from across the world. Today's auction focussed on European and British art, and as Tony entered the building, he was surprised by the number of people already there. Waiting for a few moments, he approached the desk.

'Good afternoon, sir.' The receptionist smiled at him.

'Hi, Tony Blackreach.'

Looking down at his list,

'Ah, yes,' he said pulling out a card, which he handed to Tony.

'Have you been with us before, sir?'

'No, usually my agent buys for me, but I found myself in London this week, so I thought I would make the most of the opportunity and come down in person.'

'Excellent, well, pleased you could make it. If you go

through there, Mr Blackreach. . .' the man pointed at the large double doors, 'the room is on the right. There are refreshments should you so wish.'

Tony smiled. 'Thank you.'

'Also, sir, once seated, if there is a particular item that interests you, then make it known to the auctioneer, Carl, as the bidding starts; he will then keep an eye out for you as the auction continues.'

'Thank you.' Tony went through the doors and made his way into the room as directed. Passing the offer of drinks, he wandered, brochure and card in hand, into the main auction room. There was a quiet buzz in the room as people were making their way to the chairs. You could sit anywhere, and without looking around the room he walked down the centre aisle and sat about ten rows from the front. He picked a seat in the middle of the row and began looking through the brochure.

Within a few minutes the room had filled up, and for the first time he looked around: almost the whole room was, he saw, full. It was the first time he had been to an auction but had been briefed on what to expect. Each item would come up, carried by porters, if possible, to the front by the auctioneer's podium, a description given, and the bidding would start. He saw a bank of people to his left who were on phones talking, he presumed, to their clients. They would bid on behalf of them, and Tony guessed that they had either already seen the items in person or if they were avid collectors, they would just buy the pieces anyway.

Carl had come onto the small platform. He stood behind his lectern and introduced himself and what was to come. The first painting came up; it was smaller than Tony had expected. The picture in the brochure, although giving a size, didn't really match what he thought he would see. A few thousand pounds was bid, and as he watched, Carl, he saw, scanned the room and expertly directed his gaze and questions about the next bid to those who had expressed an early interest. With a small tap of the gavel, the item was sold and the next brought up. The art varied in size; some were masterpieces, from what he had read, none of which he fancied. *Why would people buy this stuff,* he thought, *when it looks old and half of it you can't tell what it is?* However, he sat, nodding occasionally and smiling at the right moment when a bid was won. To all intents and purposes, he was, if anyone looked, a collector.

He took a quick flick through the brochure again to see where they were. The one he was interested in was on page 11, and judging, at this speed, thought Tony, on in about 15 minutes' time.

A rare piece by Domenico Corvi, a neoclassical painter from Rome, was up for auction. It had come from an estate in Lancashire and was offered in hope that it would realise enough to pay off some death duties. Painted around 1750, it was one of many canvases Corvi had painted at the time, and they were greatly sort after. It would be the star of the auction, and anticipation was high. Just after 3:00 pm, the painting, carried by two porters, was brought in the room and placed on a frame. Carl began his description and started the bidding at £4.4 million. The auction began; Tony could feel his heart begin to pump. He'd never done this before, but with the air of someone who had raised his hand many times before, at £4.6 million Carl caught his bid, acknowledged him and carried on. The price went up, Tony nodding occasionally at Carl when a bid was in order. At £5.8 million there were only two of them in the room bidding.

'At 5.85 with you, sir,' said Carl looking at Tony.

Tony nodded.

'Carl's eyes went to the other man sat on the opposite side of the room.

'£5.9 is the bid.'

Having got his agreement,

'£5.95, with you, sir.'

Tony again nodded.

Six million pounds,' said Carl looking directly at the man on the fourth row; he nodded.

Swinging his look back at Tony, he continued,

'£6.1 is the bid.'

The grey-haired man in the tweed jacket who had sat next to Tony lightly touched Tony's knee. Without acknowledging the touch, Tony looked at Carl and shook his head.

Carl quickly turned his attention to the room and the other man.

'At £6 million. . . we will sell. . . at £6 million.' Raising his hand slightly, pausing for a few seconds, he tapped the gavel onto the top of the lectern. 'Sold!'

A collective murmur swept round the room. The man who had won turned in his chair and looked across at Tony. Vittorio De Luca nodded in respect. He'd been pushed, and at one point thought this treasured piece of artwork, which he had sought for many years, was going to evade his grasp. A smile came on his face. The auction, with a couple more paintings being sold, came swiftly to a close. Tony stood and along with many others began to make his way out of the auction room, purposely ignoring Vittorio.

Through the main doors, Tony paused and lit a cigarette. Standing on the pavement slightly to one side of the door, he nodded at a few people as they passed him. 'Bad luck, maybe next time,' said one; Tony smiled.

'Ah, ciao, signor.'

Tony flicked his cigarette butt into the gutter and looked at the man in front of him.

'Good afternoon.'

'Allow me to introduce myself, Vittorio De Luca,' he said holding out his hand.

'Tony Blackreach,' replied Tony, returning the handshake.

'Let me congratulate you. It's an excellent painting, and I have to say I am disappointed about not taking it home with me.'

'Si, si, it's a marvellous painting; you obviously have an eye.'

'It's a passion of mine. I have another Corvi, and this would have complemented it well. I do love the neoclassi-cal style.' Tony rambled on, and the two men prodded each

275

other for knowledge. Tony had been schooled well and was able to ask and counter anything Vittorio brought up.

'Well, it's nice to meet you, and hopefully next time we can continue our conversation,' said Tony holding his hand out.

'Pleasure, definitely.' The two men shook hands. Vittorio turned and headed towards his Mercedes, which Ciro had drawn up a few yards away. Making his way back down towards Grosvenor Street, Tony watched as the Mercedes swept past.

'I didn't know you knew him,' said Lorenc as Vittorio got into the back seat of the Mercedes.

'Who?'

'That guy there. . .' pointing at Tony.

'I don't, we've just met. How do you know him?'

'Tony something; he knew Tariq.'

'And?'

As they drove past Tony, Lorenc stared through the blacked-out windows.

'Yeah, that's the guy, deffo. I only saw him the once, but he supplied Tariq with some gear; all went smooth.'

Vittorio stared at Lorenc. 'What gear exactly?'

'Nines and some autos, plus all the ammo he needed, from what I saw. Anything you want, he'd said.'

Vittorio looked at Tony as he passed, thinking.

'So, what do you want?' turning to Lorenc.

Tony watched as the car passed him. He continued up to Grosvenor Square and hailed a cab, which circled round and picked him up. 'Charing Cross, mate.'

Dropping Tony at the entrance to the station, Tony walked in, onto the concourse, crossed it and went out onto Craven Street. Pausing for a minute, lighting a cigarette, he watched the people around him. Confident that he hadn't been followed, he made his way onto Northumberland Avenue and headed for Trafalgar Square. The Admiralty pub, overlooking Nelson's Column, was beginning to fill up. Grabbing a pint at the bar, he spotted Cyril and sat down next to him.

'How was I then?'

Cyril sighed. 'Bit eager. Need to slow down next time, old boy.'

Cyril Rogers, dressed in the familiar tweed jacket, had been the gentlemen sat next to Tony in Sotheby's. In his early seventies, he was a senior member of the council at the Royal College of Art, fine art curator at the Tate and from time to time was called on by the Crown Prosecution Service as an expert witness when they were putting someone on trial at the Old Bailey for art theft. His knowledge on Neoclassical and Renaissance artists was unsurpassed, and Leonard had been in two minds as to whether to have him help Tony. He had decided, however, on balance that Vittorio would be unlikely to recognise him. When the bidding for the painting had finished, Tony had lent forward slightly and Cyril had turned to talk to the person next to him, semi obscuring Vittorio's view.

'He asked a few of the questions you suspected he would. It pretty well went much as planned. How did you know when to stop?'

Cyril smiled. 'Experience, dear boy. I was watching him,

and he wanted that piece desperately, but we were reaching the limit to what it was realistically worth. Might have gone for a bit more but no reason to push; hope it helped.'

'It did, thanks. So. . .' said Tony finishing his pint, 'till next time then.'

The flight out of Heathrow was on time, and the short crossing into Charles de Gaulle was routine and simple. Lorenc grabbed his bag from the locker, followed the rest of the passengers through customs and onto the rail concourse. Picking up a ticket, he lit a cigarette and smoked, waiting for the train. The 30 minute or so journey into the Gare du Nord was efficient and walking out of the station into the warm but cloudy evening he surveyed his surroundings. Unfamiliar, as he had not been to Paris before, he pulled the paper from his pocket and looked at the directions in front of him. Situated in the tenth arrondissement of Paris, a densely populated area with an eclectic mix of nationalities, he noted the information; as he began to walk, he felt comfortable. His hotel was at the bottom of Rue du Faubourg on the corner with Rue de Paradis. Checking in was simple. Passing over his passport, which he would collect later, he paid the overnight fee, collected his key and made his way to the third floor.

He had been given information as to where he could eat that evening, and he was pleasantly surprised that the food was as good as he would get in his hometown. The woman and man behind the simple counter were Albanian; the conversation was easy and respectful. No one enquired as to why he was here just that they hoped he enjoyed his stay and the meal. Not wanting to sight see Lorenc glanced at his watch and decided that he would head back for the night. Up early the next morning, he vacated the hotel and grabbed a coffee and a light bite at the corner patisserie. Finishing his coffee, he waved down a cab and set off across Paris. The roads were busy. Turning right onto Rue Du Mail, the driver slowed as he approached the junction of Rue de la Banque. Pulling over, Lorenc paid the fare and crossed the road. The landmark Place des Victoires was in front of him, and he had been instructed to look for the small café with outdoor seating a short distance slightly to the right as he approached. Spotting the café, he took a seat and waited.

'Bonjour, monsieur.'

'Bonjour. Café, s'il vous plait.'

The waiter nodded, took the cutlery from in front of Lorenc away and disappeared inside. Looking at his watch, it was nearly 9:30.

The waiter, moments later, appeared with his coffee.

Sipping his coffee, Lorenc pulled a packet of cigarettes from his coat pocket, lit one up and blew the smoke out.

'Ah, bonjour, Monsieur Lorenc. Qui?'

The man in front of him dressed in a suit and carrying a briefcase held out his hand.

Taking his hand, 'Pierre Tecky?' he asked.

'Oui, comment s'est passe ton voyage?'

'I'm sorry, bro,' said Lorence. 'My French is not, you know. We good to speak English?'

Pierre smiled and nodded.

'Of course, excuse me.'

Sitting down, he ordered a coffee as the waiter appeared at his shoulder.

'I have everything you need,' he said patting the case, putting it down by his side as the waiter delivered the coffee.

'We do quite a bit of business with our mutual friend, and I was wondering if you could maybe give me an idea about the sort of other things that we could possibly use you for in the future.'

Pierre nodded. Vittorio had told him that it might be financially appealing to him if there were a few services which either Lorenc, or his brothers, had a need for, so he began to explain his potential role.

Arriving at the check in at Charles de Gaulle airport, Lorenc handed over his passport. The lady behind the counter looked at the photo, printed off his ticket and handed it to him.

'Have a pleasant trip, Monsieur Alami.' Boarding the BA flight, Mr Darous Alami of Moroccan descent settled into his seat, ordered a drink and waited patiently for the hour and a half trip to Liverpool John Lennon airport.

Chapter 26

The building was enormous. Set back about half a mile from the road, the gated complex was within the main boundaries of the airfield. Security was tight at the main entrance. An old RAF airfield had given way to BAE's massive changes on the site. They had erected several office blocks, technical departments and warehouse and research laboratories over the previous 20 years, and it had become the main site for military aircraft engineering, some assembly, but mostly research. At the heart was the newly concreted runway. When BAE took it over, they had spent just over a million pounds having the runway extended and upgraded, and it was now one of the longer runways, surpassing the Rolls Royce one at Filton near Bristol. It was a fully operational airport and boasted the latest flight control systems, medical facilities and had its own fire personnel and engines to respond to any emergency that may occur on sight.

A constant stream of aircraft landed each week, several private jets from either America or France owned by companies who were partnering with BAE on a number of projects and an assortment of RAF planes, which either needed modifications or testing. The building that Stuart Hardman let himself into, having passed through another set of security procedures, was impressive. The outer skin was of a standard corrugated clad structure, square in design but high. At the front were two rollback doors, similar to an aircraft hangar but smaller. In addition, the main difference was the heavyweight lifting gear system, which would protrude out of the top of the building when in use. The first doors, once opened, gave way to a separate set of doors, which would be airtight, sealed when in operation. The inner sanctum of the building featured a pyramid type room where thousands of cone shaped pads covered every inch of the walls and floor. This was BAE's testing bay for the Eurofighter, the Typhoon. This room allowed engineers to monitor and fine tune the stealth capability of this extraordinary aircraft. Once rolled in and hung up inside the pyramid it was subjected to intense tests, which highlighted its ability to avoid detection using a variety of stealth technologies that reduce reflection and emission of radar, infrared, visible light, radio frequency spectrum and audio. The systems that ran these sensitive tests were highly classified, and few knew of their precise nature or of their capability.

Stuart Hardman had been working on the system for a couple of years, and as he entered the black room lit by only a few exit lights, he walked down a ramp, which dropped out of sight of this main room, picking up a set of headphones and throat mic as he went. The headphones and mic were the only way people could communicate with each other in this area as sound did not travel, there was no echo, and most of the time it was in pitch darkness, so for the new people who worked inside it took a few days to adjust to this strange, eerie place. There was a ring walkway on the inside of the main floor that contained a plethora of sensors, all linked back to the main systems in another building on site. These were all hidden, so when a test began the only thing that could bounce back any type of signal was the Eurofighter itself, a cleverly designed room, state of the art technology and one of only three set ups in the world.

Stuart had graduated from Cambridge with honours; his thesis had been on the predictability of cloaking aircraft flying at supersonic speeds at the Karman line some 62 miles above sea level and detected only by satellites. He had explored this in greater detail when he was given the post of under head of development at BAE. It grieved him that over the last few years he had been parked at this position with no possibility of being made head. 'Lack of interpersonal skills' was the reason they had given on several occasions when promoting others past him. In his eyes, he had virtually designed the whole of the stealth capability for BAE with no thanks. Every night in his flat on the outskirts of the Wirral he would pour over his designs, making slight modifications, corrections, and pushing the technology at his disposal further and further for greater results. They disliked that he took sensitive documents home with him, citing that he could be burgled, and they would be stolen and fall into the wrong hands. He'd scoffed at the time. If only they knew, he thought. It hadn't stopped him; they knew he was doing it but were tired of the arguments they'd had with him, and it was unrealistic for him to stay at the site 24 hours a day as he had once done to prove his point.

The threat Stuart saw was from China: they were becoming a dominant force across the world both economically and militarily. It worried him that no one was taking any notice of this giant as their commercial companies were buying into seaports across Europe, Asia and Africa, thus making the potential of refuelling of their warships easier. The money, they were spending in Africa on infrastructure, creating roads, railways and airports, easy staging points, thought Stuart, for an attack on the west. Plus, their ability to dominate the south China sea and armaments could now reach well into Asia and Russia. He'd raised it a few times but had been told that BAE were not a political organisation and had no interest in what China were doing, that, they said, was down to the politicians. Andrew had been right of course. They had met at Cambridge and had formed a bond. Similar thinking had led Stuart to believe that the only people capable of stopping the march of China was Russia. The two men had kept in touch over the years, meeting regularly to discuss both their work and how it could benefit others and it had been Andrew who had introduced him to Sergio. He was looking forward to meeting Andrew again and their next meeting was at the Farnborough air show, which was later that week.

Sergio glanced at his watch: 11:00 am and time for his daily stroll. It would take him about an hour, a routine he'd set up when he first came to the UK a few years ago. Every Tuesday and Friday, the route the same, picking up his jacket, he locked his office door, nodded to his secretary and made his way out of the building.

'Fine day today, sir,' said the doorman.

'Makes a change, it's normally raining.' The doorman laughed.

The gravel driveway took him to the main gate where the security guard let him out. Turning left, he headed towards Hyde Park. Following the footpath, it took him to the edge of the Serpentine. Strolling casually, he watched as a group of ducks were being fed by a couple of young children, mothers chatting away to each other with a careful eye on the kids. One left her pram momentarily and pulled one of the children back from the edge of the lake.

Carrying on, he circled the water and picked an empty bench. Pulling a packet of cigarettes from his pocket, he lit one up and leant back against the hard woodwork of the ornate seat, glancing around as he did so. It wasn't unusual for him to be followed. It had become less and less now over the last couple of years as it seemed that the security services had lost interest in him. Working for the First Directorate, he had been with the military since leaving school. The First Directorate, known as the GRU, a throwback to the USSR days, unlike the FSB, was part of the general staff of the armed forces and was not controlled directly by the president; that was the role of the defence minister, Algregor Ivanov. They were deployed world-wide with the sole intention of protecting both the security of Russia but also to gather strategic information that would help the growth of the country. A seasoned spy himself, he almost always spotted his tail and went to great lengths to lose them should the need arise; today however was not one of those days where his talent was needed.

The litter bin to the side of him was beginning to fill with rubbish; from what Sergio could see, there was a mixture of McDonald's cups, empty bags and a few crisp packets beginning to spill out of the top. That, though, was not what was of interest to him, but the red crayon mark near the bottom of the bin was. An old but very simple method of indicating that one of his informers wanted to meet. As it was Friday and this bin, he knew which one it was. Finishing his cigarette, he stood and with a brush of his jacket, which enabled him to take in anyone standing out from the crowd, he rounded the park, through Serpentine Walk, crossed over and headed down towards Harrods. At Harrods, he turned left into Hans Road and ambled down towards Hans Place, passing, as he did, the end building on his right. Pausing before crossing, he looked at the brickwork. Noting it was clean, he crossed over and sat again on a bench in the garden, this time pulling out his newspaper, which he began to read. To the casual observer he was just another man relaxing and making the most of the decent weather. Paper finished, he deposited it in a litter bin, noting again the cleanliness of the bin casing; nothing here for him today.

Circling the park, it was nearly midday, and as he came onto Pont Street, he hailed a cab.

'St Georges Square, Pimlico,' he instructed.

The driver nodded and set off. Paying the taxi driver, Sergio entered the small coffee house, ordered coffee and a sandwich, picked a booth and sipped his coffee. He was very confident that he'd not been followed; looking at his watch it was fast approaching 1:00 pm, the time of his meeting.

Stuart sat down, coffee in hand.

'How are you?' said Sergio.

Stuart grunted, it had been a long journey down and it had been uncomfortable on the train.

'Fine, as I could be, you?'

'Very well. How are your projects progressing? As expected, or have you had delays again?'

'Those morons are still getting in the way. They don't understand me or how the system can be sensitised with a bit more work.' Sergio nodded.

'It must be frustrating for you.'

'Here,' said Stuart pulling out an envelope from his pocket. These are the latest stats from the tests I've run, and I've also included the new design of the trigger relay switch that I've been working on. It's tested and works fine; your guys should be able to get it going now.'

'Thank you. I'll pass the information on. We are very pleased, as you know, about the help you are giving us, and, of course, if you need anything, and I mean anything, the offer is always there.'

Stuart nodded. 'I know, thank you, but I'm fine.'

The conversation lasted for a few more minutes; both men finished up their coffee and with a brief handshake Stuart left.

Sergio slid the document into his jacket, ordered another coffee and waited. The minutes passed, and with no activity he grabbed a cab and went back to the embassy where he went immediately to the control room and asked for the contents of the envelope to be sent urgently across to Moscow. His day had not ended, however. Spending the rest of the afternoon at his desk, 6:00 pm came round quite quickly, and Sergio headed out.

Gabrielle cleared her desk. Sheila had convinced her to stay, well, until the end of the year anyway, then if she still wanted to leave she would help her with references for a job in Europe. Locking the files she was working on in the drawer and securing the main filing cabinet, she was one of the last to leave. Brushing her hair in the mirror in the ladies, she fished around the bottom of her handbag for her ruby lipstick. Suitably made up, she adjusted her blouse slightly and left the office. Friday night, she had decided to treat herself to a drink on the way home. Every other Friday night she would drop into the wine bar near Leicester Square. It was a big bar and, on a Friday, busy, but not overly so, mostly office workers having a drink like her before they made their way home. Picking up her glass, she settled into one of the many four-man booths dotted around the edge of the main bar. Semi secluded and comfortable, she sipped her wine, trying to decide whether to have a Chinese or Indian that evening. Deep in thought, she didn't really notice the man approaching the booth until he slid in on the opposite side of her.

Startled, she looked up. 'It's taken,' she said quickly, not wanting company.

'Hi, Gabrielle,' the man said holding up his hand briefly.

'My name is Sergio, and the man over there. . .' he said pointing to the bar, 'said for me to introduce myself to you.'

Gabrielle spun a quick look; her eyes widened; she swallowed involuntarily. Femi was stood at the bar grinning at her.

'Don't worry,' said Sergio quickly. 'He's not coming over, in fact, he's just about to leave,' he said, turning his head towards Femi.

They both saw Femi feign a salute and walk out of the bar.

'Who are you? What do you want?' said Gabrielle looking back quickly at Sergio. 'I can't help you. I don't know what he's told you, but I can't. . .' The words were pouring out of her mouth.

'Don't worry. Don't worry. I don't want anything, OK,' said Sergio soothingly patting her gently on her hand.

She withdrew her hand swiftly. 'Don't touch me.'

'Sorry, sorry, I didn't mean to upset you. Please excuse me.'

'What do you want?' said Gabrielle, tears beginning to prick at her eyelids.

'Nothing, absolutely nothing. I just came to tell you that he. . .' pointing briefly at the empty space Femi had occupied, 'is out of your life, forever.'

Her eyes wide, she stared at Sergio.

'I just wanted to say hello. I don't want to upset you. I just wanted to tell you that you are free of him, OK. So don't worry, you will never see him again.'

'I don't know what to say,' said Gabrielle.

'Then don't say anything,' said Sergio rising. 'Enjoy your drink. Relax. Everything is fine. Femi is gone. OK, I'll leave you now. We may see each other again, but only if you want to.'

Picking his drink up, he looked down at Gabrielle. 'I just wish,' he said quietly, 'that we could have met before that disgusting imbecile had met you. Anyway, I'll leave you now. Have a nice evening; it's a pleasure to meet you.' Sergio smiled at Gabrielle, turned, finished the small glass of beer he had and left the bar.

Chapter 27

Izzy picked up the file; picking through the photos inside it revealed very little.

'Bill,' she said. Bill looked up. Izzy nodded, clicking off from an email. Bill walked over and sat in front of Izzy at her desk.

'What's going on?' It was more a rhetorical question than one that Bill needed to answer. 'What are we missing?' Looking through the photos in her hand she began to put them in front of Bill.

'Nothing is happening. The Kodras are just floating around. No real activity, and I see from the latest scene report from Simon that no one has visited the house.' Looking up at Bill, she raised her eyebrows.

'Don't know, boss, it's strange. It's gone quiet, none of them are doing anything, so they've either had the stuff and it's now in play somewhere or they are waiting. We got nothing to show from any of the surveillance.'

Izzy shook her head. 'It's not right. All the indications were that they were on board with the Italians, which, we guess, is what the factory is for, and the house, what?'

'Coke, maybe,' said Bill. 'They're not living there, and as I say, no one had visited.'

'The DCI is looking for results now; he's signed off on the overtime.'

'Yeah, but to be fair, boss, that's only been three days so far, so a bit early, and we've got this weekend for a change, so something might happen then.'

Izzy ignored the comment. She too knew it unrealistic to expect quick results, but with more targets being set and conviction rates falling, everyone was under pressure to deliver.

'OK, let's look at this from a different angle. Let's say you are Rinori and you have loads of coke. Just for now, we'll talk about the heroin in a minute. So, loads of coke coming, and we know his crew is getting bigger all the time, which means they are either selling direct or it's muscle.'

'If I'm Rinori, I am not wasting my time on selling a few grams of coke. It has to be kilos of the damn stuff to make it worth my while, so I get a massive delivery in.'

'How much?'

'Dunno, let's say 200 kgs or more. So it's a lot, but instead of cutting I'm selling it wholesale. Maybe I do this every month or, depending on supply, every couple of months.'

'What about the money? Where does that go?'

Bill shook his head. 'Well, the Chinese used to bag it and send a container back to Macau. Maybe they are doing the same.'

'I can't see them delivering the coke to the factory, that's too complicated. They must have more setups somewhere else. It's not the house, that's a dead cert, maybe for their own use but that's all. Still doesn't explain where the money is though.'

'The only container we've seen is at the factory.'

'Are they combining then, maybe coke and heroin money? If the spaghetti chain is a front, then the cash comes back, and they then send it out.'

'The lorries we've seen in and out are all legit, so if this is a heroin distribution point, it still leaves the problem of how.'

'Umm. . . just guess work though. When was the last time they were at the bottling place?'

Bill picked through the file. 'Not since the first visit.'

'Unless they go at night.'

'Well, we've got the place covered now, so that will show up.'

'Or they have ditched the coke in favour of the heroin.'

She started looking back over the reports and photos.

'For fuck's sake,' said Izzy resignedly.

'We done?' said Bill making to stand.

'Yes, keep on it,' she said looking at the details of the factory.

'Hang on. . .' She kept reading; Bill sat.

'How many bottles of olive oil does a restaurant go through?'

Bill shook his head.

'Why have a bottling plant? It cost a fortune to put in, and I can't see that bottling a few hundred every couple of weeks or a month or so makes any sense.'

She looked up at Bill.

'Would you spend tens of thousands on some kit then

go to the expense of getting a few pallets of bottles in then filling them with olive oil? Surely you would just buy the bottles full and just deliver to the restaurants like you would pasta or veg or whatever.'

Genti left the estate at 7:00 pm and set off for Chigwell.

'We all good?' said Karim.

'Yeah, man. Let's do this.'

The two men in the Audi swept off onto the main road and headed out. It was an easy journey, and it took them just over an hour and they arrived at the estate. Pulling up at the roller doors, Karim jumped out, unlocked the side door and then began rolling up the main metal door. Genti reversed in, and the door came down.

'Give us a hand,' said Karim bending down to pick up one of the boards that covered the pit. The two men shuffled the heavyweight board out of the way, and Karim jumped down. Opening the boot of the Audi, Genti turned and waited as the first packages began to come out. Placing the wrapped money neatly into the boot, he covered it with a rug. *Bit pointless,* he thought, *but Rinori had said to do it.*

'That it?'

'Yeah, that's the lot for now.'

Replacing the boards, opening the roller door, Genti pulled the Audi out and waited for Karim. Checking his gun in his belt, flipping down the glove compartment, he saw there was another Glock there as well. With Karim on board, they set off; the next destination was Kidbrooke. Arriving, the process was the same: straight in, into the pit, remove the packets of cash, secure the lockup and head back. This time, however, they headed over to South Stifford, and within the hour they were pulling up to the gates of Orsino's factory.

The shipment was due in today, Friday, and Rinori wanted to see how the operation worked first hand. Looking at his watch, it was coming up to 10:00 pm. Grabbing his jacket, he nodded at Grail and the two men, and checking the coast was clear, got into the waiting Audi. Gam was driving, and as they weren't expecting any trouble, the other gang members hadn't been needed. Pulling up to the gates of the factory, the gated compound was locked. Grail unlocked the gates and the car shot off round the back of the building. Grail, looking up and down the road, seeing nothing unusual, locked the gate and followed the car.

'Where's the money, bro?' said Rinori.

'Safely locked away downstairs,' said Genti. He'd been a couple of times over the last few weekends, once with Orsino to walk him through how the locks and cabinets worked. The vault now only contained their money. Vittorio's millions had gone on the last container, secure now in Europe.

Orsino walked through the door.

'Buonasera, signor,' he said looking at his watch.

'They will be here in a minute; let's go into the factory.'

He followed Orsino down through the locked doors into the bottling plant and then into the loading bay.

'Ah, I see the barrels are here, buono, buono,' he said pointing at several barrels.

They could hear voices and turned as several people entered the loading bay.

Orsino went up to the first man.

'Mario, buonasera.'

'Ciao, ciao.'

'Let me introduce you.'

Introductions made, 'Get Alfonso to take the woman through. Would you like to go with him?' he asked pointing to Rinori.

'Genti, you go.'

'OK, we will show you the process,' said Mario.

'I will leave you now,' said Orsino. 'Ciao.'

'Gezuar,' said Rinori with a thumbs up.

Mario's team split up; one jumped onto a small forklift, his partner opened the lid, and the barrel was lifted and poured into the vat. The procedure followed with the other barrels, and the bottling plant burst into life.

Rinori watched as three barrels were moved to one side; these were flipped over and the contents poured into the grate. The sweet-smelling olive oil now filled the room. The packages began to spill out, and a man with rubber gloves collected them and placed them onto the table where they were wiped dry. Rinori watched the operation, which was now in full swing. The bottles were being filled with olive oil; coming off the conveyor belt they had been labelled and were stored in boxes. The packages of heroin, wiped clean of oil, were now being taken through to the lab. As Rinori walked through he saw Genti closely watching as each package was opened, weighed and then passed to the next person, who poured the contents onto a tray and then passed it up into the middle of the long table. Each woman had several plastic bags next to her, marker pens and a sheet of paper. Each scoop of heroin was mixed with the cutting agent, weighed carefully, bagged, sealed and marked. The process was streamline, efficient and quick. Just over five hours later, all the heroin had been cut; not a gram remained on the table. Mario searched each woman before allowing her to leave the room. The plastic bags had been sent upstairs and incorporated into the delivery pallets for each restaurant.

'So, you see, ittta very good, si?' said Mario.

Rinori nodded. 'We stay the same, OK. We'll be over with the next one. Genti,' he said pointing to his cousin, 'will come over on a regular basis for downstairs, you know.'

'Si, si, no problem.'

Izzy closed the door to the conference room. It was bigger than the meeting room they had been in as there were now a lot more officers involved with the case. Bill, along with Simon and Claire, were now team leaders and each had four other officers to assist. Craig, still new to the department, floated between them all to pick up on any slack or anything that cropped up that was overly complicated. Taking her place, she opened up her file. She looked at her watch: 8:00 am Monday morning. How quickly things change over a weekend. She'd also had a call from the DCI who wouldn't be attending but would like to see her at ten.

'Thank you everyone. Bill, update,' she said looking at Bill.

'No change during the day at the factory. The only delivery was on Friday afternoon of a small container. He was onsite about an hour and then left. We tracked him back to Dover where he went over. Enquiries made said that he was empty on the way out. The extra surveillance has worked in our favour. Late Friday, me and Craig tailed Genti and Karim to two lockups; these are the addresses,' he said handing out sheets. Standing, he walked over to the whiteboard and pointed at some pictures, which had been taped on.

'This one is at Chigwell and this one Kidbrooke. They went into both and were in about 10 minutes each. From there they went over to the bottling plant at Stifford. When we got there Simon and Claire were already there. Simon. . .' he said sitting back down.

'We picked up Rinori and a couple of his guys just after ten, who we followed straight over to the plant. As we watched, Orsino also arrived. He left about 20 minutes later, but interestingly we got a few photos of this white minivan,' he continued, pointing to the picture on the board. 'We think there were about 10 or 12 women inside. Apart from Orsino, they were there for several hours. The van left first at just after 4:30 am, and then we saw Rinori and Genti leave about 5:00 am. We followed; they all went back to their flats.'

'I followed the van,' said Bill, 'to a block of flats in Peckham. Couldn't get close, and I don't know what flat they are in, but Craig followed the guy who drove the van who then went over to a house about a mile away; these are the photos of him,' he said pointing to the whiteboard.

'Right,' said Izzy. 'Progress, looks like we've been lucky at last. OK, we need to ID the guy at the house. Get his name and see who owns the house and also the flats. Need a complete flat by flat breakdown of who's who in there. Simon, you and a couple of the guys get on that, OK?'

Simon nodded.

Craig, we need more daylight photos of the lockups, who owns what, how long, etc. Get on to Land Registry, and while you are over there ask about, but be careful, see how often they get used.' Craig nodded, making notes as he did so.

'Claire, I need you to get some authorisation. Get in touch with customs. We need to know how often that lorry comes across and what the paperwork says it carries; also, if they have ever been stopped. Get the name of the driver just in case they use a different vehicle each time; odds are it will be the same driver.'

With a few more instructions, Izzy closed the meeting. They would reconvene on Wednesday morning for further updates. Gathering her file, she left the room and climbed up the two floors to the DCI's office. Knocking on the door, he waved her in.

'Morning, Izzy.'

'Morning, gov. Just had the progress meeting downstairs,' she said sitting down in front of him, running through the events of the weekend and showing the photographs that had been taken. Paul nodded a few times and made a couple of notes.

'The extra hours have paid off; we need now to cover this

lot 24 hours a day. We need both the units, the house and the factory plus time at the apartments where the members are living. I suggest we keep the surveillance to the main targets. There are too many in the gang now to cover them all and that means more chance of getting spotted. I have enough people, just need your approval.'

'How long?' Money was always an issue. He'd been with the chief on Friday, who was concerned about the amount of overtime his departments were pulling and so far, bending the DCI's ear with little or no results. He had several operations on the way, some closer than others, so he was under pressure to get an outcome.

'It'll be a few weeks, but I think they've now had their first delivery of heroin. Unfortunately, we were a bit late on the ground to mount a raid. We'll know more about the setup later this week.'

'So, where's the heroin now?'

'It will have been loaded onto the delivery trucks and gone to the various restaurants.'

The DCI sighed. 'So you've let a load out onto the street?'

'Yes, sir, but we didn't know it was coming. I'm having the manifest checked and it should show us how often it comes across; in which case we can prepare.'

'Well, it doesn't look good allowing goodness knows how much heroin to get away from you.' Izzy just looked at him; there was nothing she could say. He was being unreasonable, of course, but pointing it out to him probably wasn't a good idea.

'I need your permission, sir, to get SO19 involved.'

300

Chapter 28

Vittorio put down the phone, turned and picked up the beautifully decorated gold leaf inlaid cigarette box. Flipping the top, he selected a cigarette. Placing the box back, he picked up an extremely rare 1950s Dunhill table lighter, gold topped with aquatic carvings on the subtle green Lucite panels. Lighting his cigarette, he walked to the window and looked absentmindedly out. The news he had received was slightly disturbing. He'd known for a long time that he may well become a person of interest to the police, hence the reason he kept his affairs extremely tight. Everything on the surface, everything that you could touch, feel, look at was legitimate. Both he and Ciro had spent every year that they had been in the UK scrupulously ensuring the cleanliness of any business transactions they did or places they visited were, as far as they could be, beyond suspicion.

His basement was a secret; if it had been of interest then he would have had a visit well before now, so his paintings were safe. His dealings abroad were infrequent, and whilst anyone digging would know that his name was affiliated with the Italian families, linking and proving any wrongdoing were two different things. His recent meeting with Genaro Salucci had been in Brussels and had been conducted in private at a residence of a friend. The painting had been delivered to the freeport in Hull, and it was just a matter of time before he would arrange for it to be brought to London and hung in his gallery. However, he thought, given the recent news he may leave it there for now, safe, secure and sealed, away from prying eyes.

Pressing the button on the wall, he squeezed the life out of his cigarette and looked up as David entered the room. His long-term butler, they had been together for over 25 years, both in this country and his homeland.

'Yes, sir?'

'Is Ciro around?'

'I'll ask him to join you, sir.'

'Thank you, David, and can you pack. We will be going on vacation tomorrow back to the villa.'

Surprised at the suddenness, 'Yes, sir, of course.'

Closing the door, Vittorio began to rerun the conversation he had just had and the options open to him.

The conversation had been with Aronne. He had been photographed talking to Tony Blackreach, who was a suspected arms dealer. It was thought that it was by an opportunistic off-duty police officer capturing Tony on film, so the families thought it best for now if Vittorio went on vacation for a few months. He'd not been implicated, but an association at this time was to be avoided. It made sense, of course, distancing himself from anything untoward, thus attracting little or no attention. The information had been given to Aronne by a Shane Fonda, a Met police officer who was married to one of Aronne's brother's daughters and had been a great source of information to the families for years.

'It seems Signor Tony is as elusive too,' said Vittoria to Ciro as he entered the door.

'Have you had any information from our friends abroad?'

'Just spoken with Aronne, who has a photograph of me and Mr Tony Blackreach outside Sotheby's. Have you been able to source any further details about him?'

'I was on my way over. That confirms the call I had earlier, which indicated that he has been dealing for some time. Russia at the start then he broadened his model to include Africa. He used to go under the name Tony Bishop and now is Blackreach. Not sure if that is real, I'm still waiting on confirmation, but it appears that he is well connected and supplies a good deal of arms. I'll know more soon,' said Ciro.

'OK, well it's unlikely we will meet him again, however, as we leave tomorrow for the villa for a few months.'

'Si, capo,' said Ciro leaving the room.

Vittorio looked at his Blackberry. He'd had confirmation that the first shipment of heroin had arrived into the UK, and Orsino had sent a message saying that it had been at the factory, packaged up and sent out. It appeared the Albanians were happy with the process. Early that morning, he had been on to the banking system and seen the money come in. With a few keystrokes, various amounts had been syphoned away to numerous accounts across Europe. Once there, he had tracked them into the Cayman Islands then back out to banks in Asia and eventually transferred to individual ones in Switzerland. He had communicated with the families that their money was now on tap to do with as they wanted. Checking his other messages, he looked at his watch and decided that a coffee was in order; it was a bit later than normal but his last one for a while.

Femi chucked the half-eaten burger onto the table; he wasn't in the mood. He looked as the others munched theirs; George looked up.

'You OK, bro?'

'This Tony is bugging me. He's paying way over the odds for these scratches. Thirty-eight grand is too much; he would never have paid Tariq that before. He agreed too easily.'

'We asked around but haven't yet had any info to say that he's a crud.'

Femi shook his head. It was an old feeling, one that he had grown up with on the streets as a kid, and it had served him well. Femi shook his head again; he wasn't happy.

'Do you think he wants to take over?'

'How would he know where to get them from?'

'If he takes us out and then gives them money they'll talk. It wouldn't take him long to get back to Oparei, and if he offers that shit more money then we're fucked,' said Femi nodding. *This is beginning to make sense now*, he thought.

Looking over, he asked, 'Where are they now?'

'Oparei has got them; they are on their way. Be end of next week, Thursday, when they get in late,' said George.

Femi lit a cigarette, stood and walked over to the window. *This is all wrong*, he thought.

'I'll be getting the new van on Monday,' said George finishing and joining Femi at the window.

'What about the guys?'

'Yeah, man, they'll be down tomorrow. Got three of them coming just in case.'

'Take the boys, go down to Dawson's. Do a complete search of the site, OK, but be careful. Make sure we can get in and out with room to spare, OK? Everyone brings the autos; we are not fucking around, OK?'

George nodded. 'When you telling Tony boy, Saturday?'

'No, I'll ring him next week. Get the bags.'

George walked into the bedroom; he reached into the wardrobe and pulled out three large holdalls and lugged them back into the main room where the men were sat.

'Where you want?'

Femi indicated the table.

'Sayo, get the suitcases.'

Sayo sighed, rose, wiping his mouth, the grease from the burgers dribbling onto his fingers.

Tipping the contents from the holdalls onto the table, the bundles of twenties and fifties spilled across the tabletop. George piled them on top of each other.

Sayo meanwhile had brought in two suitcases, which he unbuckled and opened. Femi threw some clothes into each and then began to count the money. The packs were already in wads of £1,000, and as he lobbed each one to George, he packed them neatly between the clothes in each suitcase. Three hundred between each suitcase, Femi counted the remaining 150, and putting this back into the holdall he gave it to Sayo.

'Take it over to Windsor.'

'Cono, go with him,' said Femi.

Cono nodded, picked up some keys from the table, grabbing the remains of his burger and chips as he went, and left.

Zipping the case and collecting his passport and another set of keys, he pushed the first case towards the door.

'Come on, Junk.'

Looking at George, he said, 'We'll be back Saturday, OK.'

The journey down to Dover and then on to Paris would take them the rest of the day. It was his third trip this month. His meeting with Pierre was late tonight, and after an overnight stay they would catch the ferry back Saturday morning and arrive at the flats again sometime Saturday afternoon.

Izzy put the phone down, a small smile on her face. She knew it would be a custodial sentence but was unsure as to how long. It wasn't as good as they had all expected, but a couple of years was better than nothing.

'Bill!' she called, and as he looked, with a quick wave of her hand, Bill smiled, crossed the office and sat down.

'Well, how did we do?'

'Three and a half.'

'Not bad. Could've been longer, but at least she's gone.'

The trial of Sihana had taken months. She was the last one of the Shehu gang to go to trial and the last one to be sentenced. The Crown had pushed on several counts, but in the end illegal gains from prostitution got her the sentence. The women they had found had been put into various halfway houses and were well out of her reach. She had maintained that they had nothing to do with her and it was hard to prove otherwise as all the women had given statements saying it was the first time they had seen her.

'Two minutes,' she said looking at her watch; it had been a few days since their last update meeting.

Rising, she grabbed several files, walked over to the coffee machine, poured herself a drink and then headed into the small meeting room followed by Bill, Claire, Simon and Craig.

'No Wayne?'

'He's onsite at the factory.' Izzy nodded.

'OK, quick round up, Bill. . .'

'The man in the van has been identified as Mario Santoro. He's the son of Orsino Santoro, the main Genovese Spaghetti House boss who's been at the factory. He owns the house, and they also own several flats in the block we saw them drop the girls at, these are the addresses of the flats. . .' he said handing out a sheet of paper to each.

'We have a team at the flats on surveillance. Mario works in one of the local restaurants near the borough market and hasn't been back to the flats. He was born here in the UK but went to school in Italy, came back when he was around 18 and then went to Bristol Uni where he studied business management. We think he then went straight in as a manager at the restaurant. He's not married, but we also think he's got a girlfriend, who works at the restaurant; we saw them together. . .' passing photos around. 'They had drinks at a bar then back to his house.'

'Craig, how we doing with the lockups?'

More pictures followed of the units and the areas around them.

'They are owned by a French company. Purchased about a year ago, the locals say they see a car occasionally, but the units are not used on a regular basis. I tried a quick look round the back of both, but no windows. I did some digging at the council, and they used to be let out to various companies: garages, scaffold company, engineering company, etc., some for a few years, but nothing of interest. They were empty, both that is, for a few months before our boys got them. I did see though that at Chigwell a guy was installing a new camera out the front. Nothing at the other one, but I'll check up on that tomorrow.'

'Claire?'

'Yes, got information back from customs, very interesting. The lorry that they use has been used on the same run for the last couple of years, every four weeks or so. Very little on the driver as most of the time they just get waved through. Occasional stops in the last four years but paperwork always in order. They did open it once but nothing unusual. They have asked if they need to stop and search.'

'No, get back to them and ask them just to let it through again. I'll get the approval today. When's it due again?'

It's coming in Friday week, the 14th. Or it should do if it follows the same time schedule, and I can't see why it won't.'

Pierre put down the phone and smiled; it had gone through. He didn't think there was going to be a problem, but until it was confirmed then there was always a possibility. The planning authority had passed the plans. When he was at the site, he had run through them with the planning officer, and although there were a few new changes the actual building size didn't really change at all. A new link fence around the factory, a sign – which he always thought strange that you needed planning permission for a sign – a new driveway, turning area and car parking modifications to the offices and a new roof, the only real difference was the change of use from heavy industrial to light industrial use with permitted development. The paperwork would be with him shortly, and the database would be updated accordingly in the next week or so.

Dialling the number, he waited. Looking at his watch, it was just after four. He hoped they would still be there.

'Ah, oui. Bonjour, Monsieur Fleury. S'il vous plait?' Lighting a cigarette, he waited.

'Bonjour, Fabrice. Pierre, ça va?'

Smiling at the response, he replied,

'All good this end. We have planning, and I've just signed your contract, so I will courier this over now. Are you OK to start on the 27th as planned?' Listening, the conversation continued for a few minutes.

'Excellent, Fabrice, have a good weekend.'

Placing the receiver, Pierre slid the document into an envelope and pressed the intercom. Geraldine came through the door.

'OK, if this can go straight away, thank you.' Rising, he picked his jacket off the seat. 'I'm away now; have a nice weekend.' Today, his extra marital activities in cinq à sept would have to wait. Leaving the office, he trotted down the stairs, into the basement and got into his Citroen. Hitting the button, the gate lifted to the entrance and Pierre swept onto the road and headed for Gare du Nord.

Parking and walking through the huge concourse, pushing past hundreds of people, he glanced at the large train information boards and saw the train he expected would arrive shortly. Standing by the main ticket exit he spotted the two men.

'Bonjour, bonjour.'

'Hi.' Femi smiled, shaking Pierre's hand.

Greetings over, Pierre led the two men, with suitcases in tow, walked through the station and into his car. Settling in, Femi took the offered cigarette from Pierre, and they set off back to Pierre's office.

Chapter 29

The lorry left the industrial district of south Genoa and headed onto the main artery around the beautiful town and picked up the signs for Milan. It was a simple trip, and one he'd made every few weeks or so for the last five years. It was early in the morning, and after a while he made quick work of the ring road around Milan and powered the lorry up a short incline and then onto the motorway to Como, where he paid the Swiss toll. Once in Switzerland, the start of his journey then took him through the relatively flat Swiss countryside, which quickly gave way to the stunning views of the Alps. The traffic was now getting busier, and as the road went into single lanes he was, as always, in a long line of similar trucks to himself. The approach to the St Gotthard tunnel at San Gottardo was slow, and eventually the queue came to a halt. Lighting a cigarette and pouring himself a drink from his flask, he expected to wait around 30 minutes before the crawl to the toll booth and then into the tunnel itself. A traffic light system at the entrance to the tunnel alternated between letting a dozen or so lorries through then a group of cars. It worked well but was always congested. The minutes ticked by and then he was next in line. Paying the toll, he waited for the green light and entered the tunnel. At 17 km long, a single lane, it would take about 20 minutes to get through as the speed was controlled. He had the option in the beginning, years ago, to go through the Mont Blanc, but the queues were horrendous and the cost considerably higher. This way added more miles to his journey, but it was simpler, cheaper and quicker. Hitting the air conditioning button on his dash he felt the cool breeze fill the cab. At the centre of the tunnel the outside temperature would regularly hit 38 degrees; too hot for the windows to be down, and it was a blessing, he thought, having the air con. Out the other side the traffic eased, and after a couple of miles he pulled into a station, parked up and grabbed a bite to eat and a nap.

Waved through at the border to France, he side-stepped Strasbourg and headed west towards Nancy. Making good time now, the run up to Calais would take him about six hours, arriving early evening. Settling down for the night, his journey had been uneventful, as expected. Setting the alarm for 6:00 am, it would give him plenty of time in the morning to catch his ferry at 7:00. The ro-ro left on time. His paperwork in order, the lorry was strapped down as they were expecting the channel to be a bit choppy this morning. He made the most of the lorry drivers' facilities on the boat, and less than a couple of hours later he climbed back into the cab and waited patiently for the others in front to drive off through customs and onto the M20, which would take him on the motorway all the way to his drop off point in South Stifford.

*

'Target vehicle acquired, heading north M20, repeat North M20.'

The unmarked police car picked up the lorry as it left the port of Dover; the second police vehicle was a truck, and they both followed him onto the M20 and radioed in. They would be joined later by a third and fourth vehicle to take over once he hit the M25.

Izzy put down the phone.

'We're on, just left Dover heading this way,' she said to the group occupying the conference room. Nodding to Sergeant Harris of the Specialist Firearms Unit, she said,

'Over to you.'

Surveillance at the factory consisted of several vehicles, one on the road near the junction of the M25 where it joins the A13 and another further in, hidden from site but it had a clear view of any vehicles entering the industrial area. There were also two others at the other end of the estate covering the back road that led onto it. An old builder's van was parked a few hundred yards from the main entrance and with blacked out windows afforded the occupants an excellent view of the main gate, sufficient for recording any activity. All the vehicles would be changed over on a six hourly basis just in case, plus it was claustrophobic in the confines of the van, and everyone needed a break; fortunately, the team now had enough officers to keep surveillance up to the level needed. They all watched, anticipation gaining as the lorry came off onto the A13 and then into the estate. Slowly pulling into the factory, the gates open for the day, it weaved its way around the back and proceeded to unload its cargo. Finished, he left and retraced his journey back to the port. His homeward ferry would be tomorrow morning, or so he thought.

It was now a waiting game. Izzy, Bill and some of the team were at the office in radio contact with Wayne and Claire, who were on site. Craig and others were at Rinori's flat with several officers parked outside watching for Genti and his cousins. She looked at her watch; it was going to be a long day if it went as planned. The DCI was in the control centre along with the DSUPT's assistance. When it got close, he would attend and become the officer in charge. Leaving the room, she poured herself a coffee, sat down at her desk and began to go through a mass of emails and reports that had been piling up. There was nothing else she could do for now, it was out of her hands, and she prayed that all the bases had been covered.

Rinori looked at his watch; Genti yawned.

'Come on, let's go,' said Rinori.

Downstairs, the two men got into the big sporty Audi. With Karim driving and Grail next to him, smoking, he cracked the window to get some fresh air. The others weren't needed tonight as none of what they were about to distribute would be taken back and put onto the streets by them.

The journey was quick, and as they pulled up to the gates of the factory Grail jumped out and unlocked the gate.

'I'll wait for the girls,' he said.

Rinori nodded, and the car drove round to the side office by the factory entrance.

Working their way through, they got to the loading bay and saw the various drums of olive oil waiting to be opened and used.

Rinori went through to the cutting room and then into the small office where the ledgers were kept. He'd been through them and was pleased at the detail they contained. Picking one out of the drawers, he placed it onto the table leaving it for Mario to fill in as each of the bags were cut and placed for distribution to each restaurant.

Hearing talking, he walked back through and saw Mario had come in with the girls.

'Hi, bro.'

'Ciao.' Turning, he nodded at the girls, who walked through into the lab with Genti following. They seated themselves and waited.

'Carry on,' said Rinori lighting a cigarette, and he stood back as he watched the first of the barrels being opened and the contents began to be poured into the large vats that would fill the bottles. The machines started, and with more oil being poured, the bottles started to chink themselves along the production line. Meanwhile, another of the barrels had been moved, tipped and opened; the oil flowed into the grate and the men began to pick out the polythene covered packages.

The process was repeated. It was a smooth operation, and whilst the last barrel was being emptied, Mario had gone through the to the lab where the girls had made a start on slitting open the first of the heroin and began to weigh it out.

*

315

Izzy and Bill pulled up several hundred yards from the factory. They had waited until they'd had confirmation that Rinori and his men were on route. Wayne and Claire were already there as they had tailed the gang from their flat.

The briefing earlier had been in two parts: the first was by Izzy confirming the delivery of the olive oil, and during the second part the operation was handed over to the special firearms team, who would lead the raid on all the locations that were known to them.

'Machinery started,' came over the radio.

The two officers had arrived at midday. Dressed in overalls and hi vis complete with hard hats, they had made their way onto the roof of the abandoned adjacent building and had a good view of the loading bay and entrance to the factory. Waiting for several hours, they had updated command of the arrival and departure of several delivery vans, staff and later, when night had fallen, the arrival of the gang. Detailed radio information had been given to command centre as the men arrived and again when the small minivan with the girls in it turned up.

'Target 4, gate locked, and he's heading for the factory.'

The DSUPT waited.

'Target 4 smoking, not in building yet, repeat, not in building.'

'Come on, go inside,' said DCI Roberts listening to the reports in the command centre. The DSUPT had arrived and was in contact with all the teams across the city awaiting the order to raid.

'All targets inside.'

Grail had finished his cigarette, flicked the butt away and went through the office door.

'Go!' said the DSUPT into the radio.

Cutting the wire at the back of the factory, the men squeezed through and quickly crossed the lorry turning area to one of the back entrances.

At the front, the gate was cut open and the two Transit vans rolled quietly down the tarmac, coming to a halt just before the edge of the building. This was where it was going to either be a straightforward entry or the gang inside would be alerted to their presence. Sergeant Harris had laboured this point at the briefing and said that this was a part of the operation that was completely out of their control.

Luck, however, was on their side. Rinori had forgotten about the live pictures being beamed into the factory. If someone had been sat in the office, they would have seen the grainy black and white TVs, four in total, covering the back and front begin to show shadowy figures creeping along the edge of the building towards both the back and main entrances to the loading bay. Suddenly, one of the outside security lights came on, illuminating the group; it was always going to happen and now speed was of the essence. Quickly positioning themselves by the fire exit, the lead with ramming baton in hand waited for the signal; nine men were behind him ready to burst in and down the stairs as soon as the door was sprung open.

Sergeant Harris tried the outside door handle of the office; the lights now were covering the whole of the car park and they were in clear view of anyone coming outside.

317

The handle gave; Grail had not locked it on his way in. They had studied the floor plan of the building, so they quickly and quietly went through the office part up to the door to the bottling area. Looking at his watch, he waited.

It was 12:45; the second hand clicked through.

Timing was everything; taking a deep breath he hit the button on the throat mic.

'Go! Go! Go!'

The officer at the fire door smashed the metal baton into it; the noise was deafening. The tactic was effective; the door burst open, and the men streamed as fast as possible, guns locked, down the stairs. At the same time, Sergeant Harris rushed through from the office door. His weapon shouldered, he scouted the large room in front of him. The noise of the machinery from the bottling process drowned out the shouts from the police, which made entry across the factory floor easier for him and his team. The team rushed into the room, spread out and before long most of the men operating the machine they were on had been overwhelmed, flung to the floor and held down. Crossing the large floor, he spotted the door next to the lift shaft and ran through followed by a dozen or so all focussed on the possible trouble ahead. Raiding two separate locations on the same site at the same time was always going to lead to possible skirmishes with the target gang. Unsure as to the level of resistance they might have encountered in the bottling area, as fast as they were securing it, they were still several seconds behind PC Johnson, who was going down to the basement where it was thought the main bulk of the gang would be.

*

PC Johnson burst through the door and turned right followed by his wing. The second and third men through the door went straight ahead towards the centre of the room and fired. With the gunshots reverberating around the metal clad room, the two who were pulling out packages from an oil drum saw the police and knelt quickly with their hands in the air, watching as several others from the firearms team came rapidly through from the staircase following the plan they had set and vied left and right, covering the room as quickly as they could. Grail was quick off the mark. He'd been stood near the door when he'd heard the crash, grabbed his gun from his belt and shouted to Rinori and ran towards the stairs on the other side of the room. Twisting as he did, he saw the heavily armed team come through the door and fire in their direction. The two men following Sergeant Harris into the room returned fire and were more accurate than Grail, who caught three bullets in the chest, which spun him off the ground and into the door. The second officer fell to the floor as one of Grail's bullets had hit him in the leg.

'Officer down. Target four neutralised,' radioed his partner immediately.

Genti, who had been with Mario in the lab, grabbed the ledger and raced into the office where Rinori was sat at the desk. He chucked it to him and shouted,

'Raid!'

Rinori caught the ledger and threw it down the stairs behind the filing cabinet, hit the button and the cabinet rolled back into position. Rinori, hearing the gunshots and shouts from the police, had nowhere to go. He'd been in this position once before back home when he had been raided at his cousin's house. Taking the gun from his belt he put it on the table, knelt and clasped his hands behind his neck; trying to fight yourself out was not an option. Genti, who wasn't armed, had knelt in the doorway of the office giving a second or so for Rinori to lock the cabinet in place before the police came through. Genti had, like Rinori, been on the receiving end of a raid before and waited as PC Johnson approached him.

The girls in the lab screamed as the officers, guns pointing in their direction, came swiftly into the lab.

'On the floor! On the floor!' they bellowed in their ears as they went down both sides of the table. Mario, who had watched in surprise as Genti had grabbed the ledger from him and was still trying to make sense of what was happening, was taken aback, and it was a few seconds before he grasped exactly what was going on.

'Down! Down!'

Genti lay forward on his stomach, as he was bound, and as PC Johnson stepped over him Rinori heard the click of the cabinet as it locked into place. The commotion had drowned out the sound to PC Johnson, and as he looked at Johnson, Sergeant Harris was on his shoulder.

'Target one and two detained,' came over the radio.

Karim was coming out of the toilet when he saw across the bay area the black clad, armed teamed emblazoned with caps and the distinctive white and blue badges. About to pull his gun, he was brutally slammed into the wall and thrown to the ground. With a gun pointed directly into his eyes, his own gun was torn out of his waistband, he was spun over and felt the heavy knee on his back as he was handcuffed.

'Target three detained.'

Izzy and her team drove through the gates, up the tarmac and parked outside of the loading bay. They had heard over the radio that the raid had been completed and had waited for the ambulance to arrive before they went inside. By this time several other vehicles and SOCO had arrived, and it also came over the radio that the DCI was on his way.

Lights were on all over the factory now, and as Izzy worked her way through the office and into the loading bay someone had switched off the bottling machine; the smell of olive oil hung in the air.

'Everyone accounted for,' said Sergeant Harris as he came over to Izzy.

'Sorry about your man. How is he?'

'He's fine, just a graze.'

'We OK to go through?'

'Yeah sure, Grail is by the door.'

Izzy nodded. She watched as the first batch of girls were being led across the floor to the outside vehicles. Mario along with Rinori and the other gang members were safely tucked away in the vans and heading for Paddington nick.

'Let's have a look then.'

The stairs led to the bay where one of the barrels was still lying on its side as an officer, clad in overalls, was picking up packages and putting them on the nearby table, being photographed as he did so.

'Heroin?' enquired Bill.

'Looks like it. Thank God we got it right,' said Izzy.

Watching them for a moment, the two then went into the lab, where several other people were photographing and counting those bags that had been completed, waiting to be put onto the delivery vans and carefully weighing the remains of the heroin which hadn't been.

'Through there,' said one of them.

Izzy walked into the room and looked around.

'Not much in here,' said Bill.

Opening a filing cabinet, he shuffled through some files.

'Mainly restaurant orders by the looks,' he said putting some back and picking a few more up.

Izzy opened the drawer on the table.

'Nothing much here either.'

Izzy looked around the room; apart from the desk, a few chairs and the filing cabinets and a couple of wall cameras there was nothing.

'Let's go, going to be a busy week,' said Bill.

'Who was in this room?'

'I don't know,' said Bill. 'I'll go and find out.'

Leaving Izzy to look through some of the cabinets, picking up a couple of the folders and flicking through them she closed the drawer and headed towards the door.

'Mario was here,' said Bill pointing at one of the lads' chairs. 'Genti was kneeling in the doorway, and Rinori was in the office and again, kneeling; his gun was on the table.'

Smart boy, thought Izzy. *Knew he'd got nowhere to go so gave himself up.*

Nodding, she stepped into the lab and turned back to look at the office.

'Why two of them in here?' she asked, speaking out loud.

Going back into the office, she looked around. She stopped and looked down; she had trod on something hard. Kneeling, she felt the carpet and looked closer.

'Bill, look at this,' she said tracing the runner back to the cabinet.

'There's one this side as well,' said Bill.

Opening the cabinet, she felt around; inside she found a small button. She pressed it and with a whirl of the motor the cabinet moved.

'Fuck, watch out,' said Bill, standing back.

The two looked on as the cabinet began to slide into the room.

'Get Harris,' she said quickly to Bill.

Bill ran out of the room.

The cabinet stopped and she peered over the edge revealing the stairs.

'What we got?'

Izzy pointed to the stairs.

Sergeant Harris spoke into his radio.

'Step back over there. Don't come until I tell you,' he said to Izzy.

Three other armed officers quickly appeared and joined Harris at the edge of the stairs.

'Go!'

Carefully stepping down, the officer began his descent; two more steps and the lights came on.

Izzy and Bill waited.

Not hearing any shouting, Izzy peered over the edge just as Sergeant Harris came back into view; he looked up at her.

'You're going to want to see this,' he said smiling.

He didn't hear the loud bang at the front door, but his wife woke immediately and sat up in bed. Listening, she grabbed his arm. 'Wake up! Wake up!'

Orsino turned over, 'What?' just as the police came through the bedroom door, blinding them with torch light. Dragging him out of bed, searching him roughly, with his wife's screaming in his ears, Orsino was led away. The raid on the house in the quiet council estate was as expected uneventful; it was empty and would in the coming days be subjected to a thorough search by the drug's team. The wake-up calls were echoed around the city as dozens of arrests were made. Mostly, the gang members provided little or no resistance, and all were packed away and sent to various stations across the capital. Both industrial units were broken into, and after a short search the pits were uncovered revealing the hidden cocaine. In the morning, all 600 plus managers of the restaurant chain would be arrested and taken down to their local nick for questioning. Later, in one of the first briefing rooms, it would be confirmed by the DSUPT and the DCI that apart from a few police injuries, none of which were fatal, the operation had been a success and a credit to Izzy and her team.

Chapter 30

Pulling up to customs, the driver wound down his window and passed through his documents; with a cursory glance the man waved him on. It was unusual to get stopped as the traffic was, as always, heavy. The ferry from Rotterdam had been full and was the third and last ro-ro of the day. Landing at 9:30 pm, the 30-minute trip had been calm today. Driving out and onto the A14, it wasn't long before the container lorry turned onto the A12 heading towards Colchester. The A14 was always heavy with traffic, and today was no exception. Seeing the turning for Stratford St Mary, the driver took the slip road, followed the signs and picked up the old Ipswich Road.

A few miles south of Stratford St Mary, past half a dozen houses or so, he slowed and then spotted the gate. Junk looked up as the lorry approached. Leaning nonchalantly on the gate, smoking, he flicked the butt end away and pushed open the metal gate. The lorry swung in and drove up the grassy track to the first building. His headlights picked out two mini vans and Sayo, who was also smoking. Jumping out as Sayo approached, he walked round the back, cut the yellow customs tag and swung open the big metal doors.

The young girls were all huddled together frightened, many in tears. They had been in the trailer for the best part of a day. They had been given food, water and torches; several blankets had been thrown in for them and they had been told to stay quiet. When they had got into the trailer on the outskirts of Rotterdam, one girl was taken aside and beaten and thrown into the back of the container as a warning to the others.

'Come on! Get off!' shouted Sayo.

Junk had now got back, and as each one came off, he pointed to one of the two minivans.

'Get in there and shut up.'

Twenty girls got into one van, which Junk then locked, and the others into the one Sayo was driving. He moved out of the way as the container reversed and turned around, and as it did so, Junk ran down and reopened the gate. Picking him up in his headlights, he waved as the driver swept past him and saluted Sayo, who was close behind as he too got out onto the road. Sayo headed south; he would join the M25 then head up to Birmingham where this consignment of girls was destined to be used. Junk, a few minutes behind Sayo, crossed over the M25 and headed down the A12 and right onto the outer ring road. Following that until Tottenham, he then headed south and then right onto Marylebone Road. Carrying on, he turned just before Paddington, up the Edgeware Road, left into Elgin Avenue and headed down for Hormead Road. Slowing as he did so, the six-bed roomed semi-detached house had the downstairs lights on. Tooting his horn as he arrived, Abeo and George came out. Pushing the girls as quickly as possible from the van up the stone steps to the house, Benj shoved them into the downstairs living room at the back of the property. Femi was smoking a cigar as they came in. Clutching their bags, some more nervous than others, this was not what they had expected.

Femi stood up as Junk came into the room with George and Abeo grinning. He pulled the first girl towards him; she was short, so he towered over her.

'I like you,' he said passing to the next, then the third; he stopped at the fifth girl, who was crying. The slap across the face caught her by surprise and the force of it almost knocked her off her feet.

'Shut the fuck up!' he said grabbing her throat and pulling her to his face. 'You'll do, as well,' he said sliding his grip to her arm. He then pointed at the first girl.

'You, come here!'

Hesitating, she stepped forward.

'Fucking come here, bitch' he shouted, grabbing her as well.

'These,' he said pointing to a bunch of girls. 'Put them in the first two rooms upstairs.'

Abeo pushed a dozen or so of the girls out of the room and slammed and kicked them upstairs, locking the door behind him.

Benj grinned at George.

'These two are mine for tonight,' said Femi carting the two girls out of the room. 'Do what you like to those,' he said smiling, pointing at the others. 'But don't mark their faces.'

Without waiting, Benj grabbed the first girl he was next to, slapped her face hard and yanked her out of the room, pushing her into the kitchen. The girl screamed; Benj punched her in the stomach, spun her round and bent her over the kitchen table.

'You might as well get used to this,' he said laughing.

Tony had been near the telephone box most of the day. In and out of the café with coffee and then sandwiches, he was now sitting in the car as it had started to rain. Femi had said he would ring Friday afternoon. Tony looked at his watch: 4:30 pm. *Fucking bloke*, he thought.

The phone rang; Tony jumped out of his car and picked up the receiver.

'Hello.'

'Tomorrow, 10:00 at Dawson's yard.' George gave him directions, which Tony repeated back.

'OK,' he said and put the phone down. Pulling some change from his pocket, he dialled and spoke to Barry. It didn't give them much time, but they were expecting that as Tony had told Femi that he needed notice as he wasn't carrying around a shed load of money for days and needed to know the day before not the same day. Femi had argued at first, but then logic took over and he agreed.

George put the phone down.

'Done.'

'Done.'

*

'Right, get Abeo and Benj there early, and I mean early, OK. I want them in place and watching; any sign of trouble, we're out.'

Saturday morning it was chucking it down. Tony pulled his collar up on his coat as he waited for the minibus Mark was driving. The yard was about 40 minutes away. Cupping his hand around his cigarette, he stepped back against the doorway, trying to keep the rain from his face. Seeing Mark approach, he flicked the fag away and stepped into the van.

'Hiya,' said Mark.

'Typical, init?'

Tony sat on the front bench. A large holdall was on the floor; he unzipped it and saw bundles of money. With a quick glance over his shoulder, he saw Barry and Buster in the car behind.

'Didn't know Buster was coming. They won't like that too much.'

'Don't worry about Buster. He's on the back seat. He'll hide down when we go in.'

Tony nodded; they had agreed that the story would be that Barry was backup.

Dawson's was an old abattoir in Hackney just off Shacklewell Lane. Huge in its day, it had served Smithfield market since the turn of the century, but with prices and rules changing it had to close in the mid-1980s and was now just a barren building with five or six other buildings attached at some point during its useful life; all had suffered at the hands of vandals many times. The roofs had been blown off most of the small buildings, and along with whatever windows and doors there were they were now just shells. The main building had fared better over time but was still a wreck. Driving through what used to be the gates, Mark headed up towards the front of the building, which was set a short distance from the main road, and with a collection of trees and overgrown bushes, visibility from the road was poor. The large expanse of gravel at the front of the building used to be home to several dozen lorries, so the minibus Mark was driving seemed small. As Mark pulled up, they saw another minibus and a black Merc coming in front of the other entrance. Mark stopped at an angle; the Merc pulled up and Femi got out. Sayo, who was driving the van filled with the girls, pulled up behind him. The rain was getting worse.

Tony opened the minibus door and walked towards Femi, and as he did so Abeo and Benj came out of the derelict building, both carrying a Colt 9 mm SMG.

'Oh shit,' said Tony under his breath. Keeping his composure, he waved at Femi.

'Hey, we good?' pointing at the two men.

Femi grinned. *Caught you, try something now, you fuck*, he thought.

'Yeah, man, we good. You bring the money?'

Tony pointed behind him as the two men now stood in front of each other, Tony slightly to Femi's left, looking over his shoulder.

'You got my girls?'

'Who's that in the car, man?'

'Did you think I was coming on my own? He's one of mine just to help with the girls, OK.'

Barry had got out of the car and stood next to it with the door open.

'Tell him to come from behind the door.'

'He's fine. He'll stay there, alright.'

Femi looked at Barry, thinking.

'Let's see the money, man.'

Cono got out of the car; he too was carrying a Colt. As Tony looked at the bus, behind Femi he could see Junk and Sayo reaching for weapons. 'I want to see them.'

Femi put his hand up. 'You wait, get my money first.'

Looking over at Mark.

'Get him to bring it.'

'He's driving the bus. He's OK. Alright, money is in the car, take it easy. I'll get it.'

Femi put his hand on his gun. 'You stay here, him bring it over, bro.'

'No.' Tony looked at Femi; he was getting agitated. Benj was walking towards them; Cono had circled slightly and was slowly approaching Mark.

'Get them to show themselves,' said Femi aggressively pointing at Mark and Barry, his eyes flicking from one to the other. His hand now was grasped firmly on the gun in his belt.

'Slow down, it's fine; they're fine.' He watched as Benj was now moving outwards and gradually towards Barry.

*

'This is fucked up!' shouted Femi as he stepped back and swiftly pulled the gun from his belt and aimed at Tony and in that split second the gunshot was deafening. Abeo was the first of Femi's gang to react. In his eagerness, how-ever, the feather trigger on the Colt, in full automatic mode, caught him by surprise, and as he lifted his gun a hail of bullets streamed out, raking through Femi's body, across the gravel, drilling into the front of the minibus and then shattering the windscreen. Mark dived into the well getting covered in a shower of glass. With a quick look at Abeo, Benj fired a volley at Barry, who sunk down behind the car door, bullets tearing into the fabric of the metal panels. Sirens filled the air, and two armoured Land Rovers tore through the gates, lights blinding and sirens blaring. Sayo revved the engine of his bus, slung it into reverse, stamped on the peddle and at speed took off backwards straight into one of the Land Rovers, the crash stopping both ve-hicles. The men in the back of the Land Rover were thrown to the floor simultaneously, Junk and the girls were chucked about inside the bus and Junk ended up bashing his head on the handrail and falling down the small set of steps by the door. The second Land Rover came skidding to a halt, the back doors flew open, and half a dozen heavily armed police officers jumped out. George, on seeing them, slammed the Merc into gear, hit the accelerator and in a swirl, which sent stones, gravel and dust high into the driving rain, did a U-turn and headed out. The driver of the second Land Rover, with his men out, belted towards the Merc and side swiped him almost knocking the car over, the cattlegrid on the front of the vehicle doing its job nicely, stopping the Merc in its tracks.

Benj ejected, re-loaded and fired again in the direction of Barry then turned his gun on the police. Abeo, grinning and shouting, firing indiscriminately at anything that was moving, ducked towards the building, reloading as he went. As he got to the doorway, he swung round and emptied the mag at the cops who had fanned out. Returning fire from several of them, Abeo died in a hail of bullets. Cono, with George gone, saw Buster leave the back seat of the car, pull the gun up to his chest and fire. Mark grabbed his heckler and Koch rolled out of the vehicle, grabbed a knee, pulled the gun to his shoulder and returned a burst, killing Cono. Behind him, Buster took aim at Benj. Barry moved from behind the car door as Benj was clipping another new mag into place, fired, catching Benj in the chest, spinning him around, knocking him off his feet, dead before he hit the deck.

With ear splitting noise two more armoured Land Rovers had now arrived behind Barry, their occupants spreading out onto the sodden ground heading towards the Merc. Sayo had stalled the minibus and couldn't get it to start. Kicking and swearing at the dash, the door was rapidly kicked open, Junk was yanked out, smashed to the ground and held down as two more officers ran up the steps, and with guns in his face, Sayo put his hands up. George, semi-conscious, was ejected from the Merc, and before he could

333

react was on the gravel, face down, gun in the back of his neck. It had taken less than five minutes, and after several shouts the sirens were turned off and calm descended on the area, the rain still lashing down on everyone, although no one really noticed. A group of police officers began to search the outer buildings while others secured the rest of the area. Mark, wiping the rain from his face, gun in hand, joined Barry who had slowly walked towards the front of the minibus. Barry surveyed the tortuous scene, the bodies crumpled and lifeless in front of him. Kneeling and looking at Mark and with a slow shake of his head said,

'It wasn't supposed to happen like this.'

Chapter 31

Putting the phone down he smiled, picked a Hamlet from the table, lit it, poured himself a whisky and walked over to the window. The penthouse apartment offered grand views across the city, although Lorenc wasn't particularly bothered as he was now silently congratulating himself. It had been a couple of months since Rinori's arrest and the phone call he had just had was from Vittorio. The supply of heroin would continue at the end of the year just in time for Christmas, a time when consumption always went up. Mr Darous Alami, as he was now known, had, with the help of Pierre, purchased the property outright. The local solicitor selling the apartment on behalf of the developer was told that Mr Alami was setting up business in the UK and needed a north of England base. Liverpool fitted the bill nicely, and Lorenc had moved in.

The next few months would also allow the builders to complete his factory. Pierre had also purchased a factory and had arranged for French builders to create the new lab hidden neatly behind the laundry machines. The building was having five new industrial laundry machines installed. The contract they had won, or in actual fact taken over from the Portuguese company that was currently running it, served the Resting House chain of hotels throughout the country. With over 500 hotels, the group offered budget accommodation for mainly businessmen and women. All the laundry generated at each hotel would be washed and ironed, packed and sent back to each hotel with the addition of white powder packages secreted within the sheets for the local services manager to distribute as he or she wished. As with many services in the hotel industry, to cut costs the cleaning of each hotel had been outsourced, and a Portuguese company, which was a front for an Italian 'Ndrangheta family, using cheap labour had won the contract some years previously, and now with the deal in place with the Albanians, Lorenc was set to make a fortune pushing both substances. The only change in place was that Pierre had created a cleaning company for each county a hotel was in and a bank account to go with it. As the managers received the cash from the heroin, they would then pay this into the bank under the cleaning company's name, and every month or so it would be transferred to a holding company, which in turn moved the money across into the foreign banking system, eventually making its way legitimately back to Lorenc in the form of a salary and expenses, the money totally clean. He had decided to leave the London area alone for the time being until he had properly secured the north, and probably Birmingham, and had more of his extended family embedded into what would be a growing empire.

Pierre had been busy. Sorting Lorenc had taken time but would see a healthy profit for him, and as he landed at Heathrow, *with more to come*, he thought.

It had taken several weeks for him to secure a visit to HMP Bellmarsh, but as he arrived at the gates, showing his documentation, he waited patiently in the room until his visitor arrived. George came in handcuffed and took a seat opposite him.

'Bonjour, George, ça va?'

'Speak fucking English.'

Pierre raised his eyebrows and smiled. 'Trust they are treating you well and the solicitor I arranged for you and your friends is serving you OK.'

George grunted.

'What do you want?'

'I'm told that they have charged you with possession of a firearm, which carries a lengthy sentence if proved. Once you have served your time you will be deported. Your friends are not so lucky, firearm charges as well as trafficking, so it could be a long time before they will be joining you. Anyway, don't worry about money, there is plenty, and I will make sure your solicitor provides for you whilst you are here. Once back in your own country, I will, via Bala, again, make sure there is money for you to survive, OK?'

Pierre looked at George, 'Assuming of course you and your friends are, how shall we say, forgetful, when talking to the Police'

George nodded.

'In the meantime, the property in Windsor, I need to know where the keys are. The police have been in touch with regard to the other properties but do not know about this one. Do you remember where they are?'

337

George shook his head.

'The police have never mentioned it. They have asked about all the others but not Windsor; the keys, I don't know.' George shrugged his shoulders. 'Femi. whenever we came back, he took them, so I expect the police have them somewhere. There is money there.'

'Yes, I know, Femi told me earlier this year. Where abouts is it?'

George told him and how to get it out from under the floorboards.

Pierre nodded. He hadn't known about the money, so this was very much a bonus. The keys, he thought, will just be put into evidence and lost forever.

'Don't speak about it, OK, and make sure your friends don't either; as I say, the less the police know the better.'

The police had come to his office with a list of documents showing the purchase of the flats. They had to sort to find out where the money had come from, but Pierre had covered his tracks, and although, yes, he had acted on behalf of the buyer, he had no knowledge of what they were for. He had arranged the purchase of many foreign properties over the years, and these were just a few of them. Without firm evidence, the police enquiries were going nowhere.

Pierre left Bellmarsh, made a call to a friend in Paris, booked himself into the hotel in central London and waited. The next day he would, along with Jules his locksmith, go to Windsor and search the house, have the locks changed and then arrange for the house to be sold. The money would find its way into Pierre's own account. With no one having a complete understanding of Femi's affairs, the house contents and sale would be lost, giving Pierre a sizable return for all his hard work, thought Pierre smiling to himself.

Izzy sat down in front of the DCI, who was reading the report. Looking up, he closed the file and smiled at her.

'Excellent work, Izzy.'

'Thank you, sir.'

'You and the team have done well. All the way up to the tenth floor everyone is very pleased with the result. I see we have charged all the managers of the restaurant chain with intent, only 40 or so with possession, and it's been closed down. Orsino and his son will be going down for a long time. As for the gang, off the streets. I know you have been looking for Lorenc the last few weeks, any news?'

No, sir, he left for France and hasn't been back. We don't know where he is, but after all his family has been arrested, it's very unlikely he will return; we have an Interpol arrest warrant out for him.'

'De Luca is also not in the country,' said the DCI referring to the file.

'We have very little if anything on him, sir, not enough to charge him with anything anyway.'

Jackson nodded. 'OK, well if he comes back then pull him for questioning. So. . .' leaning back in his chair, 'you are having a few days off, well deserved.'

Yes, sir, Monday to Wednesday that's all. It's been a busy couple of months, but now everything is handed over to the CPS, I'll be looking at the Yardies when I get back.'

*

'Good, OK. Pass my pat on the backs to the team, and see you next week,' he said, rising.

Izzy walked into the bar. Friday night, it was busy; she liked the place, the buzz and the music. Ordering a glass of wine, she looked around. As always, all the tables were taken. As she left the bar, wound her way through some people, she spotted a small table near the wall. There was a bloke sat on his own drinking, but the way he was sat it didn't appear as if he was with anyone. She wandered over; her feet were killing her, so she took the plunge.

'Anyone sitting here?' she said pointing to the opposite side of the table.

He looked up. 'No, help yourself.' He was sat at an angle facing the bar, so when she sat, he wasn't looking directly at her.

Settling down, she sipped her wine and sighed, placing it on the table.

'Busy week?' he asked.

She smiled. 'Yes.'

'Always is, isn't it? Couple of drinks, something to eat and then back to work,' he said picking his pint up and taking a swig.

'I've got a couple of days off, which makes a change.'

'Nice one, going anywhere?'

'No, just sorting stuff out.'

He nodded. 'If you are waiting for someone,' he said, 'I can always leave you to it and stand at the bar. I don't mind.'

'No, no, that's OK, just me.'

He smiled at her. Looking at him she said.

'I'm Izzy by the way.'

'Tony, Tony Blackreach.'

The conversation continued, friendly, easy and interesting; Izzy relaxed.

Tony looked at her. He knew she came in here and had been in a few times the last couple of weeks looking for her, more curious than anything else. If she hadn't come over when he saw her come into the bar, he would have made some excuse to stand next to her. Leonard had told him to take a month or so off. 'Go relax,' he'd said, 'have some fun somewhere.'

That day was still vivid in his memory. Femi had pulled the gun, and in that instant Rob had fired from the rooftop of the building. As a highly experienced sniper, gaining his spurs in the Iraq war, he was under strict instructions from Leonard that if Femi pulled a gun shoot him.

Rob had been on the roof under tarpaulin cover since 2:00 am waiting and watching. The bullet had blown Femi's head apart. Not hesitating, Tony spun on his heels and dived towards the bus, crawling under as fast as he could. The bullets from Abeo's weapon spitting near his heels, he dragged himself further under and prayed that they couldn't see him. After the noise had died away, Barry had helped him up, gave him the keys to the car and told him to disappear. They didn't want him on site to be seen or spoken to by any of the police, it would just complicate the situation, so he'd left, got back to the hotel and stayed there until Leonard rang him.

Chatting to her was fun, and he liked the way she looked and carried herself. They got another drink and the conversation ranged from music to films to books.

'Fancy something to eat?' said Tony looking at his watch.

Izzy looked at him, pulling her fingers through her hair thinking.

'Why not?'

The two left. Holding her arm they crossed the road and went into the local Chinese; ordering, they sat at a table near the window. The evening went quickly, and Izzy found herself relaxed and enjoying herself more than she had done for a long, long time, but the evening was soon drawing to a close.

'Do you need a cab, or can you walk from here?' said Tony.

'I'm just round the corner, so I'll walk.'

'OK, I'll walk you back.'

'That's OK. I'm fine, really.'

Not wanting the evening to end,

'I insist,' he said, smiling. 'There's bad guys out there.'

She laughed. 'OK.' The walk back to Izzy's apartment took about 15 minutes, and as they approached,

'This is me,' she said.

'I've had a lovely evening,' said Tony.

Izzy paused, lent forward and kissed his cheek, holding his hand.

'Me too.'

Turning, but not letting go of his hand she hesitated, thinking. Tony hadn't let go either and squeezed it gently.

She turned back to him.

'Would you like to come up for a coffee?' she said with a smile on her face.

'Love to.'